Battered Pride
Melissa Maygrove

Truelove Press

Battered Pride

Truelove Press

Magnolia, Texas

www.truelovepress.com

This is a work of fiction. Names, characters, businesses, places, events, and incidents are either the products of the author's imagination or used in a fictitious manner. Any resemblance of characters to actual persons, living or dead, is purely coincidental.

First Edition

Paperback ISBN: 978-0-9960397-8-9

Cover by Carrie Butler

Editing by The Write Word

Passion knows no prejudice.

Chapter One

Late November 1851 Southern California, west of the Colorado River

Hatchoq placed his bare feet carefully, soundlessly, as he stalked the wayward member of his clan. He had followed Mahwat for many miles at a distance, over desert that offered no cover, using a white man's telescope to keep his quarry in his sights. Now he hid among the same groves of scrubby trees his clansman used to close in on his prey.

Sunlight filtered through the scraggy branches of the mesquite trees that concealed his approach. Despite the shade, beads of sweat trickled down his face and burned his eyes. He ignored the sensation. As boys, they had been trained to disregard pain, and they were equally matched when it came to tracking and lying in wait.

Until today.

Mahwat crept through the trees, distracted by greed, unaware he himself was being hunted. Step by silent step, he edged closer and closer to the lone wagon they had ferried across the river the previous day. He wanted the travelers' horse that they had refused to trade, but he would take more than that. He would ravish the woman after brutally killing her man. Then he would kill her, too.

Mahwat had grown cruel as he aged, and he hated the *ko*, their clan's word for whites. He could not harm them at the river, in view of other clansmen who helped settlers cross, unless he was defending himself—trading with whites was a source of supplies and had prevented starvation at times. But alone, he did as he wished.

These particular ko had not challenged him for land, nor did they pose him any threat. They were simply passing through. They did not deserve harm.

Hatchoq cringed. That was a white man's thought, one he had learned from his mother. But one with which he agreed.

The woman, called Rebecca, possessed the courage of a warrior. She had survived alone in the wilderness for many months. And the man, Seth, had spent much to rescue her. Although Mahwat did not agree, they had traded fairly for their passage.

Hatchoq would ensure their safety.

His breath caught when a serpent slithered onto his foot. Snakes rarely slept in these lands. The cool scales slid slowly across his ankle, but Hatchoq kept his body motionless and his gaze locked on Mahwat. Whether the serpent had poison mattered not. He would wait and let it pass. Movement might get him bitten and, worse, give his presence away.

Mahwat moved forward soundlessly, the distance between them growing.

Hatchoq remained calm. The disadvantage did not stir feelings of doubt. An ancestral spirit had come to him in a dream and promised victory.

Still, he grimaced at the bitter taste of betrayal. He was going to kill a man who had been a childhood friend and more. He was going to kill his half-brother. Kinship wrapped a hand around his heart, but his conscience removed it and cast it aside.

Mahwat paused at the edge of the copse and lowered himself to one knee. His hand caressed the knife lashed to his waist, and the muscles of his back tightened. He was preparing to attack.

The snake crawled off Hatchoq's foot and into the brush, so he crept closer.

Mahwat's attention remained fixed on the couple in the distance, napping in the shade of their wagon. His muscles coiled tighter. He rose to a crouch and began edging toward the open expanse.

Hatchoq slid his knife free and increased his pace. His only choice was to grab Mahwat from behind and strike without hesitation. If his first cut did not kill, it would be a fight to the death. One he could very well lose.

With bated breath and soundless steps, Hatchoq closed the distance.

Mahwat's fingers curled around the handle of his knife.

Hatchoq sprang forward, yanked Mahwat's head back by his hair, and drew his knife across his neck so deeply the blade met bone. Blood spurted into the air then subsided into a warm cascade that coated his arm.

The cry of an eagle pierced the air as Mahwat's body jerked and slumped against his.

One of Seth's horses whinnied and pranced where he was tied. Seth remained motionless, but Rebecca stirred.

Hatchoq dragged Mahwat's body back amongst the trees. His chest swelled with victory around an aching heart.

He had taken the life of his father's favored son.

Hatchoq wiped the blood from his knife and returned it to its sheath. The killing was justified—for many reasons—but no matter how much he despised Mahwat, he would not humiliate him by taking his scalp. He hoisted the body over his shoulder and carried it back to his brother's horse. Once Mahwat had been secured across its back, Hatchoq collected his own horse and led both animals back to the river. He risked being spotted, but the horses were thirsty, and his brother deserved to be mourned.

The eagle followed, soaring high above him, and watched Hatchoq swim his brother's horse across and send it on its way. Was it proud of his bravery, or did it judge him for taking the life of his kin?

Hatchoq stood on the bank as the corpse-laden animal loped in the direction of their clan. The river's current had washed away the blood, but his choice had forever marked his future.

He could never return to his people or his home.

Chapter Two

Southern Oregon Territory, One month later

Eva McCabe tapped the edge of the wooden sieve until the last bits of flour disappeared through the holes, leaving only weevils behind. She crossed the room and tossed them into the fire, smiling at the satisfying sizzle. She was probably descending into madness, but clinging to the few minor victories that dotted her days was the only thing keeping her from cursing God and giving up.

Christmas should have been spent drawing up plans with her husband for the house he'd promised to build in spring. Instead, she had spent it alone in a dank muddy hovel, save for a trip to his grave.

Be grateful for the things you have.

The one-room dugout Keith had built earlier that year was small, with greased paper windows instead of glass, but it had a stone hearth and a wood façade. He'd hewn a sizeable root cellar deep into the hill behind the kitchen. He'd also finished the barn.

The structures would satisfy the housing rules of the land grant. The problem was meeting the condition of cultivation. Keith had only plowed a fraction of the fields before his death. She'd have to farm the grant alone.

The land would become hers if she succeeded. But if she didn't prove up by November of 1854, she'd forfeit all 640 acres.

Eva added water and yeast to the flour, and kneaded the mixture into dough, then set the loaf near the fire to rise. Aiming a frown at the sod ceiling, she covered the dough with a cloth to protect it from falling dirt and bugs.

She paused in front of the small mirror by the door and tucked a loose strand of hair behind her ear. Her Scottish husband had often referred to her as his fair English beauty. She wondered what he'd think of her now that mourning him had left her gaunt and pallid.

A scarcity of food compounded the problem. The rations from the trip were gone, and Keith's planting had been limited to the few fields he'd been able to plow. After a meager spring harvest, they'd spent their last few dollars to buy seed and some pantry goods for winter. Keith had been murdered before he could plant the Fall crop.

Eva fastened on her black crape hat but eschewed the veil, as she did most days in this isolated place. She pulled her coat on over her widow's weeds and crunched through the snow to the barn. She milked her cow, took the pail to the dugout, and returned.

"C'mon, girl," she said to Guinevere, as she led the lean Jersey out into the pasture. Grazing on the dormant winter grass helped conserve feed. "God willing," she muttered, "neither of us will starve before spring."

Eva fastened the gate and returned to the dimly lit barn. Mac McKinnon, her neighbor to the east, was boarding her oxen for the winter. He'd taken her horse to be shod and would return him later in the day. After Keith's death, Mac had stepped in and helped her to the point his own farm suffered.

She'd be damned if she'd let him muck her stalls.

Eva picked up her husband's work gloves and ran her fingers over the worn leather. Her heart ached for Keith so much it beat a constant throbbing in her chest. He'd been sparing with physical affection, but he was an excellent provider who'd been faithful and kind. And he'd extended that kindness to everyone he met.

Keith was the personification of *turn the other cheek* and *love thy neighbor*. A natural peacemaker. It was why her hatred burned day and night toward the savage who'd murdered him. The brute had tortured and mutilated a man who—by his very nature—was incapable of doing anything to deserve it.

Eva put on the gloves and reached for the pitch fork hanging on the wall, but paused at the sound of hoofbeats in the distance. It was too soon to be Mac. He wasn't due for several more hours.

Someone grabbed her from behind and clamped a hand over her mouth before she could draw a full gasp. Her arms were pinned to her sides, and the wall of muscle against her back was hard as steel.

Eva's heart pounded as the stranger dragged her into the shadows, behind a tarp-covered wardrobe standing in the corner. She struggled and tried to scream.

"Shh!" he said, tightening his grip until her lips pinched painfully against her teeth. "Be silent—if you want to live."

Eva stopped fighting and nodded her head as much as his grip would allow.

The hoofbeats reached the yard and stopped. It sounded as if riders were dismounting. There had to be at least two.

Maybe it was Mac after all. He'd be leading her horse and riding his. And if his brother-in-law, Connor, was with him, that would account for a third horse and a second rider.

She'd wait until she was sure, then she'd kick and fight and make as much noise as she could. Mac was tall and musclebound. If anyone could free her, it was him.

"Shhh," the man breathed into her ear more softly than a whisper. He didn't let go, but his grip eased some, and his breathing slowed. So did the beating of his heart. It had been pounding as hard and fast as hers when he'd first grabbed her. Now she could barely feel its rhythm through her back.

Eva's pulse slowed, too. His calmness was contagious.

The rumble of male voices grew closer. "Where'd he go?" one of them asked.

The voice wasn't familiar, and it had a southern lilt. Mac and Connor were Scottish and spoke with an unmistakable brogue.

"He came this way—I saw him," another man said. Also a stranger, and also from somewhere in the south.

"Go check the house," a third barked. "We'll check in here." He sounded like a northerner, and he sounded mean.

Eva began to tremble. She was incapacitated and outnumbered. And she didn't have her knife or her gun.

"Shhh," her captor breathed into her ear again.

Maybe he was a criminal on the run. If she stayed quiet and helped him evade capture, he might leave without harming her. She could hope.

Two sets of boots tromped into the barn and went in different directions. The tack room door creaked open, and the ladder to the loft groaned under someone's weight. Footsteps sounded and paused, as if someone was checking each of the stalls. Then both sets came straight for the wardrobe.

The tarp flew off and landed in a heap to the side, mere inches from where Eva was hiding.

She flinched, but her captor didn't. His heart kept a slow, steady rhythm, and his breathing all but ceased. His grip tightened again, but there was something gentle about it, as if it were a hug meant to comfort rather than a callous prelude to harm.

"Check inside," the mean one said.

The wardrobe wobbled on the packed dirt floor as its doors were roughly pulled open.

"The house is empty," the other southerner said from the entrance of the barn. "Y'all have any luck?"

"Nah. He ain't here."

"He has to be," the mean one replied. "Where else could he have gone?"

Someone kicked the wardrobe, shifting it so far it struck Eva, though her captor's arms took the brunt of the blow. She held her breath, hoping the bang of the boot strike had covered the sound of the piece bumping into something solid.

"Damned injun," the mean one spat.

Injun? The man holding her spoke perfect English.

"They're crafty sons o' bitches, that's for sure," one of the southern men said.

"Hey, Jay," the other interjected, "didn't Whitey say a widow woman lived here?"

"Yeah. He did."

"Maybe we can find her instead."

His lascivious tone made Eva want to vomit.

"Don't be an idiot," the mean one scoffed. "The place is deserted."

"He's right. The stalls are empty. She probably went into town."

"But there's a cow in the pasture and bread set out to rise. She'll be back."

"Shut up and get moving," the mean one ordered. "There's a cave a few miles from here. Perfect place for an injun to hide."

Bootsteps retreated from the barn, and a saddle creaked with the mounting of a rider.

Eva struggled against her captor's arms. Why wouldn't he let go?

"Not yet," he whispered.

She relented with a sigh. Then her whole body went rigid.

Someone had returned to the barn. A single set of booted feet slowly paced the interior, pausing from time to time.

Eva's hands turned clammy. The pounding of her heart was like thunder in her ears. Could he hear it? Had he heard her breathe?

What if he'd had time to sort out the sounds from before? What if he'd come back to look behind the wardrobe?

The wardrobe's doors squeaked on their hinges, and the latch gave a soft click, as if they had been pushed closed gently.

Eva prayed and held her breath.

"You got away this time," the mean man said in a voice that was deadly calm, "but I'll find you."

His footsteps faded away. After more creaking of saddle leather, a chorus of hoofbeats pranced in the dirt, picked up speed, and pounded out of the yard.

Eva waited this time. Then—when she felt as certain as she could be that the men were gone—she struggled again.

Her captor didn't release her, but he loosened his grip and guided her out of their hiding place. The hand covering her mouth slowly fell away.

She filled her lungs with air but decided not to scream.

The man removed his arms from around her as cautiously as he'd lowered the hand from her mouth. "Thank you," he said as he backed away.

Eva turned around and gasped. The man who'd grabbed her *was* an Indian. He was naked except for a pair of leather pants, and black hair hung past his shoulders. His chin was marked with blue lines—some kind of tattoo—and similar lines encircled his biceps.

The urge to vomit came back stronger. He could very well be the savage who'd murdered her husband.

Eva snatched the pitchfork off the wall and aimed it at his heart. She lunged at him and made a stabbing motion.

The Indian held up his hands and took a step back. "I did not come to harm you."

"Liar." She lunged at him again.

His eyes narrowed. Then, hands still raised, he took a cautious step to the side.

She turned, too, so that the sharp prongs stayed squarely aimed at his chest.

He sidestepped again and again, until they'd circled around, his back to the open barn door. The bold savage locked gazes with her for a long moment.

He was probably buying himself time to think of a way to overpower her.

Eva gripped the pitchfork tight to steady her shaking hands. She lunged at him and growled, "Your kind isn't welcome here. Get off my land!"

His eyes flinched with a wounded look. Then he turned and walked away.

Eva watched the Indian leave until he was out of sight. She tossed the fork aside, hurried into the dugout, and dropped the bar on the door.

What if it was a trick? What if he circled around and came back?

What if the men who were hunting him did?

She grabbed her Colt and peeked out a torn corner of paper on her kitchen window. The only predators she'd encountered since her husband's passing had been wolves, coyotes, and an occasional snake. Now she'd have to guard herself against a much worse threat.

It had taken a few hours of peeking out at a deserted yard and happily grazing cow between chores to calm Eva's nerves enough to venture back outside. The waxen winter sun had dropped until it was nearing the tree line, which meant Mac would arrive soon. Eva armed herself and headed for the barn.

She shook out the tarp and covered the wardrobe then cleaned the stalls, all the while looking over her shoulder. The sound of horses coming up the drive made her flinch and want to hide. But she couldn't live in fear if she was going to run this farm alone and claim her land.

Eva returned the pitchfork to its place on the wall and walked close enough to the open door that she could see who was approaching.

Her bated breath whooshed out. It was Mac and Connor.

Both men hailed from the same small town in Scotland, but they couldn't be more opposite. Mac stood so tall he had to duck through doorways. He had red wavy hair that extended to his beard, green eyes, and muscles so large they strained the seams of his shirt. His brother-in-law, Connor, was short and thin with straight brown hair and pale gray eyes.

Mac trotted up with her bay gelding in tow and dismounted. "Evenin', lass."

"Mr. McKinnon."

Mac smirked at the formal address. By Scottish standards, they'd been friends long enough to dispense with it, but the use of Christian names for anyone other than close family went against her deeply engrained English etiquette.

Connor remained in the saddle and tipped his hat. "Mrs. McCabe." He'd been lame from birth. He could ride for hours in relative comfort, but any amount of walking pained him.

Eva aimed a smile his way. "It's nice to see you again, Mr. McDougall" She meant every word. Connor had come west with Mac to help him make improvements on the land before sending for Mac's wife, Allison, his sister. His infirmity relegated him to chores typically reserved for women, but he applied himself well and without complaint. When he wasn't wincing in pain, a pleasant expression almost always graced his slender face.

His eyes told a different story.

They'd been dulled by years of childhood ridicule, of longing for a farm and family of his own, and the shame of being unable to provide. Such a fate often turned men cruel or drove them to sloth or drunkenness. That Connor had remained kind and productive despite his lot earned him her undying respect.

Mac led her horse to its stall and gave him his feed.

"What do I owe you?" she asked when he came out of the barn.

"No' a thing."

"Mr. McKinnon..."

He ignored her and retrieved something from behind his saddle. He held out a limp mass of fur with long ears. "I got ye a bawdy."

Eva's mouth watered. Meat was a luxury, now that she didn't have Keith around to hunt. "Thank you. I'll make soup and share it with you," she said as he handed over the hare.

"Nae need. Connor got one, as well. Crack shot, he." Mac paused and looked her over. "Ye seem a wee bit aff."

She shrugged off his comment. Mac did too much for her already. If she told him all of what had happened, he would spend so much time checking on her safety he wouldn't be able to run his farm. Or he'd talk her into forfeiting hers.

He made a face and gestured at the knife tethered to her waist, then at her sagging apron pocket weighted down by the Colt. "Whit spooked ye, lass?"

Eva sighed. Mac was persistent. If she didn't tell him something, he'd keep pressing her. "Some men came around, looking for an Indian. They didn't find him, so they left."

His eyes took on a sympathetic curve. He'd helped bury Keith and knew every heinous detail. "Some settlers dinnae want land grants given tae Indians. A few are roamin' around, tryin' tae run 'em aff." He placed a hand on her shoulder. "Connor an' I are no' far. If ye feel threatened, fire a shot, an' we'll come tae yer aid."

"Thank you. And thank you for the wild onions you left on my porch the other day."

Mac paused before mounting. "I dinnae bring ye onions." He raised a brow at Connor.

Connor shook his head.

"Must've been Mr. Kramer, then." Dwight Kramer was a bachelor whose grant bordered hers on the other side. "I appreciate you taking Sir Galahad to be shod. I wish you would let me pay you."

Mac swung into the saddle and turned his horse around. "I have clothes tha' need mendin'."

"Bring them by."

He gave a nod and nudged his horse into a trot.

Connor touched the brim of his hat and did the same.

Eva skinned the hare and prepared the meat for cooking. She saved the pelt. It could be traded for supplies to help her make it through winter.

Guinevere was lowing at the gate by the time she set the pot of soup to simmer on the stove. It was milking time.

Eva placed the loaf of dough into her bake kettle and covered it with coals from the fire. The yard was still deserted as far as the eye could see, so she tucked her Colt in her apron pocket and led Guinevere to the barn. If she was going to stay and claim her land, she couldn't let the threat of interlopers keep her from her work.

The act of filling the pail with milk was calming. Her cow was insistent on their meeting times, but she was docile once the milking began. "Thank you, girl," Eva said with a pat to the Jersey's thigh. She hoisted the pail of milk and waddled sideways out of the stall.

An approaching horse in the distance drew Eva up short. She couldn't see well enough to identify the rider, though he was too small to be Mac; and if it was Connor dropping off the clothes, he was coming from the wrong direction.

Eva carried her pail to the porch of her dugout and freed her hands to defend herself.

As the horse trotted closer, she could make out a face. Dwight Kramer, the man whose land bordered hers on the west, had come to call.

"Evenin', Mrs. McCabe."

Eva pasted on a pleasant smile. "Good evening, Mr. Kramer."

"Dwight, please."

She let the comment go unanswered. He'd grown friendly since her husband died, and she'd rather not encourage him. "What can I do for you?"

"I heard there was an injun out this way, and I wanted to check on you."

"I'm well, thank you."

He lifted his face and sniffed. "Smells good. Whatcha cookin'?"

"Rabbit stew. I used the wild onions you left on my porch."

"Onions? Oh, right."

If she had a dollar to spare, she'd bet it on the timing of his visit—that it wasn't by chance. Dwight often showed up just in time for supper. "Would you like some?"

"I don't want to impose."

Yes, you do.

Eva got control of her unkind thoughts. Dwight didn't mean any harm. He'd been a good neighbor, especially after Keith's death. "It's no imposition. I'll fix you a bowl."

He insisted on carrying the milk pail and followed her into the dugout. She'd rather eat on the porch in full view of God and man, but a deep chill now gripped the air when the sun went down.

Besides, Dwight was a gentleman. And widows were granted some latitude, especially out here on the barely settled frontier.

While he put the pail in the root cellar, she ladled up two bowls of soup and buttered the hot, crusty bread. "I'm afraid water is all I have to offer," she said as they sat down at the table, and she placed her napkin in her lap. It wasn't entirely the truth, but her stores of coffee and tea were so low they'd soon be gone.

He tucked his napkin in his collar and smiled. "Water's fine."

Dwight wore his mousy brown hair parted in the middle and combed to each side, in a blunt horizontal line at the level of his earlobes. She itched to take the shears to it every time he took off his hat. But dimples that appeared in his cheeks when he smiled and eyes that twinkled with mischief more often than not mitigated its unattractive style. No matter how sad Eva was, or irritated that he'd showed up unannounced, he always had her laughing by the time he left.

Dwight had an endless supply of silly tales to tell. Whether his stories were truth or fiction was up for debate.

Eva bowed her head and blessed the meal.

Dwight offered up a hearty amen and dug right in.

She hid her ravenous appetite beneath her manners, except the rule of pausing to make conversation. Thankfully, Dwight seemed too hungry to care.

He sopped the last drops of soup from his bowl with his bread then sat back holding his stomach. "That was tasty. You're an exceptional cook."

"Thank you. I'm glad you enjoyed it." She hoped he wouldn't ask for seconds. It was an unchristian thought, but starvation was a real possibility during the harsh winter months to come, if she didn't ration her food. "I noticed someone mended my fence on the far side of the field," she said to change the subject. "Was that you?"

Dwight shook his head. "Nope." A dimple appeared in one cheek. "Though I'd claim responsibility if that would make you think better of me."

Eva grinned. He probably *would* take credit for just about anything if he thought he could get away with it.

He wiped his mouth and laid his crumpled napkin on the table. "Have you given any more thought to what we talked about last week?"

"Some." He'd asked her if she would forfeit her grant to some friends of his, in exchange for them paying her travel expenses back to North Carolina. "It's tempting."

"The surveyor would have to split your land between the two of them, but it could be done."

"Don't you want me as a neighbor?" she joked.

"You're a fine neighbor. I just hate to see a woman trying to run a farm alone."

Eva tilted her head in concession. Even she doubted her ability to hold up to the task. "Mac McKinnon offered another solution, and I must say I'm seriously considering it."

"What's that?"

"He suggested I raise cattle or sheep instead of crops. It would satisfy the rule of cultivation without more plowing. I'd only need to plant enough for feed."

Dwight raised his brows. "It could work, I suppose. Except you'd still have work to do, especially once your herd got large."

"Mr. McDougall had a fix for that. I could earn money as a teacher or seamstress. Come spring, new settlers will be arriving by the day. They'll need teachers for their children, and the bachelors will need someone to make and mend their clothes. It would be a quicker source of income than growing a herd. Then, with the money I'd earn, I could hire men to run the farm and eventually prosper from that, too."

"Sounds awfully ambitious."

"Maybe. But, even if I forfeit, I can't travel till spring. I have the winter to make up my mind."

"That, you do." Dwight rose. "Thank you for supper." He put on his hat and coat. "Is there anything you need done before I leave?"

"No. But you're kind to ask."

"Well, goodnight, then."

Hatchoq sat by the stream on the widow's land and tossed bits of roasted salmon to the cats that had gathered. The cave the man had mentioned when he'd cornered Hatchoq the previous week was not the only place to hide.

A portion of the waterway curved sharply through a grove of trees and bush so thick that, even leafless, it provided cover. So did the hole he had dug in the side of the bank. A mass of tangled branches concealed its entrance, and the thick walls of earth kept him from freezing on nights he couldn't sneak into the widow's barn.

He would have to find a better solution. The temperature had been mild, but heavy snows would return. So would the men hunting him.

He should have fled these lands already, but the woman's plight softened his heart. She toiled in the fields, stumbling under the weight of heavy equipment until she was weary. He had decided to camp on her land and provide whatever help he could without being discovered.

Some of the settlers wanted him dead, yet he couldn't convince himself to leave.

The cats sank into a crouch and flattened their ears. They backed up several steps then scattered. Whatever had alarmed them was between Hatchoq and his hidden hole.

He willed his breathing to slow. Panic never won a battle.

There was no time to bury the evidence of his presence, but that could be an advantage. If the predator was an animal, food would distract it. Either way, he would need to make a quick escape and leave no tracks. But in which direction?

Hatchoq tossed dirt onto the small fire and scooted backwards, into a thick mass of brush. He had left his horse in a clearing to the south. The animal would not give his position away; it had been trained to remain silent under almost any conditions. But if Hatchoq didn't reach him before he was spotted, they'd both be captured.

He looked up at the trees and eliminated climbing. The limbs were too small to support a tree-to-tree traverse, and the barren branches offered little concealment.

To the east and west of the stream lay wide-open pastures and fields. Going south and getting on his horse was his only option.

Step by silent step, Hatchoq picked his way through the woods. When he had put some distance between him and his abandoned camp, he paused to listen. He hoped for the growls of a wolf or a panther. But instead, he heard muffled voices.

He would be forced to trade invisibility for speed. The remains of the fish would make the men pause to search the immediate area, but they would not stay there long.

Hatchoq snapped some twigs and left some tracks in an eastward direction, as a ruse, then backtracked and turned south. He moved slowly at first, so as not to leave any evidence, then he increased his pace. The only chance he had was to reach his horse before the men reached him.

He could hear them getting closer, but they were forced to stay out of the thickest part of the trees because of their horses. Hatchoq ignored the gouge of thorns and branches as he sped forward, trying to gain ground. The brush ahead was thin, so he paused to listen.

One of the horses was nearly even with his location. But it was to the west of the stream, on the neighboring farm.

He closed his eyes and called upon the power of the spirit. The men would have the path to his horse blocked within minutes. He could reverse course and run back to his hiding place in the wall of the bank. But, now that they had found his camp, the men would continue to search there. He would be trapped even if he was not discovered.

If he had his arrows, he could covertly fell them one by one, but he had left his quiver tied to his horse. He could fight the men by hand, even outnumbered, but his knife was no match for their guns. The only way out was to do something they didn't expect.

Hatchoq eased to the eastern edge of the thicket until he had a view of the widow's pastures. The men had all passed him now, one to the west, and two to the east—her side. He waited until they went farther then crept out onto the snow-dusted clearing. He crouched low and moved slowly. He would not risk hiding in her barn again, but if he could make it to one of the structures, he could use it to shield his movement and keep going.

The woman's cow raised its head and mooed.

Hatchoq froze. He held his breath and looked over his shoulder.

The two men on horseback gave no notice, so he kept going.

A few steps more, and he would be halfway to the barn. The men would likely find his horse, but he could sneak back at night and retrieve it. He just had to escape and hide until then.

The woman's horse walked out of a shelter in the next pasture. He paused then tossed his head and whinnied.

Shouting erupted from the men—he had been spotted. They turned their horses and spurred them into a gallop.

Hatchoq changed course and bolted for the horse. He could use it to get away. He had enough of a lead, and he had befriended the animal during his many nights sleeping in the barn.

His long stride ate up the ground between them, the men's cries urging him on. He leapt over the fence and raced toward freedom. The men were closing in, but once he was mounted, he could move faster than all of them. The widow's horse was young and strong and would be running without the weight of a saddle.

Hatchoq had mere seconds to hoist himself onto the horse's back and gain control if he had any hope of outrunning his enemies. He reached the animal and grabbed for its mane.

The horse blew and balked.

Hatchoq lunged for a second try, but the horse sidestepped again, making him lose his balance. He cursed the ko and his own misjudgment as his body hit the dirt. Horses raised by whites were trained to be mounted from only one side.

"Get him!" one of the men shouted.

The other dismounted and grabbed Hatchoq as he scrambled to his feet.

Hatchoq fought with all his might. If he could break free, he might get another chance to mount the widow's horse and ride away. He could leap onto its back faster than these ko could climb back onto their saddles.

The man who had grabbed him landed several painful blows. Hatchoq let him think he was winning, then he feinted a punch with his left fist, followed by a solid strike with his right. His opponent's gaze went unfocussed, and he swayed. The second man stood a few feet away, keeping his distance.

The third man was nowhere in sight, but crossing the stream would have delayed him.

Hatchoq decided to make a run for it. He turned to flee and found himself staring down the barrel of a gun.

He held up his hands and took a step back. "Let me go. I will leave these lands."

"Lyin' injun. You should'a left when we chased ya the first time."

The gunman was squinting into the late afternoon sun, so Hatchoq used that to his advantage and weaved sideways.

The gun fired with a deafening blast. Searing pain sliced through his left shoulder. Someone behind him knocked him to the ground. The man who'd shot him kicked him hard in the stomach and the ribs.

Hatchoq curled up on his side, trying in vain to draw a breath. All three men were kicking him now, landing blow after blow. The one in front bent down and swung the gun. White light exploded inside Hatchoq's head. Then the pain ebbed, and everything turned black.

Chapter Three

The walk home from Mac's farm wasn't long. Mac and Keith had built their dugouts near the dividing line between their grants on purpose. Eva had returned the mended clothes, but instead of feeling glad that she'd repaid a debt, she felt confused.

Both Mac and Connor claimed they hadn't fixed her fence. They'd also denied leaving cooked meat and tanned animal pelts for her to find. And she'd already ruled out Dwight.

Other settlers in the area were apparently responsible. Word of her husband's death had had four months to spread. No harm had been done, and nothing had been taken. According to Mac, she should accept the gifts and be grateful.

Eva paused and glanced around as she emerged from the path. The pop of gunshot had sounded to the west while she was visiting. The men had debated investigating but decided it was someone hunting, probably Dwight.

Guinevere was waiting for her by the gate. She put the cow in the barn and did the milking, then went in search of Sir Galahad. Winter weather fueled his spirits, and he liked to play hard to get.

"Gally," she called, from the edge of the pasture. "Come on, boy. Time for your feed."

He appeared in the distance, prancing toward her with his characteristic cold-weather flair.

Eva went inside the gate, halter and lead line in hand.

He came up to her, but then he backed away and tossed his head.

"I know you'd rather stay out here and frolic." She reached up with her free hand and stroked his broad neck. "Easy, boy. Let me put on your halter."

The horse cooperated, albeit grudgingly.

"One of these days," Eva said as she led him back to the barn, "when I can afford more horses, and you have friends to huddle with in your shelter, I'll be able to leave you out." He would've been fine by himself tonight—mild temperatures were still holding—but a change of routine on the cusp of a blizzard wasn't wise. If she gave her stubborn Gally an inch, he'd take twenty miles.

Sir Galahad shied when they neared the barn. He could be headstrong, but this wasn't like him.

Eva stopped and stroked his muzzle. "What's wrong, boy? Don't you want your feed?"

After some petting and crooning, he followed her in.

Eva got him settled into his stall. One space over, Guinevere lay, resting on a bed of straw. "Goodnight, Gwenie."

The log box by the hearth needed refilling, so Eva detoured to the woodshed on the side of the barn. She came to heel-digging stop and gasped. The same Indian who had grabbed her lay before her in a bloody heap. By the looks of it, he'd been shot and beaten. His whole body was covered in lumps and bruises, and deep red stains tainted the ground all around him.

The band of men hunting him must've caught up with him. But why had they left his body here?

Once she got over her revulsion, Eva picked up one of the logs and nudged his foot.

He didn't respond.

She tossed the log aside and hugged herself, torn between anger and unease. She had enough work to do without burying a savage. He didn't deserve to have a final resting place on her land, and the ground was too hard to dig a grave anyhow.

It was cold, and she was tired. She'd leave him there tonight and ask Mac for help in the morning. With any luck, wolves would drag his body away.

The ground glistened with frost the following morning but no new snow. Eva milked Guinevere and turned her and Sir Galahad out to graze. She still resented having a body dumped on her farm, but time and rest had cooled her anger.

Haltingly, she ventured to the woodshed. She'd fallen asleep, listening to the wolves last night. That wasn't unusual. But they had sounded awfully close. If they *had* carried him off, she hoped they'd taken all of him.

She braced herself and rounded the corner.

What in the world?

The Indian hadn't moved—his body looked the same as it had the night before—but every barn cat she had was on him! Some were lying on top. Others were curled up next to him, tucked in the curves and valleys of his lifeless form.

For a moment she feared they might have been feasting on his corpse, but every single feline looked as if he or she had been peacefully sleeping.

The cats ran when Eva neared, save a couple who stood their ground and meowed until she shooed them away.

"Oh, Mac," Eva muttered. "I hate to burden you with this after all you've done for me." For a moment, she considered asking Dwight instead, to save Mac another interruption to his day.

No. The situation called for discretion. Mac and Connor were the only people she knew without a doubt she could trust.

Eva took her gloves from the pocket of her apron, pulled them on, and buttoned up her coat. The air was calm, but the walk to Mac's house would be a cold one.

A strange sound sent a tingle over her skin. It sounded like a groan.

It couldn't be. He was dead.

Even if the Indian had been alive when she first found him, he'd have frozen to death during the night.

Eva took a step closer and looked him over. He didn't appear to be breathing, and his skin was pasty white, even his lips. She must be hearing things.

A groan came from his direction again, and his fingers moved.

Dear God, he's alive!

Chapter Four

Eva stared at the injured man on the ground.

Part of her wanted to leave him there to die. The other part of her—the part that had replayed his actions over and over—knew he didn't deserve such harshness. He'd grabbed her and scared her, but he'd only done it to save himself. And, in the process, he'd spared her, too.

Love your enemies, do good to them which hate you.

Inasmuch as ye have done it to one of the least of these my brethren, ye have done it unto me.

Eva got a piece of oilskin from the barn and rolled him onto it. It took all her strength to slide him along the ground, to the dugout. She didn't have a plan beyond bringing him in out of the elements and bandaging his wounds, but she needed to get him warm and hidden. She needed time to think.

The Indian groaned, and his eyes fluttered open for a moment when his body jostled over the threshold. She feared what he might do if he awoke, but his injuries appeared severe enough to make him weak.

Eva placed him in front of the fire and put some water on to heat. She dabbed his wounds with a moistened cloth and washed off the dirt and the blood. A large lump stood out from the side of his forehead. Bruises and scrapes covered his body.

As the fire warmed him, blood began to run freely out of the bullet wound in his shoulder, from holes in both front and back.

He was so pale. He couldn't stand to lose more.

She put pressure on the holes and held it firm until the bleeding stopped, then she tied bandages in place. When she rolled him part way over to check his back, he moaned as if he were in pain. Boot-shaped bruises covered his ribs, so she bound them.

None of his limbs appeared misshapen. That was good. But now that his skin was warming up, his cheeks and the tip of his nose had turned a dusky pink.

Eva checked his hands. The same odd hue covered his fingers. Some of his toes were also affected. Having lain out in the cold all night, he'd be lucky not to lose them.

A pang of guilt pinched. She should have looked closer the evening before, instead of walking away in anger.

Eva placed a folded cloth beneath his head and covered him with a blanket. There was nothing more she could do for him but watch and wait.

She went about her chores, glancing at him from time to time.

He slept so soundly she worried that he might have died. More than once, she lifted the edge of the blanket to assure herself he was still breathing.

By late afternoon, the Indian still showed no signs of waking, so Eva saddled Sir Galahad and rode to Mac's to ask his advice.

He dropped what he was doing and immediately followed her back.

She showed him where the Indian had been dumped then took him inside.

Her patient hadn't moved.

Mac walked to where he lay and looked him over. He nudged him with the toe of his boot a little too firmly for her liking.

"*Mac.*"

"Jus' makin' sure he's no' pretendin'."

Eva pointed to the lump on the Indian's head then lifted the blanket and exposed his bruises. "He had boot marks all over his ribs, so I bound them."

"Whit's th' bandage fur?"

"He was shot in the shoulder."

"Did ye take tha bullet oot?"

"It went all the way through."

She invited Mac to join her at the table and poured him a cup of weak tea.

He narrowed his eyes at the Indian. "I ken why they beat 'im, but I cannea fathom why they dumped 'im here."

Eva stirred her tea, unnecessarily, and fidgeted with the saucer. She needed to tell Mac the whole story, even if it made him angry. "He's been here before."

"Tha Indian?"

Eva nodded and looked up at him through her lashes. "I told you a group of men came looking for him...but that isn't all of the story."

Mac sighed and sat back in his chair. "Oot with it, lass."

"When I went to the barn to muck the stalls that day, the Indian grabbed me from behind. He covered my mouth and told me to stay quiet."

The muscles in Mac's jaw clinched tight, and she could hear his teeth grinding together.

"He dragged me behind the wardrobe and held me there while two men searched the barn. A third man searched the dugout. They were looking for him, and also me."

"Ye? Whit in God's name fur?"

"Someone had told them a widow woman lived here. The way they spoke..." Eva felt her cheeks heat. Then the warmth drained from her face. "Their comments were crude. If they had found me..."

His face flushed red. "Did they say who told them aboot ye?"

"Someone named Whitey."

Mac closed his hands into fists and opened them a couple of times, as if he was trying to keep his anger under control. "I dinnae ken any *Whitey*." He released a measured breath. "Keep goin'"

"After the men left, he uncovered my mouth and let go of me. I didn't even know he was an Indian until I turned around and saw him. He spoke English."

"Did he say anythin' else?"

Eva's face warmed again, but this time with shame. "He told me he hadn't come to hurt me, and he thanked me."

"Fur whit?"

"For not making noise and giving him away."

"An' he left?"

Eva nodded. "I chased him with the pitchfork. But, looking back, I didn't need to." She fiddled with the handled of her cup then met Mac's gaze. "He kept me safe, and now he needs help. What should I do?"

Mac stayed quiet for a long moment. "He cannae defend himself, an' willny be able tae fur some time. I dinnae ken why he was dumped here, but I can assure ye he wis left fur deid. Tha men ridding this land o' natives dinnea take prisoners."

"We have to hide him—at least until he heals."

"Aye. He's better aff if everyone thinks he's deid." Mac scrubbed his hand across his beard. "We shuid move 'im tae ma house."

The thought was tempting, but— "His injuries are too severe. I don't think he should be moved. Not yet."

He eyed her with a brooding frown.

"Maybe in a few days," she offered, "if he survives."

"Vera well." Mac stood. "I need tae go turn tha soil an' cover tha blood. I'll stable Galahad an' milk Gwenie while I'm oot there."

"Thank you."

He cast a stern glance at the Indian and left.

While he was gone, Eva looked her patient over. His lips were beginning to crack, and his tongue was dry. She filled a cup with water and spooned a small amount into his mouth.

Nothing happened at first, but then his throat moved with a swallow.

Eva dribbled more water, a little at a time, until the cup was empty. She followed that with a small amount of broth.

He drank it, but he never woke.

She wrapped up some fresh bread to send home with Mac, for his trouble, then she sat in the rocker and wondered at the will of the Almighty. Why had He taken her husband? And why had He allowed this native to end up here?

Mac stooped through the door and stomped the snow from his shoes. "I'll be stayin' tha night."

"You don't need to do that."

"I dinnae want ye here alone if he wakes."

"You saw the place where he lay, all the blood. If he even wakes at all, he won't have the strength to sit up, much less harm me."

"Well, let me send Connor, a' least."

Eva gestured at her straw tick bed. "Where is he going to sleep? Which one of us will take the rocker or the floor? Connor's leg pains him enough." She stood and placed her hand on his forearm. "I'll be all right. I'm capable of defending myself against an invalid, should it come to that."

Mac looked as if he wanted to argue. He glared at the Indian then blew out a breath. "I'll bow tae yer will, but I dinnae like it, lass. Ye keep yer gun at tha ready, and dinnae let yer sympathy fur tha man stop ye from usin' it."

Eva startled awake from a sound sleep. Her fingers curled around her gun, as her gaze focused on the Indian in the pale morning light.

He still lay in front of the hearth, motionless, except for the faint rising and falling of his chest.

The fire had burned down to embers, so she got up to tend it. Cold air chilled her when she pushed aside the quit. She might have noticed sooner, but she'd slept in her clothes. On her way to the wood box, she lifted the corner of the torn paper window and looked out. The land glistened with a thick blanket of new-fallen snow.

What if she'd left the Indian outside a second night?

She shuddered at the thought.

Eva went and stood at his feet. She needed to move him, but where? There wasn't a good place to put him that gave her access to the fire. She wanted to be able to see him if he moved, but she needed to keep him hidden.

After a long moment of deliberation, Eva dragged him to the empty span of floor between the far side of the bed and the wall. Sod provided better insulation than the wooden walls of the kitchen, and the space was out of the line of sight of the door. She wouldn't be able to see him unless she walked around the bed, but there was enough space beside his pallet to kneel and tend to him.

She got the fire going and built up one in the stove. After fortifying herself with bread and tea, she gathered some supplies and lit a lamp. The room had warmed enough to uncover him.

The bandage on his shoulder was partially soaked with blood, but it had dried. She'd leave it for now. Changing it might start the holes bleeding again. The color of his bruises had deepened, and the skin on his fingers and toes was beginning to blister. She prayed it wouldn't turn black.

Eva brought a spoon of water to his lips and paused. Something was different about his face. She put the spoon back in the cup and brought the lantern closer. A shadow of whiskers covered his jaw. She gently touched the stubble and the blue lines tattooed on his chin.

The Indian sighed.

Eva jerked her hand away and picked up the cup. She wanted him to recover, but the thought of him waking made her shiver.

Gwenie was anxious for her milking by the time Eva made it to the barn. Sir Galahad wasn't much calmer. Before she'd filled the pail, he was whinnying and pawing. "Be patient, Gally. I'm almost done."

Eva wagged the bucket of milk out of the barn and came face to face with a riderless horse. Heart racing, she looked in every direction. Noone was there.

She set the pail down and eased closer. The horse remained calm, so she walked up to him and stroked his nose. His coat was mostly chestnut with white markings, and he wore a simple bridle made of rope. His saddle was unlike anything she'd ever seen. It was covered in tight, furry buffalo skin and didn't have a pommel. She felt the fur pad underneath. It looked like bear.

Something was sticking up on the other side. She rounded the horse and found a bow and a leather quiver of arrows.

Eva glanced around again. She led the animal into a barn stall—saddle and all. His bridle didn't have a bit, so she gave him water and hay.

A small drawstring bag hung beside the quiver of arrows. She loosened the rawhide strip holding it in place and tucked the bag into her apron pocket. The horse was likely the Indian's, but she couldn't be sure. Maybe the bag held clues to the identity of its owner.

Galahad was still in a taking, so she led him to the pasture and let him run free.

"Go tromp through the frigid snow all you like," Eva muttered as she went back for the cow. "I prefer a chair by the fire." She turned Gwenie out then carried the milk to the house.

Her patient was sleeping where she left him.

Eva knelt by his pallet to give him more water and wrinkled her nose. He smelled. The odor reminded her of the sick room where her uncle had languished for weeks after an apoplexy. Until the Indian either died or awoke, she would have to change his bedding and wash him.

Eva rushed through her breakfast of cornmeal mush and milk so she could look through the items in the drawstring bag. She carefully poured the contents onto the table. Out came several coins, a handful of pretty beads and stones, a heavy item wrapped in cloth, a second one in a cylindrical leather case, and several smaller bags that tied closed just like the large one.

The leather cylinder held a small brass telescope, like a sea captain would use. The item wrapped in the cloth was a long thin piece of flint with a sharp edge on one side. She rolled it back up and opened the bags one by one. They contained dried leaves and herbs, some she recognized and some she didn't. She refastened them and peered down into the nearly empty pouch.

A few more items were stuck inside. She reached in and pulled out several feathers. Some were solid brown. Others had pretty stripes of white and black or rich shades of light-brown that reminded her of deer skin. Eva set them aside and lifted the last item out, a folded piece of paper. She carefully spread it open.

A colorful chalk drawing of a fair-skinned woman smiled up at her. Wavy blond hair framed a heart-shaped face, prominent cheekbones, and a slender nose. Everything about the woman was pretty, but Eva's gaze was drawn mostly to her eyes. Faint lines feathered out from their corners, and her light-blue irises were encircled by a dark rim.

Sir Galahad whinnied, and Eva heard someone walking in the yard.

She hurriedly put the items back in the bag and hid it in her sewing basket then stowed her Colt in her apron.

"'Tis only me, lass," Mac called.

Eva's whole body sagged with relief. She went to the door and let him in.

"Where is he?" Mac demanded before she could get a greeting out.

"I moved him to the far side of the bed."

Mac walked over to where the Indian lay. "How wis yer night?" he asked her in a kinder tone.

"I was able to get some water and broth in him, but he still hasn't woken."

"No' at all?"

She shook her head.

Mac rubbed his bearded chin with his fingers. "One o' ma cousins wis out fur a week after hittin' his heid."

"I'm worried he might lose his fingers."

Mac lifted the blanket. "They hevny turned black."

"Not yet."

He lowered the blanket and made a face. "Fetch me some rags an' a bucket tae wash 'im with. An' some fresh beddin'."

"You don't have to do that. I can–"

"A bath wis whit woke ma cousin, an' he came up swingin'. I dinnea want tae risk it."

Eva did as he asked then busied herself making a new pallet out of an old quilt, while Mac stripped the Indian of his leather pants and gave him a passable scrubbing. He tossed a towel over the Indian's hips when it came time for her to help roll him and change his bedding. Her gaze lingered on the Indian's muscular abdomen and broad chest. Even bruised as he was, his body commanded attention.

"Eva?"

She mentally chastised herself for gawking and jerked her gaze to Mac. "Hm?"

"Let's put a piece o' oilcloth under 'im, an' a towel."

Mac rolled him again so she could place the layers beneath his hips. That would keep her from having to change the entire pallet every time, which would save work on laundry day.

He sat back on his heels when they were done. "I still think I shuid move 'im tae ma house."

Eva held a few choice words behind clenched teeth. *He means well.* "Not yet."

"Ye must keep 'im hidden. If anyone asks aboot 'im, say I carried 'im aff an' dumped 'is body over tha falls."

"I will." She stood and motioned for him to do likewise. "I need your advice." She led him to the barn and showed him the horse. "He wandered up this morning without a rider. I think he belongs to the Indian."

Mac examined the horse's tack and the bow and arrows. "Aye. I wouldna bet against ye."

"I can feed him for a time and put him in the pasture with Gally, but what do I say if someone asks about him? I haven't a need for another horse." *Or the means to buy one.*

"First, we need tae hide 'is saddle. That would be a worse thing tae be seen with than tha animal." Mac looked the horse over again. "I see no brands o' marks. I'll put 'im with ma lot an' say he's a gift I bought fur ma wife."

"What if the Indian wakes up? He's going to want his horse."

"We'll worry aboot that then."

Mac removed the saddle and carried it to the tack room, careful not to spill the arrows out of the quiver. Then he retrieved the rope bridle and bearskin pad. They placed a stack of crates in front of the saddle stand and covered it all with a tarp, so the shape wouldn't give it away. "That should do," he said, brushing the dust from his hands. "Kindly loan me a bridle tae lead 'im home."

Eva chose a leather bridle without a bit and handed it over.

"Connor'll be crossin' yer land tae go fishing. Dinnae be surprised if he stops by with some salmon."

Eva fed the Indian thin potato soup along with meat broth and water for two days, and he still wouldn't wake. She began to think his injuries might be worse than she feared, that she was only postponing the inevitable. But how did one know when to give up? How long could a person sleep like this and still regain a productive life?

Mac said his cousin had slept for a week.

She should give this man that long, at least.

Eva busied herself with chores. Mac had brought flour that morning and asked her to make extra bread while he and Connor went hunting. Sunlight gleamed off melting snow today, but a winter storm was coming. He wanted them all to be prepared.

She set the loaves by the fire to rise and retrieved some dried corn from the cellar to make soup. A rustling sound made her pause. The Indian was moving. She set the pot down and walked to the end of the bed.

Eva eased forward until she could see him, but she stayed out of his reach with her hand resting on the hilt of her knife.

His arms twitched under the covers, and his head moved back and forth, eyes closed, as if he was in the throes of a disturbing dream. Now and then, he would mumble, but the sounds didn't make any sense.

"What's wrong?" she asked.

He quieted some but didn't answer.

"Are you in pain?"

The Indian started mumbling again, his eyes still closed, and his voice breathy and rough. Occasionally, she could make out a word, but they didn't make sense.

"*Inchen... nyahwat*," he said then groaned. "I... I..."

"You what?"

"I killed him." His face went slack, and he fell back into a sound sleep.

Eva stood there, staring. He was delirious. He didn't know what he was saying.

A tingle ran over her skin at the sound of an approaching horse. Mac and Connor weren't due back for hours.

She hurried to the kitchen and peeked out the window. *Dwight.* Eva's mind raced to come up with plausible excuses to keep him from coming inside.

She yanked on her coat and stepped out of the dugout, closing the door behind her, as if she were going to the barn. She pretended not to notice Dwight until she was halfway across the yard. "Hello, Mr. Kramer."

He reined his horse to a stop and touched the brim of his hat. "Mrs. McCabe."

Eva shielded her eyes with her hand. "What can I do for you?"

"I have news," he said as he dismounted, "and coffee," he added pulling a bag from his coat pocket. "Do you have time for a cup?"

"I'm sorry. I don't," she said with an apologetic smile. "Too much to do before I get snowed in."

"Oh. How can I help?"

Eva debated giving him a chore. The sooner he left, the better, but she could use the assistance. "I was headed to the woodshed," she lied. "Would you fetch some wood and stack it on the porch?"

"Yes, ma'am." He handed her the bag of coffee, strode to the shed, and loaded his arms with firewood. "I'd be happy to take it on inside," he said as he carried it toward the dugout.

"That won't be necessary." Eva hurried ahead of him and stood in front of the door, pointing. "The wood box is full. Just stack it here, under the eaves."

Dwight did as she asked and made two more trips. "Is that enough?"

"More than enough. Thank you."

"Are you sure you can't spare a few minutes for some coffee?"

"I truly can't."

Dwight scratched the side of his head below his hat brim. "I don't mean to be mulish. What I have to say is... Well... You'll want to be sittin' down."

Eva gestured to a bench Keith had built and placed beneath a nearby oak tree.

Dwight went with her, waiting for her to sit first and leaving a respectable distance between them when he joined her. "I overheard something while I was in town. I debated whether to tell you, but I think you need to know—for your safety."

Eva braced herself. "All right."

"A group of men were bragging about chasing an Indian. They said he'd been camping on your land."

Eva wasn't sure whether to feign surprise, feign fear, or admit prior knowledge. She kept her expression neutral with a hint of concern. "Go on."

"They described him as having long black hair and tattoos on his arms and chin. They didn't say whether or not they caught him, but they were sure he was the one who killed your husband."

A thick lump of emotion clogged Eva's throat. She swallowed hard and found her voice. "How would they know?"

"The Indian dropped something while they were chasing him. I couldn't hear them that well, but I think they said *watch*."

Eva blinked back tears and kept her composure when she'd rather fly off in a rage. Keith's scalp hadn't been the only thing taken. His pocket watch was missing from his body, too. "Thank you for telling me," she said in a quiet voice. Speaking in a near-whisper was the only way to keep the emotion out of it.

"I know this must upset you, but I worry about you. Living here is dangerous, especially for a woman alone." Dwight turned his body so that he was facing her more. "Maybe you should think about going back to Wilmington. My friends are still willing to take over your claim and pay all of your travel expenses."

Eva gripped the bag of coffee tightly in her hands and stayed silent. She was so angry she'd barely been able to make sense of his words. "I don't want to leave."

"You might not have a choice. Well, not entirely. I inquired about claim laws. Widows can't inherit. You'll have to forfeit Keith's half of the claim, regardless."

"Truly?"

Dwight nodded. He removed his hat and tugged at his collar. "The only way to keep the entire claim is to marry."

Eva let out a rueful laugh. "So, wedding one of the many suitors lining up to court me is the only way to keep my land." She swept a hand in the direction of her empty yard. "Tell me, Mr. Kramer, which one should I choose?"

He cleared his throat. "Me."

Eva's mouth dropped open before she could control it. She snapped it closed.

"My timing is less than ideal, but the offer is sincere. Your claim is twice the size of mine. You can't farm it alone. I could talk my friends into taking over my claim instead, and that would free me to prove up yours. Or, rather, ours."

Eva was speechless.

"Please tell me you'll think about it."

"...I will."

Dwight settled his hat back on his head. "I am sorry for heaping all this on you."

"No need to apologize. I prefer plain speech." Eva rose and held out the bag of coffee.

"Keep it. It's the least I can do." He started to walk away and turned back. "I hope you won't wait too long to make up your mind. If that Indian returns—"

"He won't. The men you spoke of must've caught up with him."

"Oh?"

"Someone killed him and left him on my land. Mr. McKinnon carried his body away and threw it over the falls."

Eva tucked the bag of coffee into her pocket. "Good day, Mr. Kramer." She turned and made a beeline for the dugout.

The lie she'd told was about to become truth.

Chapter Five

Eva yanked the Indian's head back and held her knife to his throat, her hand trembling, his pulse tapping against the gleaming tip.

Thou shalt not kill.

She gritted her teeth and growled out her rage. The savage who'd mutilated her husband had murdered him without a second thought, viciously. The Bible also said an eye for an eye. She should slit his throat and gut him, just as he had Keith.

Thou. Shalt. Not. Kill.

Eva grabbed a lock of the savage's hair. With a tortured cry, she began sawing it off in clumps and flinging it into the fire. She should have stood firm on her first instinct. She should have left him in the snow to freeze.

Her blade nicked his neck, his cheek, his ear, but she kept cutting. If she couldn't disgrace him by taking his life or his scalp, she'd do the next worst thing.

When she'd shorn his flowing black locks to a ragged line above his shoulders, she stood back and seethed. The scent of burning hair filled the room like a banner of victory. But it didn't avenge what the savage had done. Nothing could.

Eva gagged on the stench. She clutched her stomach, ran outside, and vomited. She'd taken this traitor in and cared for him. Now she was stuck with him until Mac returned from his hunt. She'd drag him back outside if she hadn't already told Dwight he was dead.

She had no choice but to force herself to make it through the day and give the Indian over to Mac. If he didn't kill him himself, at least he'd get Keith's murderer out of her house.

Eva sheathed her knife and went back inside. She fixed some coffee for herself but gave nothing to the Indian. He mumbled a few times in his sleep throughout the day. She ignored him and did her baking. She could barely stand to look at him and only glanced in his direction as often as she must to ensure her own safety.

The sun set on Eva pacing the yard. Mac and Connor hadn't returned, and it wasn't like them to ride after dark.

She went back inside and paced the tiny confines of the dugout. If she were strong enough to lift the savage onto a horse, she'd carry him off and dump him. She wanted him out!

She marched over and kicked him hard in the leg.

The Indian grunted and opened his eyes.

Eva stumbled backward. He was looking straight at her.

He tried to sit up but grimaced in pain and lay back again. He ran his tongue over his dry lips and cleared his throat. "Where am I?"

Eva's chest heaved with fury even as her heart raced from fear. "In my house—the house of the widow whose husband you killed."

A crease appeared between his brow. "Kill?"

"Yes. My husband. You mutilated him."

"I did not do it," he rasped.

"Yes, you did."

"When did he die?"

"Four months ago."

"Where?"

"You know where!" She snapped her arm out straight and pointed. "Right out there in his field."

"It was not me."

Eva's fists balled at her sides. "Don't lie to me!"

"I am not," he said in a scratchy voice and attempted to moisten his lips again. "I was not in these lands then." He grimaced and pushed himself up on his elbow. "I need water."

The urge to draw her knife and cut his lying throat made her entire body tremble. Eva filled a tin cup with water and threw it at his chest.

He picked up the cup with his blistered fingers and drank the few drops that hadn't spilled then held it out to her. "I am thirsty. Please."

Eva snatched it from him and filled it again. She shoved it at him, sloshing it.

He took it from her and drained it with audible swallows. He handed her the cup and wilted back onto the pallet.

"I can't believe I took you into my home," she grumbled as she returned the cup to the kitchen.

"I did not kill your husband." The Indian's voice was weak, but his words sounded honest. If she didn't know otherwise, she'd think he told the truth.

Eva added a log to the fire then put on her coat. She stepped outside and listened for horses in the distance. The storm was closing in. Flakes of snow had already started to fall. Surely Mac and Connor wouldn't risk making camp on a night like tonight.

She was about to give up and bar the door when a ball of light immerged from the forest and danced toward her, across the pasture. Equine knees and hooves flickered in and out of view, lit by the faint glow.

"Hullo," Mac called. He lifted the lantern and waved it as the horses neared.

Connor did the same behind him.

Eva met them in the yard, bouncing on her toes as much from the frigid air as from excitement. She'd never been so glad for homecoming. "How was your trip?"

"See fur yerself," Mac said as he swung down from his horse. He patted a fine buck tied behind his saddle and pointed to another on Connor's horse. "Show 'er tha bawdies."

Connor reached down and lifted a cluster of hares too numerous to count. "Mac'll claim 'tis due tae his skill," he said with laughing eyes, "but it be mine."

Eva grinned. Connor rarely bragged. But then, hunting was one of few activities that didn't make him feel inferior.

"We'll skin 'em an' pack 'em in salt tonight," Mac said. "Then I'll hang tha meat tae smoke on tha morrow." He stepped closer, and his gaze locked with hers. "How's tha patient?"

"He woke up."

Mac looked as if she'd slapped him. "He dinnae harm ye, did he?"

"No."

He grasped her by the arms and set her aside in his haste to get to the dugout.

"Wait," Eva said. "There's something I need to tell you."

Mac turned around and placed his body between her and the door.

Eva motioned for Connor to join them. The muffled groan that came from him when he dismounted broke her heart.

He pulled his walking stick from a scabbard on his saddle and headed their way.

She waited until he hobbled over to where they stood and lowered her voice. "Dwight Kramer paid me a visit. Don't worry," she added when Mac opened his mouth to speak. "I kept him outside. And I said what you told me to say about disposing of the Indian's body. I *had* to. Mr. Kramer overheard some men in town who claimed they'd chased the Indian on my land." The men exchanged a look, and she braced for their reaction. "They said he murdered Keith."

Fury lit Mac's eyes. "Give ma five minutes with tha bastard. I'll return tha favor."

Connor put a hand on Mac's arm and said something to him in their language that calmed him a little. Connor turned to Eva. "Ye said he wis awake. Can he speak?"

"Yes."

"Did ye confront him with tha information?"

"Of course, I did."

"Whit did he say?"

"He claims he didn't do it."

Mac growled.

"Patience, *bráthair*. Dinnae rush tae judgment. Dinnae trade yer future fur a momentary taste o' revenge."

That banked the fire in Mac's eyes, but he still seethed. He turned and shouldered his way into the dugout.

Eva hurried in behind him.

Mac kicked the Indian's leg. "Wake up."

The Indian jolted awake with a grunt and stared up at Mac with round eyes.

"Ye murdered ma friend. Tell me why I shuidny do tha same tae ye."

The Indian looked over Mac's shoulder, at her, then back again. "It was not me."

Eva glared down at him. "Liar. You confessed it in your sleep. You said 'I killed him'."

The Indian frowned and stared absently into the air.

"You mumbled something about *inches*," Eva went on, "and then you said *I killed him,* plain as day."

Shame clouded his expression. Then he raised his gaze and looked her in the eye. "I killed a man before I came to these lands, but he was not a white. I did not kill your husband."

Mac glared at him with narrowed eyes. "Get up. Ye're comin' with me."

"*Mac,*" Eva and Connor said at the same time.

He gave a dismissive wave of his hand. "I willny kill 'im. I plan tae toss 'im on 'is horse an' send 'im on 'is way."

The Indian pushed himself into a sitting position, but it was clear he was too weak to stand.

Eva looked up at Mac. "He's not well. Sending him out in this storm..." The sudden wave of compassion surprised her, but Mac's plan was tantamount to murder.

"An' dinnae forget aboot tha game an' tha horses," Connor said. "We'll be lucky tae sleep t'night as it is."

Mac grumbled something under his breath. "Vera well. Ye an' Eva start skinnin' tha bawdies. I'll tend tae 'im."

Eva put some water on to heat and set out some towels. "He hasn't eaten. There's corn soup on the stove."

She followed Connor out and glanced back as she closed the door.

"Mac willny harm 'im," Connor assured.

Eva hung the men's lanterns on the porch to light a space for them to work. "I almost did."

"Aye, but ye settled fur a scalpin' o' sorts."

"I wish I'd stuck with my original plan."

"Are ye sure aboot that?" He untied the cluster of hares while Eva brought crates for them to sit on.

"Mr. Kramer's story was very convincing."

The corner of Conner's mouth lifted. "Dwight Kramer is a passable fellow, but I've known 'im tae bear false witness on occasion. Petty things, mind ye. Nothin' that would get a man hanged."

"He has a slippery side," Eva conceded, "but he's a good neighbor. He told me the men described the Indian's tattoos and said he'd dropped an item belonging to Keith when he was fleeing."

"Whit item?"

"His pocket watch."

Connor studied her for a long moment in the light of the moon that was cresting the tops of trees. "Yer anger is plain tae see, but so is yer doubt. Dwight made a damning case against this Indian, yet yer not sure ye believe it. Why?"

Eva exhaled a tired breath. "Because he kept me safe when he could have harmed me."

"And...?"

"And because I sense he's telling the truth." Tears stung the backs of her eyes. "But what if I'm wrong?"

"Whit if yer not? No man deserves tae be condemned on hearsay."

Eva busied herself skinning hares.

The day had left her weary, but she'd work through the night if that's what it took. A few more hunts like this one, and they'd have enough pelts to trade for supplies and enough meat to last till spring.

Connor finished his pile and eyed the two deer he was unable to lift, much less hang. He gritted his teeth and pushed himself up from the crate with the help of his walking stick. "I'll go hurry them along. We need tae salt these bawdies down."

Eva finished her lot soon after and entered the dugout.

Connor was seated in the rocker, and Mac was rummaging around in the cellar.

The Indian sat on his pallet, propped against the wall, eating from a bowl. He paused and watched her as she crossed the room to the cellar.

"I found yer barrels," Mac said, "but I cannea locate yer salt."

She pointed to the salt box sitting in the corner.

Mac ruffled the side of his hair and gestured in the Indian's direction. "Was that yer handiwork?"

"It was either that or his throat," Eva muttered.

Mac chuckled. He carried the barrels and the box to the kitchen and checked his watch.

"Ye can hang tha deer high an' butcher tomorrow," Connor said.

"Nae. I want it done."

Once both deer had been butchered and all the meat covered in brine, Eva dished up some soup and served it with one of the loaves of bread. "You can take him," she said to Mac, indicating the Indian. "I don't want him here."

"Vera well, but it'll have tae wait till mornin'. His shoulder bled when I changed tha bandage, an' he cannae ride. I'll fetch 'im with tha wagon when I come fur tha meat."

Eva nodded and accepted her fate,

"Mac has tae go tend tha animals," Connor said, "but I'll stay tha night."

"Ha. Whit's left of it," Mac remarked between bites.

"You don't have to do that,' Eva said to Connor.

Mac speared her with a look that squelched any urge to disagree. "Aye. He does."

Eva opened her eyes to a silent, cold room filled with paper-dulled sunlight. She took in her surroundings before moving a muscle. The fire had burned to a pile of embers. Connor was snoring on the bed to her left, and Mac was nowhere in evidence.

She curled her hand around the Colt in her pocket and stood up from the rocker. Blue eyes met hers from across the room.

The Indian was sitting against the wall, wrapped in a blanket. "Good morning," he said softly.

Pleasantries wouldn't reach her lips for him, so she gave a single nod. She added wood and stoked the fire, all the while watching him out the corner of her eye.

She risked turning her back to light the stove and put some coffee on to boil. He was still sitting in the same place, gazing at her placidly, when she brought him a cup of water. Even so, getting close enough to hand it to him sent a nervous ripple through her skin.

He took a generous sip of the water and cradled the tin cup in his hands. The redness was leaving his skin, and the blisters had turned to scabs. "Where is my horse?"

Eva set a chair close enough to the Indian's pallet that they could converse without waking Connor. "What does your horse look like?"

"He is brown and white."

"Mr. McKinnon took him to his farm, to care for him."

"What about my pants?"

"They're here, under the bed."

He drank the rest of his water and handed her the cup.

Eva couldn't stop staring at his eyes. The morning light drew his irises tight, turning them the color of Forget Me Nots. The pale disks stood in sharp relief to outer rings of midnight... which might as well have been iron manacles, the way they held her captive.

She'd seen those eyes before. They were the same as the woman's in the drawing.

Eva put away his cup and dug in her sewing basket for his bag. "Is this yours?"

"Yes."

She handed it to him and sat back down. "We hid your saddle in my barn."

He opened the drawstring and peered into the bag.

"I looked through it," she confessed, "trying to determine if the horse belonged to you. And because I was curious."

He removed one of the small bags of herbs. "May I have some hot water?"

Eva brought a cup of steaming water to him then poured herself some coffee and buttered them both some bread. "I saw the drawing," she said as she served him and sat back down. "Who is the woman?"

He added some of the dried leaves from the bag to the cup of hot water. "She is my mother."

That must be how he knew English so well. "You have her eyes."

He blew into the cup and took a cautious sip.

"What did you put in the water?" she asked when he didn't respond.

"Herbs to help me heal."

They ate their bread in silence, save for the crackling fire and Connor's soft snoring.

"I am called Hatchoq," the Indian said. "What is your name?"

"Eva McCabe." The surname brought Keith to mind and snapped the few strands of rapport that had started to form. Whether or not Hatchoq had killed her husband, she could never consider *any* Indian a friend.

Eva returned the chair to the table and called Connor's name until he roused. "I'm going to the barn to tend the animals," she said as she pulled on her coat and tied a knitted wool scarf around her head.

Connor winced and scooted himself to the edge of the bed. "I can do it fur ye," he said in a sleep-roughened voice.

"I appreciate the offer, but"—she lifted her chin in the Indian's direction—"he's awake, and I could use some fresh air. There's bread and coffee on the stove."

A thick blanket of snow coated the farm. The skies had cleared enough to let the sun through, but a dark bank of clouds lined the horizon to the north.

Mac drove up in the wagon as Eva was crossing the yard to milk Gwenie, puffs of white coming from his horses' nostrils with every breath.

"Good morning," she called as he climbed down. "Or should I say good afternoon?" It took all she had not to laugh.

"Ye're aff yer heid."

"And you're late. Have you had breakfast?"

"No' yet."

"Go join Connor."

He went inside then appeared in the barn a few minutes later, a thick slice of bread in one hand and a steaming cup of coffee in the other. "Tha storm'll likely snow us in fur days. Shall I send Connor tae stay with ye?"

"That's not necessary," Eva said from the milking stool. "I can manage." She had plenty of wood, and she'd fasten a length of rope to help her find her way to the barn. "Just stack some wood inside the dugout, in place of the Indian's bed, before you go." She paused and looked up. "You *are* taking him with you, aren't you?"

"Aye. I'll hide 'im till he's well enough tae ride."

Mac polished off the bread and saluted her with his cup. "Where'd ye get the coffee?"

"Mr. Kramer gave it to me." Eva carried the pail of milk out of the stall. "He tried to talk me out of proving up the claim on my own. He said two of his friends were willing to pay my way back to Wilmington in exchange for my claim."

"Does that interest ye?"

She shrugged "I told him I'd think about it."

He took the pail from her, set it aside, and placed his hands on her shoulders. "Yer family tae me an' Connor, but neither one o' us would blame ye fur givin' up yer claim."

A sad smile curved Eva's lips. How she wished Keith was still alive. They would have had such fun, farming and raising children alongside the McKinnon's.

She slipped out from under Mac's hands and got the fork to muck the stalls. He took it from her and took over, so she sat on a crate. "I still haven't given up on the idea of raising cattle instead of crops, although Dwight thinks that's futile, too. And even if I were successful, I'd have to forfeit half the land."

"Whit fur?"

"A widow can't inherit her husband's portion."

"Hmph," Mac grunted.

"He did offer a third option."

"An' that would be?"

"Marriage."

Mac stopped shoveling. "Tae whom?"

"Him."

He let out a laugh. Then he turned serious and narrowed his eyes. "Do ye fancy him?"

"No." Her heart wasn't capable of fancying anyone yet.

"Did ye turn 'im down?"

Eva shook her head. "I didn't give him an answer."

"Take yer time, lass, an' do whit ye feel is best. Dinnae let anyone sway ye."

Chapter Six

The storm snowed them in for weeks, letting up for a day or two then coming back even stronger. Eva prayed every night for fair weather. Sir Galahad was fit to be tied. Even Guinevere was getting antsy. Worst of all, their store of feed was getting low.

Reading and sewing helped Eva fight boredom. Some days she relished the quiet. There were benefits to the absence of menfolk, such as not having to cook large meals or sleep fully dressed. But day after solitary day in the dugout was a taste of years to come if she decided to prove up her claim alone.

Mac paid her a visit each time the storm ebbed. During the last, he'd said Hatchoq was well, and that he'd bring him to get his saddle as soon as the storm subsided.

Anger and fear plagued Eva. Her intuition warred with the knowledge he'd possessed her husband's watch. They might very well be letting her husband's killer go. While she appreciated Connor's plea not to rush to judgment, she didn't share his optimism or Mac's gradual change of heart. After a mere few weeks, both men had unequivocally acquitted Hatchoq.

What if the Indian was lying and biding his time until he was strong.

How would they feel if he came back and murdered her?

Sunny days finally persisted. Eva trudged through the snowmelt and turned a giddy Sir Galahad loose in the pasture. His antics were so extravagant, she paused after latching the gate and laughed.

She started to go back for Gwenie and stopped herself before she turned around. Footsteps were approaching behind her. She pretended to keep watching Galahad and slid her hand into her pocket.

Her fear ratcheted higher. She'd forgotten her gun.

Eva slid her hand up and over, to her knife.

"Mrs. McCabe," Dwight called out.

She whirled around. "Mr. Kramer, you startled me!" He was standing in her yard, holding a fat dead duck. "It isn't polite to sneak up on people." Little did he know, he'd risked his life, sneaking up on her.

"I apologize," he said, walking closer and lifting up his kill. "I went hunting this morning, and I thought you might like some fresh meat after that storm."

"I hope you're not giving up your only bird." Especially if he expected her to cook it for him.

"Nah, I got three."

Eva held the bird up and looked it over. "That's a nice one. I haven't had duck in a while." She laid it on the makeshift table she used for butchering. "Would you like a cup of coffee?"

"I wouldn't turn it down."

Eva started toward the dugout then remembered Gwenie. "I need to let the cow out first."

"I'll do it."

Eva brought the cups out and met Dwight coming back from the pasture. Mac had said he would send Connor to scout before bringing Hatchoq, but she'd try to keep Dwight outside if she could. "I can't get enough of this sunshine," she said, sitting on Keith's bench and inviting him to join her. "I hope you don't mind."

Dwight sat and took a sip of his coffee. "Not at all. I was going a mite batty myself." He looked sideways at her with a hopeful smile. "Should I take your choice of location as a sign?"

The steam curling around Eva's cheeks felt hotter. "Your offer—both offers—are tempting, but I haven't made up my mind."

Dwight took another sip of coffee instead of responding, and she wondered whether it was to restrain irritation or cover disappointment.

"It's a big decision," she added.

"It is," he conceded.

She smoothed a wrinkle in her black crape skirt, wishing she'd put on her veil when she went to pour the coffee. "And I'm still in mourning."

He stared at the ground and nodded. Then he looked up at her. "I'll understand if you don't want to marry, but please give my friends' offer some serious thought. This is a dangerous place for a woman alone."

Dwight rose and set his cup on the bench. "Thank you for the coffee, Mrs. McCabe."

Eva watched him go, feeling a pang of guilt for all the times she'd had an unkind thought. Dwight wasn't perfect, but he was trying his best to help. "Thank you for the duck," she called to his back.

He kept walking, raised a hand, and waved.

Eva finished her coffee and went to work, butchering. One by one, the barn cats gathered along the periphery. Now and then, she tossed them scraps.

She paused and cocked her head toward the sound of hooves in the distance. Connor must be doing his reconnaissance.

She continued cutting the usable parts from the carcass. If Connor took his time, she could make duck stew before they arrived. She could feed him and Mac, and, though it irked her, she could send Hatchoq off with a full belly. It was the Christian thing to do.

The barn cats flattened their ears and slinked off to hide at the sound of approaching horses.

There was no clatter of a wagon.

Connor must've found the area deserted. The plan had been to conceal the Indian and his saddle under a tarp until he was far enough away to put it on his horse without being seen.

In any case, the stew would have to wait. Hatchoq wouldn't starve, though. Mac had likely loaded him down with enough hard tack and pemican to last for days.

Eva rinsed her hands and walked out to greet them. Her smile fell as they came into view.

Three strangers were riding up her drive.

She squared her shoulders and lifted her chin. Bravado was her only weapon. Her gun was still in the dugout, and her knife was yards away, on the butchering table. "Good morning. What can I do for you gentlemen?"

One of them smiled. "I have a few ideas."

Eva's blood ran cold. She'd heard that voice before, in her barn. He was one of the men who'd chased Hatchoq.

The second man smirked, but the third one eyed her with a bone-chilling glare.

Eva fisted her hands to steady the shaking. "Get off my land."

"Or what?" the first man said in his southern drawl. He swung his leg over his horse and dismounted.

"Or my neighbors will send you to meet your maker. They're due to arrive any minute."

He started walking toward her. "I didn't see anyone," he tossed over his shoulder. "Did you, Jay?"

The second man shook his head. "Nope. Not a soul." His familiar southern lilt made Eva nauseous. The last man had to be the mean one.

What was she going to do?

The men were tall and muscular. She couldn't fight off one of them, let alone three.

Eva began backing up slowly and thinking of things to say. If she bought herself enough time, she could get within grabbing distance of her knife.

Southerner number one kept advancing, and southerner two—Jay—dismounted.

The mean one stayed on his horse and glared, the corners of his lips turning up in a sinister curve.

Eva's heart beat so hard she could hear it pounding in her ears. Even if she reached her knife before they reached her, there was no hope of fighting them off. Tears gathered in her eyes as realization landed like a boulder in her gut.

The only way to save herself was to take her own life.

She increased her pace when her whole being wanted to savor her last few moments on earth. Every second counted if she was going to draw the knife across her throat before one of them snatched it away.

The sound of a rifle being cocked echoed to her right. "Stop right there."

Thank God! It was Dwight.

All three men looked to him, and the southerners lifted their hands.

"You have two minutes to get out of my sight," Dwight told them, "or I start shooting."

The southerners backed away and got on their horses.

"Go on. Git!" Dwight barked as they turned their horses and spurred them into a gallop. "If I catch you on her land again, you're dead."

Eva nearly crumpled to the ground with relief.

Dwight set his gun aside and rushed over to her. "Did they hurt you?"

She shook her head and blotted her eyes with her sleeve. "They would have if you hadn't come along."

"It was providence, I guess. One of the ducks came loose from my saddle shortly after I left, but I didn't notice till I got home. I heard them when I came back to get it." He tilted his head and studied her. "Are you sure you're all right?"

Eva pulled herself together and dried her eyes. "Yes. Thank you, Mr. Kramer."

He hadn't scolded her or pressed her for an answer to his offer, but reproach lurked amid his concern.

Maybe he was right. If she were smart, she would forfeit her land and go back home.

But *this* was home. It was all she had of Keith.

Dwight hadn't moved, despite her reassurance.

"Mr. McKinnon will be by later," she said to nudge him along. "In the meantime, I'll keep my gun handy."

He picked up his rifle and tipped his hat. "Good day, Mrs. McCabe."

Eva sheathed her knife and gathered up the meat and organs she'd cut from the duck. She dumped it on the table, barred the door, then sat down and cried. Really cried. Not the bridled little trickle she had shed in front of Dwight.

What if he hadn't arrived when he did?

She'd be dead or wishing she was.

Once her bouts of sobbing subsided, Eva got up and occupied herself with the mindless motions of cooking. She seasoned the duck and added what few vegetables she had to the pot. The potatoes and carrots were spongy but passable. She went through four onions before finding one that wasn't completely rotten.

The state of her root cellar weighed more heavily than Dwight Kramer's admonishing gaze. She needed to make up her mind. Spring would be here soon.

Eva slid the pot of stew to the back of the stovetop to cool just as a wagon pulled into the yard. It was likely Mac, but she looked before assuming.

Connor led the way. He waved from atop his horse. Hatchoq's horse trailed behind him on a lead, and Mac was driving the buckboard, sitting next to a man she didn't recognize.

Eva went out to meet them, puzzled and a bit perturbed. How were they to speak freely with a stranger in their midst? And why would Mac risk anyone seeing the Indian or his saddle?

"Greetings, lass," Mac called.

"Mr. McKinnon... Mr. McDougal," Eva said with a nod to each. She smiled politely at the stranger. "Who's our guest?"

"I told ye," Connor said to Mac, looking awfully full of himself.

"Aye," Mac replied. "Ye did."

Eva planted her hands on her hips. "What are you two going on about?"

Mac hooked a thumb in the direction of the stranger. "Look closer."

She didn't know what good it would do, but she looked the man over again. His shirt and trousers were that of a typical farmer, unembellished and worn. A straw hat covered most of his hair, and he had a full dark beard.

When she focused on his face, the stranger didn't flinch. He held her gaze and waited.

Eva narrowed her eyes as she cataloged each detail. Tan skin. Aquiline nose. His features seemed familiar, yet she couldn't place him—until she looked into his eyes. Forget-me-not blue encircled by midnight.

The stranger was Hatchoq! And if she hadn't known otherwise, she'd have thought he was white!

Amusement twinkled in his eyes.

"Shall I pick yer jaw up fur ye, lass?" Mac asked.

"Catchin' flies, she is," Connor added with a chuckle. "Ye owe me a whisky, *bráthair*."

Eva snapped her mouth shut and invited them in for lunch. She needed to sit down.

Hatchoq followed the men in and removed his coat and hat. Someone had repaired her ragged cuts. His hair was neatly shorn and combed back. It was several inches long on top, but short enough at the sides to show his ears. He flashed a smirk in her direction and sat at her table without invitation.

Eva let his boldness go without comment. Instead, she frowned into the stew pot as she dished it up. When she served the food and took her seat, the men tucked into their meal with gusto.

She stared at her steaming bowl. She didn't have an appetite.

"Is it tha company?" Mac asked.

Eva looked up at Hatchoq then cut her eyes to Mac. "No."

"Whit, then?" Despite the serious question, mischief glittered in his eyes. "I get a wee bit nervous when tha cook willny eat her own food."

She took a small bite to assure him he had nothing to fear, then she turned her attention to Connor. "Did you see anyone during your ride this morning?"

"I dinnae go. *Isaac*, here," he said with a nod to Hatchoq, "could ride through tha middle o' town an' no' raise any brows."

Well, hadn't *they* become fast friends.

"His saddle would," Eva grumbled.

"Aye," Mac agreed. "He could say he acquired it in a trade, but tha quiver an' bow..."

"They never saw 'im ridin'," Connor countered. "Only on foot."

Mac shook his head. "It's too risky." He looked at Eva with gentle eyes. "I hoped ye might be willing tae sell me a saddle."

The only extra she owned was Keith's.

Eva aimed a contemptuous glare at Hatchoq then cut her eyes back to Mac. If it got the Indian off her land and out of her life, it was worth it. "You can have it."

"Are ye sure, lass?"

Eva nodded. "What do I do with the old one?"

Mac sat back in his chair. "That's been a topic o' discussion. Tha quiver an' bow could be concealed in a bed roll easily enough, but tha saddle..."

Sadness seeped into Hatchoq's expression. It was clear he didn't want to part with it.

"We could burn it," Eva said with a perverse sense of delight.

All three men shot her a look of appalled revulsion so severe she flinched with shame.

"That willny be necessary," Connor said. "If Isaac is unwilling tae part with it, he can send us a note when he gets settled. We can crate it up an' have it shipped."

"I'm not storing it *here*," Eva spat like a spoiled child.

"Ye willny have tae," Mac said with an edge of longsuffering to his voice. "I'll take it with me today." He studied her then glanced back absently, toward the window. "Did ye take Gally fur a ride this mornin'?"

"No. Just turned him out in the pasture."

He looked to Connor then her. "I saw fresh tracks. Did Dwight come calling? Is that whit has ye stirred up, lass?"

That man was too perceptive by half. "Dwight brought me a duck early this morning."

"And," Mac pressed.

"And it's a good thing he was near." Eva ignored the three sets of eyes that had narrowed on her and picked at her food. She set her spoon aside. "After he left, I heard someone riding in the distance. I thought it was Connor, so I didn't pay any mind. Half an hour later, horses rode into the yard. But it wasn't you."

Eva slid a hand below the level of the table and pressed it to her queasy stomach. "It was the same men who chased Hatchoq the day he hid in my barn. I knew it as soon as I heard their voices."

Connor's eyes went wide, and Mac swore under his breath.

Hatchoq's eyes lit with alarm, but a look of fiery determination quickly replaced it.

Mac fisted the edge of the table. "Did they threaten ye?"

Eva nodded.

"Whit did ye do?"

"I reached for my knife—"

"Ye dinnae have yer gun?"

"No, but Dwight had his rifle. He heard them when he came back to get a duck he'd dropped, and he chased them away."

"Ye need tae make up yer mind, lass. Either take Dwight as yer husband or take tha stage back tae North Carolina."

"She could stay with us," Connor offered.

Eva shook her head. "Thank you, but no. If I leave, someone will steal my claim. I might barter it, but I won't give it away for free."

Connor frowned. "We need tae send *Isaac* on 'is way. Tha farther from here, tha better."

"Aye."

"No," Hatchoq said.

"Yes," Connor countered. "I'll be sad tae see ye go, but it's no' safe fur ye here."

Hatchoq speared him with a look that could cleave a boulder. "It is not safe for *her*. I will stay."

Eva's mouth dropped open.

"I dinnae—"

"*No, you will not*," Eva barked, glaring at Hatchoq. "Just who do you think you are?"

He glared right back. "The man who brought this threat onto your land."

"So?"

"So, *you* are the one in danger. They think I am dead."

Eva scoffed and looked to Mac.

Mac tilted his head and raised a brow. "He has a point."

"You can't be serious!" The one thing she would *never* choose is letting the Indian stay. She'd rather abandon her claim.

Connor looked at her cautiously. "Ye have tae admit 'is argument has merit."

Eva shot to her feet and threw her napkin on the table. "No!" She stormed out the door without her coat.

Mac followed her out and came to stand beside her at the paddock.

She crossed her arms over her chest and kept staring straight ahead.

"I understand yer animosity," he said. "Truly, I do. But Connor an' I have had weeks tae assess this man's character. He dinnae kill Keith. I'd wager me first *bairn* on it. Hatchoq is no' without sin, but he is an ethical man."

"I didn't think injuns had any ethics."

"Eva…" Mac chided. "Ye know that's no' true."

He was right, but she stared at her feet and huffed out a derisive note anyway.

"Look at me, lass."

She pressed her lips together then grudgingly turned and faced him.

"Forget all yer problems fur a moment—all tha obstacles. Whit is it that ye *want*?"

Eva swallowed back the urge to cry. "I want to stay on my land. This was Keith's dream, and it's all I have left."

"All right, then. I have no doubt ye could prove up, but ye'll need help tae do it, an' ye need a protector. Wedding Dwight would give ye both."

"It would also give him ownership of me and my claim." Eva dropped her arms to her sides and fingered the folds of her skirt. "But then, what does it matter. I can't inherit Keith's half anyway."

"That might change. There's talk o' granting widows' rights."

"There is?"

Mac nodded. "If it comes tae pass, would ye regret wedding Dwight?"

"I don't want to marry anyone. Not yet."

"Then don't, but ye still need a protector. Seems tae me yer choices are forfeit yer claim or let Hatchoq stay."

Eva's chest sparked with indignation. "Living with a man out of wedlock would ruin my reputation."

"So, dinnae live with 'im. Treat 'im as ye would any hired hand. Build 'im a shack." Mac rested his arm on the rail and locked gazes with her. "Ye have *years* tae work yer land before it's time tae prove up. Give tha laws time tae change, if that's whit ye choose. But doon't try tae do it alone."

Eva sighed and nodded. She attempted to rub the chill from her arms, to no avail.

Mac held his arm out in invitation.

She let him put it around her shoulders and draw her against his warm side as they walked back to the dugout. "You're a human furnace. If Allison doesn't banish you from the bed in summer, she should."

"Aye," he said with a chuckle. "But come winter, she presses her frigid feet tae ma back." His expression turned wistful. "I miss those feet."

"Will you send for her this spring?"

He let out a sigh that bordered on a tortured groan. "I want tae."

"Then do."

"Allison has it easy in her sister's house, an' she's safe. I miss her fiercely, but I want whit's best fur her."

"Being with her husband is what's best. Trust me on that."

Mac opened the door to the dugout and followed her in.

Eva ignored Connor's and Hatchoq's stares as she crossed the room. She stood in front of the fire until she'd warmed herself.

"Well," Connor said when she turned around, "whit's tha verdict?"

"Hatchoq can stay for now. But not here." Eva gestured in the direction of the pasture with a flutter of her hand. "He'll need to build a shack of some sort."

"I can sleep in the barn," Hatchoq said. His confidence bordered on arrogance, and it was disquieting.

"I suppose that would work," she conceded. "If you stay, you'll be expected to work and hunt."

He gave a single nod.

"Ye'll also be expected tae come tae Eva's aid, should anyone threaten her safety," Mac interjected. "Even if it means givin' yer life tae save hers."

Hatchoq didn't even blink. He simply nodded again.

"In return," Eva said, "we'll protect your identity."

"In that case," Connor said, "ye'd better start callin' 'im by 'is other name."

Eva crossed her arms over her waist. "Calling him Isaac alone won't do. Not only isn't it proper, he'll need a surname if it's to be believable."

"I have one," Hatchoq said. "It is Shaw."

"In that case, Mr. Shaw, lunch is over. Get to work."

He didn't argue or flash her an angry glare. He got up from the table and put on his hat. "What would you have me do?"

"The stalls need mucking. You can start there."

Mac watched Isaac walk out the door. "I think ye made a wise choice," he said to Eva after he left.

Eva stared at the door. "Time will tell." She turned to her friends and smiled. "You have work to do. Go home."

Mac stood. "How much dae ye want fur Keith's saddle?"

"Keep your money. I'll let Mr. Shaw use it on loan. When his show of masculine pride wears off—and it will—he'll abandon this place on his own beloved saddle."

Connor shared a look with Mac and pushed himself up with a groan. "Thank ye fur tha meal, Mrs. McCabe. It was delicious."

"You're welcome. For all you two have done for me, it's the least I can do. Would you like me to box up the rest of the stew so you can take it home?"

"Best save it," Mac said. "Ye have a ranch hand tae feed."

For now. "If he sticks around, what do you advise I raise? Crops, cattle, or sheep?"

Mac paused before putting on his hat. "Ask Hatch—I mean Isaac—'is opinion. Not only will he be doin' tha work, he's lived aff tha land 'is entire life. See whit he has tae say on tha matter, an' then we'll talk."

Chapter Seven

Feminine footsteps sounded behind Hatchoq in the barn. He stopped filling the stall with fresh hay and turned around.

Eva stood there, dressed from head to foot in black, staring at the pitchfork and keeping her distance.

He set the fork aside and looked at her expectantly.

"Mac took your saddle, to hide it. There's one in the tack room that should fit your horse." She stood straighter and lifted her chin. "It was my husband's. I expect you to take care of it, and I want it returned to me when you leave."

"What should I do when I finish the stalls?"

"Refill the wood box in the kitchen and..." Her gaze flicked away, lighting on one thing after another as she apparently searched for an answer.

He kept his face neutral. Barely. It was hard not to smile at this dainty woman determined to be bold.

She finally made eye contact, appearing resigned and somewhat embarrassed. "I haven't decided what to do with the farm. Mac suggested I ask your advice." A bit of boldness crept back in. "We can discuss it when you're done with the stalls and the wood. Then I want you to observe how I tend to my animals this evening and see if Guinevere will let you milk her."

Hatchoq inclined his head in response.

Eva tucked a loose strand of pale hair behind her ear and waited, as if she might have something else to say or wondered if he did.

"Mrs. McCabe," he said when she turned to leave.

She looked back over her shoulder, wariness mixed with curiosity in her pale blue eyes.

"I will take good care of your husband's saddle."

She blinked then gave a subtle nod and left.

Eva looked up from her mending when the wood chopping ceased and the sound of boots approached the dugout and stopped at the door. Hatchoq—no, *Isaac*; she needed to start thinking of him as Isaac, lest she slip and give him away—must be ready for their talk.

A knock sounded. "I am finished with the wood."

"Come in." She set aside her mending and stood, smoothing the wrinkles from her skirt.

Isaac opened the door and entered then looked at her expectantly. His demeanor wasn't threatening, yet he had an air of confidence that never went away.

He'd gained weight during the weeks he spent at Mac's. His clothes hid his warrior's body, but the image had long been etched into her mind.

Eva gestured for him to take a seat at the table. "Do you prefer coffee or tea?"

He removed his coat and hat. "Whatever you are having will do," he replied as he sat.

"Tea, then." A slight shiver ran down Eva's spine as she turned her back to him. She would have to master her fear. Isaac was staying, at least for now. And, though she would be safely locked away from him at night, they would take meals together.

Eva served their tea and joined him at the table. Her eyes were drawn to his hands as he picked up his cup. They were masculine and broad at the palms. His fingers were in proportion, yet they were long and had an elegance about them.

Isaac sniffed the tea and tested the temperature with a cautious sip. He sat back in his chair and looked at her. His gaze was calm, but the fearlessness within it was unnerving.

"How much has Mac told you about me?" Eva asked.

"He said you moved here with your husband last year, and that your husband planned to plant crops and sell the surplus."

"That was the plan," she said wistfully. "I want to stay and prove up the claim, but Keith had only plowed a portion of the fields before... Mac suggested I raise cattle or sheep instead. I could produce enough feed in the existing fields to grow the herd."

Isaac didn't reply, just took a sip of his tea. His self-assured gaze wasn't the only thing unnerving. His comfort with silence was, too. But then, a man who was slow to speak could usually be counted on to give well-thought-out advice.

He took another sip of tea and set down his cup. "That plan is good. I recommend cows over sheep. Do you have a bull?"

"No. But Mac does. I would have to save money before buying cows."

"How would you do that?"

"By going to work as a seamstress or a teacher." He didn't respond, so she went on, "My husband died before he could plant the fall crop. I sold his horse, and still, I've used all my savings to make it through winter." Eva stared into her tea. "Save for the charity of neighbors, I would have starved."

"Have you considered raising horses?" he asked as though she hadn't just demeaned herself with talk of poverty.

"No. But I have no one to break them."

He raised a brow.

"I mean I didn't." And if he left, she would have to hire a replacement. But that would be the same no matter what she chose.

"I am capable of the task."

"I'd have to save money for horses, too."

He reached up and rubbed at his shoulder, the one that had been shot.

A pang of guilt hit Eva. She hadn't thought about his injuries when she'd assigned chores. Chopping wood must've been excruciating. "Are you in pain?"

"Some."

"Would your herbs help?"

"I do not need them." He lifted his cup and took a leisurely sip.

Eva downed the remainder of hers and decided to go all in. "What do you think I should choose?"

Isaac rested his hands on the table in front of his cup and interlaced his fingers. "I can plow the rest of the fields, but the seeds will be at the mercy of the rain.

"The lands where I was raised border a river. We planted in the fertile fields nearby and let the rising of the river water our crops. The best I could do here is divert some water from the stream. But I will do it if that is what you choose."

"What about cattle and horses?"

"Just as with crops, those are only worth as much as you can get at sale. But the outcome is less dependent on the weather."

"Do you recommend one over the other?"

"Cattle would be easier to raise. Horses would be more profitable, especially war horses," he added with a notable change in his tone.

"Is there a market for those?"

"Yes," he said darkly. "And it will grow in years to come."

"You sound as if you hope I won't choose that."

"My way of training horses is different. It will be noticed."

Judging by the look on his face, that wasn't all. "Is that the only reason?"

"The horses might one day be used against my people. But, as I said before, I will do whatever you ask."

Eva frowned. "Why are you willing to do so much for me?"

A look of genuine empathy softened Isaac's eyes. "Because your sadness hurts me."

He rose. "If you have no objection, I will go to the stream and fish until milking time."

"Um... No. I mean yes. Go."

Eva sat motionless long after Isaac walked out the door.

She made some corncakes to go with the fish then went to work on the list of seeds she would need for spring—seeds she had no money to buy.

She set her pencil aside and breathed a weary sigh. Even with help, proving up her land would be a grueling, uphill battle without any promise of success.

Isaac knocked on the door and brought in three gutted salmon that he'd skewered on a small branch. "I will wait for you in the pasture."

Eva set the fish aside to cook when she returned and got Gally's bridle and lead line. When she reached the fence, Isaac was already in the pasture, walking alongside her headstrong horse. "Did you put him under some kind of spell?"

Isaac paused and eyed her, obviously confused and possibly offended.

"Sir Galahad doesn't like being in the barn," she explained. "Some days, I can barely get his bridle on. How did you make him follow you?"

"I did not force him. I spoke to him, and he chose to obey." Isaac took the bridle and slipped it over the horse's head, clipped on the line, and handed it to her.

Unbelievable.

He paid attention as she instructed him on feeding Gally then went back out with her to get Guinevere.

The cow followed him just as calmly and let him milk her, as if he did it every day.

Isaac brought the pail and set it at her feet. His gaze wavered then met hers with a look of resolve. "I camped near your stream when I first arrived. Your animals know me because I have slept many nights in your barn."

The realization that he'd been that close without her knowledge sent a wave of queasiness rippling through Eva's entire body. But he'd never harmed her, even though he could have done whatever he wanted any of those times.

Numbed by a mixture of shock and relief, she picked up the pail. "Supper will be ready in half an hour."

Hatchoq knocked on the door of the widow's dugout and waited for permission to enter. She had accepted his confession surprisingly well, but that was before she had time to think it over. He braced himself for rebuke and possible dismissal.

She looked up at him with a shy smile as he removed his hat and hung it by the door. "I hope I cooked the fish properly. I usually fry them in a pan."

He peered down at the platter. They were roasted well enough.

She brought a bowl of corncakes to the table and two cups of tea then sat and bid him to do likewise. "I'm sorry there isn't more. The vegetables in the cellar have all gone to ruin."

"This is plenty." During years his clan endured drought, this would have been viewed as a feast.

As they ate in companionable silence, he matched his manners to the widow's, which brought to mind his mother. She had encouraged his father to raise him as part of the clan, but she insisted on speaking English to him and teaching him the ways of her people.

The widow was being subtle about it, but she was watching him. She'd been doing so ever since he'd returned.

Hatchoq set his fork aside and stared at her. It was rude, but he wanted to see how she would react to such scrutiny. Provoking a reaction from this woman gave him pleasure.

She blinked at him and made a quick assessment of his empty plate. "Do you need something? More tea, perhaps? If you're still hungry, I can make more corncakes."

"I have had enough."

Hatchoq picked up a piece of paper lying on the table. It looked to be a list of seeds with a tally of the cost to buy them. "Is this what you want planted this spring?"

The widow stared at him, her lips slightly parted. "You can read."

"I can also write."

Her face flushed pink. "I'm sorry. It's just... You're not what I expected."

"You expected an ignorant savage," he said without spite.

"No!" Her hand flitted from her plate to her saucer, adjusting their position on the table unnecessarily. "At first, maybe," she conceded, fingering her collar then tucking her hand in her lap. "But now that I've spent time with you, I know you are neither."

He held no animosity toward Eva—especially after learning that her husband had been murdered—but her flustered reaction gave him a moment of satisfaction.

Hatchoq handed her the list of seeds. "You have chosen well."

Her expression brightened then it wilted along with her shoulders. "By the time I can save enough to buy the seeds, it will be too late to plant."

Hatchoq took his napkin from his lap and placed it on the table. "No, it will not. Excuse me." He went to the barn and got the bundle of pelts he'd tanned while staying with Mac.

Eva was clearing the table when he returned. Her eyes rounded when he handed them to her.

She untied the bundle and examined them, flipping over a few and scrutinizing the backs.

The widow met his gaze with a look of astonishment. "It was you. *You* were the one who left the pelts on my porch. And the onions."

Hatchoq nodded.

"Why?"

"I saw you struggling."

"We were strangers. You didn't owe me anything."

Hatchoq lifted his uninjured shoulder and let it fall. "I gave it in return for camping on your land." He pointed at the pile of pelts. "They are yours now. Trade them for supplies."

Eva stared at them then at him. "Thank you, Isaac."

The sound of his English name struck his pride like an arrow but flowed like a warm summer breeze over his ears. He wished he could hear his mother say it once more, but that could never be. He'd murdered a member of his clan. He could never go home.

A gust of night-chilled wind blew through the cracks and the torn paper of the windows. Hatchoq went to the hearth and built up the fire.

He turned to find the widow standing a few feet away, staring at him.

"Why are you doing all this for me? When we first met, you were dressed as a warrior. Wouldn't you rather be with your people?"

The truth was a source of shame—that his clan would shun him if they learned what he had done, but worse, that he didn't fully want to be with them. A part of him was drawn to the ko.

Though he had denied it for years, white women appealed to him most. Maybe it was that his mother's face had been the first face he had seen. Maybe it was that she loved him without conditions. Or maybe it was a curse imparted to him by the spirits of her people. Whatever the cause, he longed to be free of it.

Wouldn't you rather be with your people?

Yes.

He'd stayed because the widow needed help. She deserved his protection. He'd also stayed because she stirred his passion, and he hated it.

Hatchoq pulled her rocking chair closer to the fire. When she lowered herself into it, he sat on the floor with his knees bent and his ankles crossed. Chairs were convenient for some tasks, but he preferred sitting this way.

"I did not plan to stay when I first came to these lands," he said. "I saw you had more work than you could do alone, so I camped here and did what I could to help." He paused before telling her more. It shamed him to speak of his defeat. "After the men beat me, I had many dreams while I slept. One vision came to me many times. I saw a doe surrounded by scorpions. When you said the men returned and threatened you, I realized you were the doe."

The widow hugged herself and rubbed her arms as if to brush away a chill. "Do you know the men who attacked you?"

"No. Only that they were the same ones I hid from in the barn."

"Did you get a good look at them?"

He shook his head. "I remember running from them then waking up on your floor."

She seemed oddly relieved.

"Do *you* know them?" he asked.

"No. I didn't realize who they were until I heard their voices. But now I know what they look like," she added with malice seeping into her tone.

"Word of my death has spread. I doubt they will return."

Her frame relaxed, though her relief was tempered with frustration. It made him wonder whether the revenge she hungered for was on her behalf or his.

The widow's shoulders tightened, and she rubbed one hand with the fingers of the other. "Why did you leave your family...? Was it because of the person you killed?"

"Yes."

She held his gaze despite the fact his answer clearly unnerved her.

"My people help wagon trains cross the river. They used me to communicate. A single wagon came later in the year than the rest. It belonged to a man who had rescued a young woman from the wilderness. He was taking her to find her family."

The widow's tension eased as he told the story.

"We traded with the man for our assistance. The negotiation went well until a member of my clan asked for one of his horses. The man was unwilling to part with it. He could not pull his wagon without the horse."

"Did they fight?"

"No. The woman offered him a box of colored chalk instead. He agreed and helped them cross, but he still wanted the horse. He had more greed than other members of my clan. He hid and followed the man and the woman after they crossed the river. If I had not stopped him, he would have killed them and stolen their horses."

"It sounds like a justified killing. Wouldn't your clan understand?"

"No." Hatchoq considered explaining why but decided against it. She would shun him just as they would if he told the truth.

She looked as if she wanted to argue the point. The way her lips pressed together to hold in her words made him do the same thing with his to keep from smiling.

"Tell me about your mother," she said.

"What do you want to know?"

"How..." The widow fingered the button at her collar. Her gaze darted away—the same way it had the times he'd caught her staring at his chest—then she looked at him again and returned her hand to her lap. "How did she and your father meet?"

"My mother married a fur trader and came west with him in 1828. She was captured by the Comanche when they murdered her husband and stole his pelts."

The color drained from the widow's face.

"My clan took possession of her in a trade soon afterward."

"You speak of her as if she's a *slave*."

"She is. But being a slave among the Mojave is better than being one among the Comanche. They would have raped her and tortured her."

The widow flinched at his blunt speech, but it cooled her righteous anger.

"My father fell in love with her, but he could not have her."

"Why?"

"The men in my clan do not marry captives. They believe it will bring sickness to the land. My father resigned himself to abide by this."

"What changed? I mean something had to, didn't it?" Her polite way of asking if he was the product of some clandestine act.

"My mother saved the life of a Mojave child who was thought drowned. This elevated her standing in the clan, and my father was able to have her. His first wife accepted his choice."

The widow's mouth dropped open. "Your father has two wives?"

"No. He divorced one and married the other."

"How awful!" A flush of pink burst across her cheeks. She fingered her collar again and drew a deep breath. "I mean it can't have been easy for his first wife."

"The Mojave do not have the same beliefs as whites when it comes to divorce. A husband or wife can choose to leave the marriage at any time."

Her face turned red, and revulsion simmered in her eyes. She didn't need to speak her thoughts for him to hear them.

Immoral, God-forsaken heathens. That's why people call you savages.

Hatchoq let the mental sting subside and continued. "I was born in 1830. Most of the clan had accepted my mother by then, but some still feared her presence. They went to the leaders while she was in labor and demanded I be buried as soon as I was born."

The widow's revulsion turned to shock then pity.

"My father pleaded with them not to harm me. No trouble had befallen our people as a result of my mother's presence, and—even though I was a half-breed—he accepted me as his son.

"The leaders granted his request and let me live."

"Are you his only child?"

Hatchoq shook his head. "He had a son with his first wife. My mother gave birth to three daughters after me."

"Were your sisters allowed to live?"

"Yes. My father accepted them, so the clan did as well."

"What about his son, your half-brother? Are you close?"

"We were when we were young."

"He must harbor some resentment toward your father... for his choice to leave."

"He didn't at first. This is the way of our people. But as my brother grew, so did his anger. When word of your government's Indian Removal law caused friction between my mother and the clan, my father showed mercy toward her, and that further angered him."

The moon had risen high enough that its light shone through the torn paper window.

Hatchoq added another log to the fire and stood. "It is late. We should rest." He moved the widow's rocker back to its usual place, near her sewing basket. "If you are not opposed, walk the fields with me tomorrow. It is time to choose what you will raise on your farm."

Chapter Eight

Eva buttoned up her coat and tied her scarf snuggly around her head before leaving the dugout the next morning. A clear sky stretched out before her, but frigid air chilled every inch of exposed skin. She stuffed her hands in her pockets and shivered as she went to meet Isaac in the yard.

His hands were bare, and his coat was unbuttoned, yet he seemed unaffected by the cold as he led her to the fields. He began with the one nearest the stream.

Isaac squatted down, scooped up some of the dark loamy soil, and let it sift through his fingers. "This field is best for carrots, radishes, and cabbage in the spring. In summer, I advise planting melons, beans, potatoes, and squash."

She nodded her agreement when he looked to her for a response. A couple of items came as a surprise, but the rest she would have chosen also.

Isaac stood and walked toward the stream, to the place where the vegetation changed. He pointed to a spot several feet before the flat land began to slope. "The water rises to here in the spring. I will dig trenches, so some of it can spill over and irrigate the plants." He turned and pointed to a spot farther down. "I will dig a deeper trench there," he said, tracing his finger along the horizon, "that will carry water to the other fields. These trenches will not help in times of drought. But when the water level is high, rain falling upstream will irrigate your crops, even if it does not fall on your land."

"That makes sense." It *more* than made sense. His plan was clever. Perhaps she'd raise grain instead of livestock after all.

Isaac led her past the paddock, to the edge of Gally's pasture, overlooking the hayfield. "If you choose to sell grain, this field can be expanded. If not, the meadow beyond could be fenced and used for grazing." He turned and pointed to a stretch of bush-covered land behind the paddock, between it and the tree line. "If you raise horses, I will need a second enclosure large enough for training. That area could be cleared and fenced for such use."

"Will one choice require more work than the others?"

"No. A grazing pasture wouldn't need to be plowed, but it would need to be fenced."

Eva gazed out over her land. Its vast beauty filled her with awe. Then thought of the effort it would take to cultivate sucked the wind from her sails. She wasn't a quitter, but she wasn't sure if proving up would be worth it.

If the law didn't change, she would toil for years to forfeit half.

Isaac began walking across the fallow hayfield at a gentle pace.

She followed, silently sorting through her options.

"You seem troubled," he said.

Eva looked up into blue eyes framed by a furrowed brow. Isaac's concern was so blatant, her next breath stalled in her chest. "No matter what I choose, there will be so much work."

"You will not have to do the work alone."

"Livestock can take ill or be stolen. Crops can fail. What if I make the wrong choice?"

Isaac stopped walking and faced her. "You cannot make a wrong choice."

"Yes, I can."

He shook his head. "Your land is good for livestock or crops."

"But—"

"You worry in vain. Regardless of what you choose, you cannot know the future."

Eva pressed her lips together and exhaled through her nose. She didn't know whether to be perturbed or relieved.

Isaac motioned in the direction they had been traveling. "Come."

He led her to the edge of the field, where it bordered the meadow. "If you choose to raise animals, your herd will be small at first. Part of this meadow could be farmed for a year or two then converted to pasture. If the crops failed, you would still have the animals. And if you failed to bring the animals to market, you could sell the surplus hay and grain."

"What if they both failed?"

Isaac's mouth curved into a taunting half-smile. "What if they both thrived?"

Eva's hand itched to slap the smirk off his face, but she deserved it. She was being a ninny. The risks of proving up were nothing compared to those she'd taken when she loaded all her earthly belongings into a wagon and came west.

"I like your idea," she said and began walking again. "I suppose all that's left is to choose horses or cows."

"Horses would bring a higher price per head."

"But they would need to be trained. Giving your identity away is not a risk I'm willing to take."

He grimaced as if he wanted to argue, but he gave a single nod instead. "I will prepare your land for cows."

"Cows and crops."

The lumpy furrows under Eva's boots smoothed into solid footing as she crossed into the meadow. Its gently rolling hills spread out before her and touched the horizon. Yellowed winter grass dotted the ground, but come spring, a sheet of vibrant green would sprout and ripple in the breeze.

"I will hunt until I have enough pelts," Isaac said from behind her. "Then we can go to Cedar Junction and trade them for cows and seed."

Eva caught her lip between her teeth. "Do you think that's safe?" she asked as she turned around.

"Hunting?"

"No. Going into town."

"I went with Mac and passed for ko."

"What is ko?"

"It means white."

Isaac lifted his gaze and looked past her. "Come. I found good land for an orchard." He led her along the edge of the meadow then turned south, toward a field that had been cleared of rocks and stumps. He kept talking as he walked, his words fading into a distant buzzing.

Eva stopped and stared at the dirt a few inches from her boots. The earth formed weathered rows that ended where she stood. Her hands started shaking. Tremors worked their way up her arms and through her chest until her whole body was trembling. This was the place Keith had been plowing when he was murdered.

Rain had long since washed his blood into the soil, but time could never wash away the memory. Eva clenched her hands and shut her eyes in vain. The gruesome sight was forever seared on her mind like a brand.

"Mrs. McCabe?"

Something brushed her arm.

Eva batted it away with a whimper.

"Mrs. McCabe...? What has upset you?"

Warily, she turned her head toward the sound of the voice and slowly opened her eyes.

Isaac had returned to stand beside her. A frown deeply creased his brow, and his gaze roamed her face with uncertainty.

She hastily brushed tears from her cheeks.

Comprehension smoothed his brow. "This is where your husband died."

"Not died—murdered. Keith was *murdered*."

The tremble of despair quaking her insides escalated to a vibration of rage. "I found him lying here, mutilated," she spat. "He'd been beaten, his fingers broken—all of them. His scalp was gone, and his innards–" She clutched her stomach and clenched her jaw to stifle a retch. "Keith was the kindest, most peaceable man I've ever known, and one of your kind gutted him in his own field. *For no reason!*"

Isaac's lids flinched.

"Well?" Eva demanded. "Don't you have anything to say? You have an answer for everything else. What's your answer to this?"

"I do not have one."

A derisive note pushed its way up her throat. "Of course, you don't."

Eva turned and walked away. The rant had given her a queer sense of victory, but nothing could bring her husband back. With every step, her anger seeped out just as Keith's lifeblood had, leaving only bitterness and exhaustion.

Eva sat in her rocker, motionless.

Isaac had followed her back from the fields silently, at a distance. He'd spoken only to say he was leaving to hunt and would be back in time for supper. He hadn't deserved her harsh words, but Eva couldn't muster an apology.

She spent the rest of the day in a senseless fog, cleaning and mending and making corncakes, then sat in her rocker and stared into the fire. Skipping lunch had left her with a rumbling stomach, but it hadn't revived her appetite. If Isaac caught something, he could roast it. If not, so be it.

A familiar knock sounded at the door.

"Come in," she called from her place in the chair. "You can stop knocking for permission when the sun is up," she told Isaac as he entered. It was as close as she could come to an apology. Besides, she was tired of answering the door several times a day.

He eyed her as he poured himself a cup of water and downed a few swallows. "I got four hares and a duck. Which should I butcher first."

"Whichever one you want for supper."

Isaac gave her his signature silent nod and drained the last of the water in the cup.

Eva rose and headed for the yard. "Let's do them all before we lose the daylight." She chose the duck and let Isaac skin the hares. "You must've gone quite a distance from the house," she said as she sliced the underside of the bird so she could skin it. "I didn't hear any of the shots."

He glanced at her sideways. "I didn't use a gun."

She set down her knife and examined the hole. He'd used his bow. "What if someone had seen you?"

"I was careful."

"You were foolish."

His lips pressed together, and he stripped the hare's skin off with a firm yank. "I can fell more game with arrows than bullets. To save your land, this is what I must do."

They finished their tasks without speaking.

"I made corncakes," Eva said as they carried the meat inside. "You roast a hare while I salt the rest down."

Isaac rinsed one of the hares as Eva did the same with the rest of the meat. He worked it onto a skewer and propped it above the fire while Eva poured salt into a barrel and added water. She stuck her hand in to swirl it around and hissed. Her whole hand burned as if it was on fire. She gritted her teeth and stirred until the crystals disappeared.

Isaac rose from his crouched position. "What hurts you?" He crossed the room to where she stood. "Did you cut yourself, butchering?"

Eva plunged her hand into a pan of plain water on the dry sink and sighed. "No. My skin is raw and cracked. It gets this way in winter."

He blotted her hand dry with a towel then took both her small hands in his large ones and examined them. "Sit at the table."

"But I have to brine the meat."

"I will do it. Sit."

He made quick work of the brining, checked on the roasting hare, and began opening bottles of herbs on the shelf, sniffing them one by one. He let out a grunt of satisfaction and set two of the bottles on the table. "Do you have... *'ahmo*?" He placed his fist in the palm of his other hand and made a grinding motion.

"A mortar and pestle?"

"Yes."

Eva pointed. "There's one in the cupboard behind you."

He set that next to the herbs then emptied some of each into it and ground the leaves into a powder. Next, he spooned a glop of lard into a cup and stirred the powder into it.

Isaac motioned for her to give him her hand. He smeared a generous coating of the lard all over one hand then the other. "Do not move." He retrieved some cloth from the rag bag then tore it into strips and wrapped her hands from her palms to the tips of her fingers. "You will leave this on all night."

Eva held up her mummy-like mittens. "How will I prepare our plates with this on my hands?" How would she do anything, for that matter?

"I will do it."

Before she could mount an argument, he'd prepared two plates with buttered corncakes and roasted hare. He even cut hers into pieces.

"Thank you," Eva said as he sat.

Isaac took a few bites then stopped. He looked from her untouched food to her hands. "I left your thumb free so you could hold a fork."

"I'm not hungry."

"You need to eat."

Eva fumbled around with her fork until she got a good grip and took a bite of hare to appease him.

Isaac began eating again, glancing at her as he did. "There will be more variety come spring."

A feast could have been placed before her, and it wouldn't have made any difference. "It isn't the food."

The corner of his mouth ticked up. "I thought you had finally tired of corncakes at every meal." She hadn't made biscuits or a loaf of bread in weeks.

"No. Have you tired of them?"

He shook his head and popped half a corncake into his mouth.

Eva cut her eyes in the direction of the pantry. "I quit making bread because I can't stomach the bugs anymore. There are more of them than flour."

Isaac set his fork down and went outside. A few minutes later, he returned with a handful of dry slender leaves and tossed them into the flour bin. "We will get new flour when we go to town," he said as he sat back down. "For now, that will help you salvage what is left."

"What kind of leaves were those?"

"I do not know the English name." He speared a piece of hare with his fork. "I will put some in the new flour. It will keep the bugs away."

Eva stood to begin clearing the table.

Isaac waved her away. "I will do it."

She returned to her rocking chair. It felt strange to sit and watch someone do her chores.

When he was finished in the kitchen, Isaac came over to her, squatted down, and reached for her foot.

She jerked her leg back. "What are you doing?"

"Removing your shoes."

"I can do it myself."

He looked up at her and raised a brow.

Eva stared down at the laces then at her bandaged hands. She'd barely managed her fork at supper. If she didn't let him help her, she'd be sleeping in her boots. Grudgingly, she lifted her foot.

Isaac loosened them both and slipped off one boot, then the other.

"Thank you."

"You are welcome."

He added a log to the fire but didn't sit cross-legged on the floor. He brought a chair from the table and placed it across from her rocker. His eyes searched hers when he sat. For the first time since they'd met, his annoying self-assurance was nowhere in evidence. "Tell me about your husband."

Eva's breath stalled in her chest. What business of his was it? "He was a good, hardworking man," she said firmly.

"There is evidence of that all over your land."

"Then why are you asking me about him?"

"What happened the day he died?"

"I told you," Eva said, pressing a bandaged hand to her uneasy stomach.

"You described his injuries. I want to know other things about that day."

"He was plowing, and a savage murdered him," Eva bit out. "What more is there to know?"

"Had he been trading with anyone?"

"Not that I'm aware of."

"What about sightings of strangers... people passing through?"

"We hadn't seen an Indian since we were with the wagon train."

"Was livestock taken?"

Eva shook her head. "The oxen were still harnessed to the plow."

"Did anyone come to the house and threaten you?"

"No. There was only one set of tracks to and from the body—moccasin tracks."

"Was anything stolen?"

Eva shook her head.

"Not even food?"

"No."

Isaac stared absently past her and frowned.

"All this is pointless," Eva said with a wave of her bandaged hand. "Indians kill whites for no reason. They murder innocent people who didn't do anything to deserve it."

"That is true."

"You say that as if it's justified."

"To them, it is."

"You *are* them."

"I... I do not agree with such killing, but I understand it. Whites believe in seeking out the persons who wronged them, that only the guilty deserve retaliation. To clan warriors, this does not matter. It is about numbers. They kill to even the count."

Eva's mouth fell open. "You're saying Keith was killed at random, to avenge some crime he didn't commit?"

"It is possible."

"*Savages,*" she growled.

Isaac flinched, and the muscles along his jaw tightened. "I said it was possible. I did not say it was likely. Most of the clans in these lands are peaceful. Even if your husband refused to trade with them, they would not have killed him. And those who might would not have left empty-handed."

Eva wanted to shake him and scream *They didn't! They took his watch and his scalp!*

She wrapped herself with her arms. "I don't want to talk about this anymore."

He rose and returned the chair to the table. "Do you need help removing your garments?"

"How dare you even suggest such a thing!" She shot to her feet, marched to the door, and yanked it open on the third try. "Goodnight."

Isaac studied her with that bold, self-possessed gaze of his, when any civilized man would have the decency to look away, shamefaced. "Goodnight."

She slammed the door behind him and lowered the bar. After fumbling with the buttons of her dress in vain, she huffed out a breath and flopped onto the bed fully clothed.

Isaac set the pail of milk on Eva's porch and turned the animals out to pasture. Holding his tongue when she referred to his kind as savages was growing difficult. He did it because grief had left her hurting and angry. To her, Indians seemed uncivilized, and some were—the Comanche, who'd killed his mother's first husband, tortured captives ruthlessly and would ride hundreds of miles to seek revenge—but they were the exception.

He had lived his entire life with a foot in two cultures, learning the ways of both and seeing the wisdom and the flaws of each. He was more like a white than Eva knew—more like a white than he wanted to be. And yet he was drawn to it. Drawn to her.

But he would never abandon the ways of his people. Not entirely. The Mojave clans were peaceful. If Eva could walk among them and see how they lived, she would understand.

Isaac paused at the dugout door. The sun was up, but the pail of milk still sat outside. He picked up the pail and knocked.

Eva opened the door, wearing the same dress as the day before, and stared at him. She often wore clothes more than once, but this was likely of necessity.

"May I come in?"

She took a step back. "I suppose." She held out her hands as he set the pail on the dry sink. "When can I take these bandages off."

"Whenever you wish." He drew his knife and motioned for her to hold out her hands.

She grudgingly complied, keeping her eyes trained on his knife.

Isaac cut the knotted strips of cloth loose at each of her wrists and began unwinding one of the bandages.

Eva yanked her hand back, her attention still fixed on his knife.

"Why do you fear me?" he asked as he sheathed the weapon. "Have I not proven myself worthy of your trust?"

Her gaze shot to his then cut away. Color rose in her cheeks as she busied herself unwrapping the bandages from her hands.

"Save those. They can be used many times. Then, when your hands are healed, I can make torches."

She handed him the mass of greasy strips and reached for the soap.

"Do not wash it off."

"But I have to make breakfast."

"The herbs have no poison." He set the strips aside and handed her a towel. "Only wipe away the excess. What remains will protect your skin."

Isaac left to split some logs. He filled the wood box then joined Eva for a simple meal of corncakes and milk.

She looked up at him with pink cheeks and her head half bowed. "My hands feel better. Thank you."

"I will wrap them again for you tonight." He gestured at the last corn cake then took it when she nudged the platter in his direction. "The ground is still too cold to plow, so I will hunt."

"With your bow."

"Yes."

Eva stared at him, her lips pressed into such a tight line they blanched.

"It is the only way to get enough pelts to trade."

"It's a perfect way to get yourself killed."

Isaac drained the last of the milk from his cup. "One dead savage is no real loss."

His words landed like a slap. Eva flinched, and her entire face went pale. "You are not a savage," she said in a pained voice just above a whisper.

Isaac took the napkin from his lap and laid it on the table. "Do you have chores for me before I go?"

"Just draw some water. It's laundry day."

"The lye is not good for your skin."

"All our clothes are dirty."

He rose. "I will make soap."

Eva hurried to clear the table. She'd started to ask Isaac how he was going to make soap in time for her to do a full day of washing, but he left before she could form the words.

The cauldron had already been filled when she reached the yard.

Isaac was pouring water into the rinse barrel. "Start the fire," he told her as he picked up the empty bucket sitting at his feet and headed for the well.

Eva shook her head as she lit the fire under the cauldron and added wood. What kind of soap could a person make in a matter of minutes? She was going to waste an entire day, washing and rinsing, only to have to do it all over again.

Isaac returned and finished filling the rinse barrel. He set the buckets down and held his hands up, moving them to indicate the shape of a square. "Get a piece of threadbare cloth from the rag bag, about this size, and"—he held his index fingers about six inches apart— "a length of string."

She did as he asked then sat on the bench and waited. Several minutes later, he returned from the direction of the pasture, carrying something in his hand that looked like a turnip.

"What is that?" Eva asked.

"It is a root used for washing and bathing." The insult of her earlier remark had apparently been forgotten, or at least forgiven. His voice had lost its sharp edge.

Isaac knelt by a large flat rock. He beat the root with a smaller rock, until it was fibrous and mushy. He rose long enough to pinch a sprig of rosemary off the bush then returned to the rock. "Spread out the cloth." He tossed the rosemary onto it, scooped up the glob of mush with both hands, and placed it in the center. Then he gathered the corners of the cloth together and tied the bundle snuggly closed with the string.

Eva followed him to the cauldron and watched as he held the bag over the steaming water and squeezed. Milky liquid began running between his fingers. As he squeezed the bag over and over, the fluid running out began to lather. When no more liquid dripped out, he lowered the bag and floated it in the water.

"That's it?" Eva asked. "That's the soap?"

"Yes." His eyes twinkled with a hint of boyish mischief. He smeared some suds on the tip of her nose then walked to the rinse bucket, dunked his hands, and swished them around until they came up clean.

Eva swiped the suds off her nose and rubbed the substance between her fingers. It was slippery. She lowered her head and sniffed. The scent was mild. Slightly medicinal.

"Stir it with the paddle for a few minutes before you add the clothes."

"Thank you for making this."

Isaac gave her one of his solemn single nods. "I will bring another root when I return. You can use it for washing the dishes and bathing."

Eva swirled the soap bundle around in the cauldron. The scent of rosemary rose with the steam and permeated the air around her. "Can I add flowers to scent the soap?" she asked as he turned to walk away.

"If their color is bland. Dark ones will stain cloth."

She'd try gardenias and honeysuckle come summer. If the soap worked.

"I will be back by suppertime," Isaac said.

He retrieved his horse from the paddock. Keith's freshly oiled saddle gleamed in the morning light as Isaac hoisted it on and adjusted the cinch. He had kept his word.

He mounted and rode around back of the dugout, up to the top of the hill from which it had been hewn. Isaac turned his horse in a slow circle as he scanned the farm. Then he returned to the yard, brought his bow and quiver from their hiding place in the barn, and attached them to the side of the saddle.

Eva frowned at him, though she knew it would do no good.

Isaac tipped his hat to her and rode away. From within the shade of its brim, he'd smirked at her. She was sure of it.

She watched him until he disappeared into the tree line then began filling the cauldron of simmering, soapy water with dirty clothes and pushing them under with the paddle.

While they soaked, she checked the flour, hoping to make a batch of bread dough. Nothing but stubborn lumps of flour remained in the sieve—the leaves had chased the bugs away.

Eva set the loaves out to rise and hurried back to check on the laundry. She had to scrub a few stubborn stains, but she would have had to do the same with lye. Isaac's root soap was cleaning the clothes. And the only thing causing her hands to sting was the temperature of the water. She moved that batch to the rinse bucket and filled the cauldron with more soiled clothes.

Boil, scrub, rinse, wring, hang on the line, repeat. Those monotonous tasks consumed Eva's day, along with baking bread and fixing herself a simple lunch. She chopped some wild onions that Isaac had dug, so she could quickly add them to whatever game he caught for their supper stew, then went to rinse the last cauldronful of laundry. She'd already brought in the thinner items that dried quickly. The rest would have to dry overnight.

Eva's hands were red from being in water all day, and they ached from kneading dough and wringing out a week's worth of garments. A relieved sigh fluttered her lips as she clipped the last batch to the line.

The sun was beginning to set, so she fixed herself a cup of hot tea and sat on the bench to wait for Isaac. A gentle breeze rippled through the clothing. It had been a long time since trousers had hung next to her dresses. It pinched her heart, and yet it made her smile.

When she and Keith had first arrived in their wagon, Keith immediately went to work, stringing a rope between two sturdy trees. He'd grumbled the entire time that he was tired of finding twigs in his clothes from laying them over trailside bushes to dry.

She missed the sound of his voice. Even his grousing when he was perturbed.

Footsteps approached on the far side of the clothes line. "Mrs. McCabe?" Dwight called, "are you there?"

"Yes." Eva glanced in the direction Isaac had gone. What would she say if Dwight saw him and started asking questions?

She popped to her feet as he swam his way through the curtain of clothes. She'd converse a few moments then pretend to turn in for the evening, so he would leave. "What brings you by?"

He smiled. "Just a neighborly visit."

After their last couple of encounters, she doubted that. Seeing her land through Isaac's eyes had caused her to realize its value.

Dwight looked around the yard then at the china cup in her hand.

The longer he stood there, the more unsettled she became. Isaac would be home soon, and they hadn't come up with a story to explain his presence. She had to get rid of Dwight, even if it meant being rude.

Eva held up her cup. "I was enjoying some tea before turning in. I'm afraid washday has left me weary."

"Mac got you doing his laundry again?" Dwight looked more closely at the trousers. "Or are those Connor's?"

"They're mine," Isaac said, riding into the yard and stopping his horse mere inches from Dwight.

Eva's gaze shot to the back of his saddle. No bow. No arrows. Just a deer and a tether of small game.

Thank the Almighty.

Dwight looked Isaac up and down then turned a confused expression on her.

"Mr. Kramer, this is Isaac Shaw, my new farm hand."

"You hired a stranger? Just like that?"

"Mr. Shaw is not a stranger. He..."

"I am a friend of Mr. McKinnon," Isaac said, looking down at Dwight. "Mac mentioned Mrs. McCabe's situation to me, and I decided to help her."

"Who's working your farm while you work hers?"

"I do not have a farm."

Dwight narrowed his eyes at Isaac then lifted his chin in challenge. "So that's it—you plan to talk her out of her land."

"No. I plan to replenish the savings that was stolen from me, when bandits robbed the stagecoach I arrived in, and use it to prove up my own claim."

"Hmph. Don't expect much in the way of wages," Dwight scoffed. "She can barely afford to feed herself."

Eva clenched her teacup so tightly she feared it would shatter.

"But she *has* fed herself," Isaac countered, "as well as her animals. Mrs. McCabe is determined to succeed, and I am willing to wait to share the profits." He guided his horse over to the makeshift butchering table.

Dwight glared at Isaac's back as he dismounted then turned to her. "Have you given any more thought to my proposal?"

Eva had to stifle the urge to spew obscenities before she could answer. "I did, but I've decided to cultivate my land and prove up my claim."

"You'd really do all that and forfeit half?"

"If that's what the law requires." Hopefully, by then, it wouldn't. But she would do it, and in no small part, to spite him.

"I think you're making a mistake."

"You've made that abundantly clear."

He frowned slightly, seeming to realize his blunder. "I mean I wish you'd reconsider. If you don't change your mind before my friends leave Tennessee, they'll claim land elsewhere."

Eva kept her face neutral and held his gaze.

"Of course, my other offer still stands."

If she loosened her tongue enough to utter more than a single word, it would turn into a screaming setdown. "Understood."

"Well... All right, then." Dwight tipped his hat. "Goodnight, Mrs. McCabe." He looked Isaac over again then turned and walked away.

"Arghhhh," she growled as she marched to where Isaac was butchering. "That man!" She snatched a skinned hare off the table and whisked it into the dugout.

Isaac finished salting down the meat and took his place at the table.

"The leaves worked," Eva said as she set the food before him. "I was able to use the flour."

He responded with a grunt, barely looking at her. Eva's ire had apparently cooled, but his had not.

"The soap you made from that root did also. My hands are a little raw from being in water all day, but not nearly as painful as they would have been if I had used lye."

"Good."

Eva placed her napkin in her lap, bowed her head briefly, and buttered herself a slice of bread. "I panicked when Dwight showed up. I feared he'd see your bow. How did you sneak it into the barn without being seen?"

Isaac was so deeply mired in his thoughts, he had to pause to make sense of her question. "I did not put it in the barn. I hid it in a thicket until I was sure we were alone." He would be wise to build a small shelter for it in the thicket and store it there all the time, but he kept that thought to himself.

She tilted her head in concession. "I still think you're taking a big risk."

Eva refilled her soup bowl and buttered a second slice of bread. Washing clothes must've given her an appetite.

Hours of hunting had left him hungry, too, but the food sat like a cold river stone in his belly.

Isaac finished eating and set down his spoon. "What proposal?"

"Hm?"

"Mr. Kramer asked if you had given thought to his proposal."

Eva dabbed the corner of her mouth with her napkin. "Mac didn't tell you?"

"No."

"Two of Mr. Kramer's friends offered to take over my claim in exchange for paying my travel expenses."

"To where?"

"Back home, to North Carolina."

Returning to her family would mean a safer, easier life, but the thought of her leaving saddened him. "Is that something you want?"

"It was tempting, but I decided to stay."

"Mr. Kramer mentioned a second. What was it?"

"He offered to marry me."

Isaac's heart stuttered in a suddenly hollow chest. "What was your answer?"

"I told him I would have to think about it."

"I do not like him."

"I don't like him at this moment, either," she said, placing her napkin on the table and rising from her chair, "but he's been a good neighbor to me."

Isaac stood and glared at her. "He wants your land."

Eva planted her hands on her hips. "So do you."

"I do not."

"You say that now, but after you've worked for months–"

Isaac advanced on her until their bodies were inches apart. "I do not want your land," he said as she stared up at him with round eyes. "But I will not cultivate it and give it to *him*."

Color rose in her cheeks. "Then don't!"

The widow trembled, but not entirely from fear. Or anger. The rapid beat of her heart pulsed the base of her throat, and her pupils expanded to fill the center of her eyes until they were as dark as the mourning clothes she wore.

Isaac stared at the flush of desire spreading over her fair skin. At her lips. He wanted her, even though his pride railed against it.

He leaned so close he could feel her breath against his face. "Do not marry him."

Her eyes blazed with anger, but it didn't conceal her lust. She placed her hands on his chest and shoved. "Get away from me!"

Isaac clenched his jaw to keep himself from kissing her and backed up.

He snatched his hat off the peg and went to the barn. He should have held his tongue. Now Eva would send him away and marry her neighbor.

Isaac rose from a restless night and tended to the animals. He fully expected the widow to throw him off her land, but he would honor his commitment until she did. Perhaps, if she would let him speak, he would try one last time to persuade her against marriage. He knew greed when he saw it. If she bound herself to Dwight Kramer, he would take possession of her farm and steal her independence.

A plate of corncakes and a tepid cup of coffee waited on the porch when Isaac brought the milk pail. As he bent over to pick them up, a shadow darkened the paper window of the kitchen, near the tear in the corner. Eva was watching.

He half-smiled. He had only been banished from the house.

He ate alone then saddled his horse for another day of hunting. Whether Eva dismissed him or not, she would need all the pelts he could acquire. This time, he concealed his weapon in a roll until he was far from the house. He had refused to admit it to her, but her worry was justified.

For the remainder of the month, he hunted during the day and tanned pelts at night, by lamplight. In between taking breakfasts and suppers on the porch, he lunched on roasted fish from the stream. He held no illusions as to why the barn cats kept him company at mealtime. Their loyalty was bought with scraps he tossed their way, but he enjoyed their presence nonetheless.

On the first day of March, Isaac brought Eva's team of oxen from Mac's and hooked them to the plow. He paused to honor the place where her husband's spirit had departed then continued plowing the earth where he had stopped. Once the fields were ready to receive seed, he would gather the pelts and give them to Eva. Her anger should be cooled enough by then to allow him to accompany her to town.

If not, he would ask Mac to do it and ride escort at a distance.

Isaac halted the team. The midday sun was hot for such a mild day. He wiped the dust from the oxen's nostrils with a cloth, so they wouldn't overheat, then rested in the shade of a nearby tree. His stomach growled with hunger, but he couldn't leave the animals to fish. He unwrapped a corncake saved from breakfast and washed it down with water from his pouch.

His hand went to the hilt of his knife at the sound of approaching footsteps. He returned it to his lap when he heard the rhythmic brush of fabric against grass. A woman's skirt.

Eva paused at the edge of the field, several feet away, staring at him from underneath the brim of her bonnet.

Isaac stayed seated and kept quiet. Mostly to appear nonthreatening, but partly to twit her English manners.

"You didn't leave."

"You did not send me away."

"I wanted to."

She took a few halting steps forward then walked over to where he sat. "Here," she said, holding out a cloth bundle. "I brought you lunch."

He took it from her. "Thank you."

She fidgeted with the folds of her skirt and took a step back. "Mr. McKinnon came to visit. He said I should give you another chance."

"Is that your choice?"

She nodded.

Isaac opened the bundle and pulled out a sandwich made of bread and cheese. He took a bite and chewed.

She stared at him then gazed out over the newly plowed field. "You're making good progress. When will it be ready to plant?"

"By the end of the month," he replied as she turned her attention back to him. "We will ride to town then and buy seed." Isaac held her gaze and watched closely for her reaction. "Whether you allow me to stay or not, do not marry Dwight Kramer."

Her nod of acknowledgement did not come as quickly this time, but she gave one.

Chapter Nine

MARCH 31, 1852

Eva ran her palm over the hides and pelts that filled the back of Mac's wagon. Deer, rabbit, mink, beaver. The stack Isaac had hunted and tanned dwarfed Mac's and Connor's combined.

"Up ye go, lass," Mac said as he lifted her onto the wagon seat. He joined her and drove them out of the yard, well behind Connor and Isaac, who led the way on horseback.

Mac glanced sideways at her, his eyes glittering with mirth. "Isaac said ye finally let 'im back in, tae take meals in tha house."

"I hope I don't live to regret it," Eva groused. "It isn't funny!" she said when Mac's chest shook with silent laughter. "That man is the epitome of impertinence."

"I would no' go that far."

"I would. He's bold and ill-mannered. He even offered to help me undress!"

Mac frowned. "When wis this?"

"A few weeks back. He had bandaged my hands with some salve he made for my skin. I let him help me off with my boots, but then he asked if I needed help taking off my clothes. I couldn't believe he would even *think* such a thing, much less ask."

Mac stared at Isaac's back. "So, it wis fur practical reasons."

"Yes, but that doesn't matter. He was raised by a white mother. He should know better." She started to tell him about the time Isaac had cornered her over Dwight's proposal, with a look so fierce she wasn't sure if he wanted to strike her or ravage her. But that was better left unsaid. Isaac had backed down and walked away as soon as she'd told him to.

Mac sighed. "Tha choice is yours, o'course, but ye'll need help tae prove up, an' Isaac is a hard worker."

That was true. He'd worked countless hours, plowing fields and tanning enough pelts to buy the seed and the cows. "He's just so... *assertive*. He goes along with my choices, but..." How did one describe a man that was all at once meek and self-possessed? Well-mannered and presumptuous? Quiet, but with confidence that bordered on insolence?

"Isaac respects ye."

"He does?"

"Aye. An' he worries fur yer safety." Mac slowed the team and looked over at her. "I tasked 'im with givin' his life tae protect ye when I brought 'im back, but I dinnae need tae. Isaac would die fur ye without a second thought."

Eva stared at the baffling man riding ahead. "Why? He barely knows me."

"I dinnae ken. I jus' ken that he would."

Eva sat straighter as they entered Cedar Junction. She scanned the boardwalks from under her long black veil, worried that Isaac's secret would be discovered.

Man after man passed by, and none of them paid him any mind. The women either. Well, a few did, but not with the skepticism Eva had feared. They looked with appreciative gazes that lingered long enough to be improper.

Mac parked the wagon near the store. He took Eva's shopping list and a bundle of letters the three of them had prepared for the post then helped her down and escorted her in. Connor and Isaac stayed with the wagon.

"I'll get a proper price fur tha pelts," Mac assured her with a kind smile. "Take yer time an' shop."

Eva closed her eyes and breathed deeply. She'd loved the smell of a general store since she was a little girl. It meant fresh food and new garments. She meandered through the aisles, perusing all the goods on display, making a mental list of the items she'd add if there were funds left over.

Yardage for clothing had already been budgeted, so she went to the fabric. Eva fingered the bright floral prints then sighed and moved to the bolts of black. Deep mourning lasted a year, and she had five more months to go. A second year came afterward, but, since fancy collars and cuffs were impractical for farming, the only thing that would change was the length of her veil. She'd endure two summers dressed head to toe in black.

For Keith, she would do it without complaint. He deserved to be properly mourned.

"I think you should buy the blue," Isaac said from behind her.

"I can't," Eva responded quietly.

"Why not?"

"Because I'm mourning a spouse. I can't wear anything but black for another fourteen months, at least." She looked up at him. "Why aren't you guarding the wagon?"

"Mac is there with one of the clerks, unloading."

"He got a good price?"

"Yes. He—" Isaac cocked his head, as if a sound had caught his attention. "Excuse me." He walked over to a rack of leather belts and began looking them over.

Eva shrugged and went back to her shopping. She'd buy black now, but with next spring's money, she'd get something with color and spend the summer making dresses.

Mac and Isaac joined her at the counter as she was making her final choices. "Ye 'ave eight dollars surplus," Mac said to her. "How would ye like tae spend it?"

"I don't know. Perhaps I should save it." She looked to Isaac, who was handing over a coin in exchange for a newspaper. "What do you think?"

Isaac frowned at the paper then folded it. "You need chickens."

A coyote had made off with their rooster shortly after Keith died, and she'd eaten all but three of the chickens over the winter.

"Aye, lass. Ye need tae rebuild yer flock."

"I can only eat so many eggs."

"Ye can sell tha surplus."

"All right."

"Anything else?" Mac asked. At her denial, he closed out the tab and paid the clerk for all the goods.

"I'll have some chicks soon enough," Mac said as they left the store. "But we'll price a lively cockerel when we visit tha man with tha cows."

"Not too lively," Eva grumbled. "I don't want to do battle every time I gather eggs."

Mac laughed and lifted her onto the wagon.

Connor had climbed into the back while they were shopping. He helped stack the bags of seed and boxes of rations as Mac and Isaac loaded them on, fire brigade style.

Eva leaned toward Connor once the wagon was packed. "You got stuck with guard duty the whole time." He'd chosen the job that pained his leg the least, but still. "Did you want to go inside and have a look around?"

Connor smiled and shook his head. "I added tae Mac's list afore we left, an' I can ride tae town anytime." He scooted carefully across the bags of grain and swung his leg over his horse, who'd been patiently waiting alongside the wagon.

Mac climbed on and took up the reins. "Ready, lass? Let's go choose yer cows."

Eva glanced back at the crated rooster sitting atop the bags of seed. "My, he's loud." The bird flapped and squawked incessantly despite the tarp Connor had laid over his cage.

"He's jus' complainin' aboot tha ride," Mac said. "He'll settle down once ye get 'im home."

The calves had been much better behaved. They were prime stock, robust and reasonably priced. As soon as Isaac fenced a suitable pasture, the men would ride to the ranch and drive them home.

But first, she and Isaac had to sow the seed.

"I'll deliver ye an' yer supplies then turn fur home," Mac said as he guided the wagon down the road that led to their farms.

Isaac's horse burst into a canter.

Eva squinted at the landscape as her farm came into view. Nothing was amiss that she could see, but Isaac's horse was impeccably well behaved, even at feeding time. He wouldn't take off in a run unless Isaac prodded him. "What's happening?"

"I dinnae ken."

Connor took off after Isaac. When the wagon caught up, Connor was scanning the farm from atop his horse, and Isaac had dismounted. A portion of the fence had been knocked down, and Gwenie was grazing in the yard.

"Where's Sir Galahad?" Eva asked, anxiously scanning the pasture. Her one and only horse was nowhere to be seen.

"Give me 'is halter an' a lead line," Connor said. "I'll search until I find 'im."

Isaac looked as if he wanted to argue, but he was the better choice to stay behind.

Mac tied off the reins and hopped down. "Have faith, lass. Gwenie dinnae get far. I doubt Gally did either."

Eva sighed and carried the first of many boxes into the dugout. The sooner they got the wagon unloaded the sooner Isaac would be free to join the search.

The men were still unloading grain and seed when she finished toting boxes, so she made a trip to the woodshed. "Oh, no!" she shrieked.

Mac and Isaac rounded the corner at a dead run, knives drawn.

"What's wrong?" Mac asked.

"Half the firewood is missing!"

Mac glanced this way and that, scanning the area around him.

"Why would someone steal wood in springtime?" Eva lamented. "They have months to chop an ample amount and put it up to dry."

Isaac knelt, touching the ground as if searching for tracks. "It was a man wearing boots."

"Only one?" Mac asked.

"Yes."

Eva peered closer. "How can you tell those prints from ours?"

Isaac rose. "They are too large to be yours, and the shape of the boot is different than mine."

The joy and optimism that had filled Eva over the course of the day drained away. Her firewood supply was at its lowest all year, so half now wasn't nearly as much as it would have been in fall. But it would take weeks to replace—weeks they didn't have.

Connor trotted up. "Yer Gally isn't beyond tha pastures. I'll go search along tha stream. It's possible tha water drew him."

Mac gestured to the space left by the pilfered wood. "Keep yer eye oot fur a thief while yer at it."

Connor gaped. "I assumed tha lass's spirited mount broke tha fence."

"Apparently not."

"Stealin' wood's a callous misdeed, but stealin' a horse can get a man hanged," Connor said with an ire-filled growl. "Tha vandal better pray we find Galahad." He spun his horse around and headed north, toward the place where the stream entered her land.

Isaac paced slowly around the yard, staring at the ground, then made his way several yards up the wagon path that led to the main road before returning. "The only fresh ruts are ours, and there is only one set of unfamiliar boot prints near the fence and the shed. Either the thief made several trips, or–"

"He had an accomplice," Mac said.

Isaac studied the ground in the yard again, concentrating on a cluster of prints left by shod hooves. "To carry that much wood without a wagon, he had to have at least one."

Mac scrubbed a hand across his beard. "Proobably handed tha wood aff tae another man on horseback."

"Or more."

Eva's insides began to quiver. Had the men who'd threatened her and beaten Isaac come back? She wrapped her arms around her middle, but it didn't help.

"Chin up, lass. Connor an' I 'ave plenty o' firewood. Together we'll all make do."

Connor emerged from the trees with Sir Galahad in tow. "Found this rebel drinkin' from the stream, jus' as I guessed."

"Gally," Eva crooned, hurrying over to nuzzle her wayward gelding.

"That's a relief," Mac said. "Lowers tha wretch tae mere vandal—someone set on thwarting a female settler, most like—but let's stable yer animals, jus' tae be safe."

Once Gwenie and Gally were settled, the men gathered at the wagon.

"Do ye think we need tae take turns at watch?" Connor asked.

Mac looked to Isaac before he spoke. "Seems tae be an act tae thwart progress, no' a prelude tae war."

Isaac nodded, but his brow was tense and brooding. "She should not be alone."

"Ach, aye," Mac agreed. "Tha farm either, if it can be helped."

"What about yours?" Eva asked. "You should go check for damage."

"She's right," Connor said. "You an' Isaac go unload. I'll stay till he returns."

Isaac made it back at dusk. He spoke a few words to Connor in the yard, and Connor mounted up and left for home.

"Was anything amiss at Mr. McKinnon's?" Eva asked when he came in the door and hung up his hat.

"All was well."

"Good," she said on a sigh. She placed two bowls of porridge on the table and dropped into a chair. "Apologies for the meager meal. It took the entire time you were gone to empty the boxes and restock the cellar."

"This will do." He ate without further comment.

She hadn't the energy for conversation either.

Isaac rose and checked the supply of firewood in the box. "I will repair the fence in the morning and chop wood."

"When will we plant?"

"That depends upon the weather."

The last few days had been fair and sunny, but Eva didn't have the strength to argue. "All right. See you at breakfast."

She barred the door and climbed into bed. Had she been anything less than completely exhausted, she wouldn't have slept a wink.

Eva turned Gwenie and Gally out in their mended pasture to the echo of trees being chopped and felled.

The thump of hooves on the ground sounded from the direction of the road.

Eva shielded her eyes just in time to see Dwight coming up the drive in a farm wagon.

He reined his horse to a stop and tipped his hat. "Connor rode out this morning and told me what happened. I brought wood."

"You didn't have to do that, Mr. Kramer."

"I had some I could spare."

"Well, in that case, thank you."

He moved the wagon closer to her barn, so he could unload. The gift only replaced a fourth of what had been taken, but it helped.

Dwight brushed the bark from his hands and removed his hat. "I owe you an apology for the way I spoke to you when I saw you last. I meant no offense."

To say none had been taken would be a lie. "Apology accepted. Would you like a cup of tea?"

"If you'll serve it outside, in this pleasant weather."

Outside where Isaac might see was what he meant.

Men and their stubborn rivalry. Little did they know they were sparring over a prize neither one of them would win.

Dwight was waiting for her on the bench when she returned. He popped to his feet.

"I assume your farm was unharmed," she said as she handed him his cup, and they sat.

"My farm? Yes. Nothing was damaged or stolen."

So, it was likely not a random crime committed by a band of ne're-do-wells passing through. But Mac had said as much.

And strangely, the attack had put her on her mettle as much as it had frightened her. Instead of cowering her into giving up, it had lit a blazing fire to succeed.

"Have you planted yet?" she asked, in an effort to make conversation.

He lowered his cup. "I finished seeding last week. You?"

"I haven't started." Eva took a sip of her tea and braced for a scold.

"You still have time."

She took another sip to hide her amusement. Mr. Kramer had definitely changed his tune since last they spoke.

But it was too little too late. He'd shown his colors. That, paired with Isaac's entreaty that persisted even when he thought he'd be dismissed, had made up her mind. She would refuse Dwight's offer of marriage, but not yet. She might be new to farming, but she was no fool.

She'd wait until fall, when the health of her herd and the fate of her first year's harvest was known. Deep mourning would allow her to put him off at least until then.

She rose and smiled kindly at her guest, who popped to his feet as quickly as before. "Thank you for shoring up my supply of firewood, Mr. Kramer. If there's something I can do in return, please let me know."

He handed her his half-full cup that still radiated its last vestiges of heat. "Nonsense. It was a gift freely given," he replied with an answering smile. "But since you offered, I must say I've missed your company. Perhaps we can share a meal sometime—when it's convenient, of course."

Of course.

"Give me time to get my fields planted, and I'll grant your request."

Despite Dwight's gifted firewood, Isaac insisted on felling, hauling, and chopping trees for two more days. He stacked pieces of the larger ones in the woodshed to cure, and he split the smaller ones and stored them in the barn to use later, when he fenced the new pasture.

Eva eyed him from across the table at breakfast. "When are we going to plant?"

"I told you," he said, barely looking up, "it depends upon the weather."

"The weather has been perfect since before we bought the seed." Well, almost perfect. Some clouds had drifted in the previous afternoon, but the sun still shone. "Dwight's fields have been planted for over a week."

Isaac stared at his half-empty plate then set down his fork. He pulled the napkin from his lap and rose. "I will go look."

That was what he'd said yesterday. And the day before.

Eva felt like screaming, but she kept her composure. "I will go with you."

His lips pressed into a tight line then relaxed. He gave her a silent nod.

She followed him out of the dugout. He paused and looked up at the sky.

"Well?" she asked.

"Come."

He saddled his horse.

So did she.

She kept pace with him as he rode to the western meadow. A few clouds hung in the sky, and the breeze had cooled some from the day before, but a little rain after seeding was good, wasn't it?

"What exactly are you looking at?" she finally asked, bewildered.

Isaac stopped and motioned for her to bring her horse alongside his. "Look," he said, pointing heavenward. "The clouds are few, but they are tall." He lowered his arm and pointed in another direction, towards a lone bird, wings spread, floating on the breeze. "The birds are flying low, and the direction of the wind has changed."

He urged his horse into a trot and led her to the bank of the stream. "The current is swift, and the level of the water is very high. Rain is falling somewhere upstream." He shook his head and frowned. "We wait."

Eva sighed and accepted his decision. "Can I help get wood for the fence?"

"If you wish."

Felling trees and hauling them one at a time by horse was backbreaking work, but it made her feel useful.

When Isaac switched to splitting the logs he had harvested, Eva excused herself to go prepare lunch.

An hour later, Isaac ducked in, soaked to the skin. "The rain has come."

No kidding. Eva giggled.

Isaac stared at her, water dripping from the brim of his hat. "Why do you laugh?"

That only made her laugh harder.

She clamped her mouth shut, causing her cackles to come out as spurts and snorts, and took him a towel. "Y– You have an odd way of stating the obvious."

He hung his hat on a peg and began drying himself off.

"Here," Eva said, handing him some clothes of his that she'd mended. "Use the cellar."

Isaac removed his boots where he stood then went and changed in private. She had steaming bowls of soup waiting when he returned. She hung his wet clothes over a rack near the stove then joined him at the table.

"Should we move the animals to the barn?" she asked.

"I already did."

Eva placed her napkin in her lap and picked up her spoon. "I guess I'm eating crow."

Isaac frowned and lifted a piece of venison out of his bowl. "This is crow?"

"No! It's deer. 'Eat crow' means admit my mistake. You were right about the rain."

"Oh." Isaac tucked into his meal.

Eva did, too. She hadn't been hungry when she'd first returned from logging, but her appetite had come in with the rain. Or maybe with Isaac. She hadn't laughed like that in ages.

Lightening lit up the paper window, and thunder crashed so loudly it reverberated through the ground.

"Listen to that," she remarked as she refilled Isaac's bowl. "It's really storming out there." Rain was falling so hard, the portion of the roof that extended beyond the hill was beginning to leak.

Isaac glanced up at the big fat drops of muddy water forming one after another then shielded his soup with his hand and kept eating.

Eva freshened her tea and joined him, but she sat in a different chair, away from the leaky spot. If she was going to eat crow, she might as well go all in. "You were the one who patched my fence, weren't you?"

Isaac looked at her as if she was daft. "You watched me."

"Not this time. The other time, before we met." His method was identical to the mystery Samaritan.

"Oh... Yes." He started eating again.

"Thank you."

He grunted an acknowledgment between bites.

Eva sipped her tea and let him eat in peace.

Once he'd polished off his second bowl, Isaac sat back and wiped his beard with his napkin. "When the fields dry out, we will plant."

"Can we gather lumber for the fence while we wait?"

"Not if the mud is deep. The horses cannot pull the logs unless they have sure footing."

Eva sipped her tea to hide her frustration. Her chance for success was ticking away with every minute. "A pie would have gone well with the soup," she lamented. "Next month, the rhubarb will be–"

A big fat snake fell onto the table with a splat.

Eva screamed and bolted from her chair.

Isaac frowned at the writhing creature. He picked up the snake, opened the door, and tossed it outside. "It is a rat snake. It has no poison."

"I don't care. I despise snakes," she said with a shudder as she wiped the mud off the table. "I try not to be ungrateful, but I will rejoice when I have a proper house." The thought of how many logs they would have to haul to build it made her weary, but she would work herself to the point of exhaustion if it put an end to falling dirt and bugs and slithering creatures.

She just needed to get the farm up and running. All her problems would be solved by sowing the seeds and fencing the pasture—including that one. If her crops and cows thrived, she could purchase milled wood instead.

Sparks rose as Isaac stoked a fire in the fireplace and added a couple of logs.

Eva eyed the precious contents of the wood box. "Do we need that? It's springtime."

Isaac brushed the dust from his hands. "The rain will make the air cold. You need to stay warm and well so you can help me plant."

He picked up his boots and sat in an empty chair to put them on.

"Where are you going?" The rain was coming down in torrents.

"To the barn."

"Why?"

"You have made it clear my presence is not welcome unless it is meal-time."

She had, and after feeding him on the porch for weeks, like a dog.

Eva's cheeks heated with shame. "Don't go out in the storm. You need to stay well, too."

Isaac stared at her for a long moment then gave her one of his nods. He placed his boots by the door and sat cross-legged on the ground near the fire.

Eva covered the soup and left it on the back of the stove so it would stay warm. She paused before sitting in her rocker. "I have a few books that survived the trip west. Would you like something to read?"

"Do you have *Gulliver's Travels*?"

"No. I have"—she opened her trunk and sifted through them—"*Pride and Prejudice, Jane Eyre, The Count of Monte Cristo*, and *The Swiss Family Robinson*." She held up the last. "If you enjoyed *Gulliver's Travels*, you might like this. It's about a family that gets shipwrecked."

He held out his hand. "I will try it."

Eva gave it to him and took note of the dimly lit room. The storm had darkened the sky until it resembled dusk. "Do you need a candle?"

"The light from the fire is enough."

She lit a candle for herself then settled into her rocker and took up her mending. The side of the dugout where her chair and bed sat had been hewn from the hillside and did not leak.

Isaac read for half an hour then closed the book.

"Don't you like it?"

"I do. My eyes need rest."

You did need a candle, stubborn man.

"You mentioned *Gulliver's Travels*," Eva said as she resumed her stitching. "Have you read it?"

"My mother read it to me when I was a boy."

"What other novels did she read to you?"

"That was the only one. Her Bible and *Gulliver's Travels* were the only two books she possessed."

"I suppose living in tents would make it difficult to own much."

"The Mojave do not live in tents. We build permanent dwellings."

He stared into the flames then looked back up at her. "When the Comanche killed my mother's first husband, she grabbed a bag that contained items of value and ran. The Comanche caught her and took most of the items for themselves. When they began throwing her books into one of the fires they'd set, she begged them to let her keep two."

"Poor woman! I understand why she would choose her Bible, but why *Gulliver's Travels*?"

"It was her husband's favorite."

Isaac rose, crossed the room, and looked out the door. The lightning and thunder had stopped, but rain fell so heavily it was deafening.

He closed the door and returned to his place by the fire. "The pastures are beginning to flood."

"The house won't." Keith had used dirt hewn from the hill to raise the floor several inches higher than the ground outside, and the yard sloped gently downward, away from the dugout. "Did your mother read the Bible to you, too?"

"Yes. She made me copy scriptures when she taught me to write, first with a stick in the dirt, and later with a slate she acquired in a trade."

Eva added more thread to her needle and resumed her mending. "Did your mother teach the other children?"

"She taught them a few English words, but she was careful not to offend my father's people. She adopted their ways to gain acceptance."

Eva stitched for a while, lulled by the sound of the rain and the crackling fire.

Isaac began reading again, but only for a few minutes this time.

"Are you sure you don't want a candle?"

"It will waste your supplies."

She gestured to the kitchen chairs. "You can put one of those over here and use the light from mine."

"Later, perhaps." He set the book on the lid of her trunk and stared ahead at nothing. His mind was churning. She could see it in the set of his brow. He'd worn the same brooding expression for days.

Eva drew the thread through and paused. "Is something bothering you?"

"Why do you ask?"

"You've looked troubled ever since the trip to town."

"It is not important."

"Liar."

He cut his eyes to her, and she smirked. His turmoil wasn't funny, but calling him on his prevarication gave her immense satisfaction.

Isaac's brow smoothed, and some of the tension left his shoulders. "I overheard something in town. I hoped it wasn't true, but the newspaper confirmed it."

"What?"

"Your government passed a bill that creates a reservation for Indians in Oklahoma. The treaties will no longer be honored."

Eva wasn't sure what to say.

"The tribes will continue to govern themselves, but forcing them to live on a small portion of land..." He sighed. "They hunt to survive. They will not be able to feed themselves if they are not free to roam their lands." Isaac went from looking troubled to looking defeated. "The tribes will not go peacefully. Men will die, on both sides."

"Could they move to another state? There's still plenty of land that hasn't been settled."

Isaac shook his head. "That solution would not last. Your government will keep taking land by force."

"Well, if the Indians would stop slaughtering settlers–"

Isaac's eyes lit with outrage. That had been the wrong thing to say.

"There's enough land for everyone," Eva grumbled. She picked up the skirt she was mending and resumed stitching.

A chill breeze blew her way as Isaac stalked past and opened the door. "Put my meals on the porch," he snapped. "I will sleep with the animals." He stepped out into the downpour and shut the door.

Chapter Ten

The mud firmed up, and the puddles disappeared two days after the storm passed. It took two more until the soil was dry enough to plant. Isaac's anger had cooled toward the widow, but even if not, he would help her cultivate her farm. She had placed her hope in his promise of work, and—unlike the white man's government—he was a man of his word.

Isaac loaded as many bags of seed as his horse could carry and led him out to the far field. By the time he'd unloaded and put his horse in the pasture, Eva was making her way up the path, wearing a simple black dress and a matching bonnet.

She stopped a few feet away.

The sight of her kindled twin smolders of anger and lust, both of which he kept hidden. "Good morning."

A cautious smile appeared on her face. "Good morning."

"Have you planted before?"

"Only the kitchen garden. Mac and Connor always teamed up with Keith and took turns, planting each other's fields."

"They cannot help this time. We are all planting late. Any delay at this point can affect the harvest."

He indicated she should walk with him. "We will plant sixteen acres of grain and twenty acres of hay," he said as he led her to the field he'd prepared for grain. "That will feed your animals and leave a surplus."

"All right."

"Together, we should be able to seed four acres per day."

A crease appeared between her brows. "That's nine days... Ten, if we rest on Sunday."

"Yes." He was reluctant to submit to the religious observance, but she would need the rest. "We will plant half the grain field first, then half the hay. When that is done, we will go back and plant the other half."

"Why that way?"

"The sooner the seed is planted, the greater the harvest. This gives both fields a better chance."

Isaac moved the two full canteens he'd brought to a shady spot then handed Eva an empty seed bag. "Put it over your shoulder, like this." Using his bag, he showed her how to position the wide cloth strap across her chest, so her left shoulder would bear the weight, and the bag would rest near her right hip.

He knelt and slit the first sack of seeds open with his knife then used a wooden scoop to fill the bags they wore.

"This is not too bad," she said, patting the bulging sack resting on her hip.

"Come." Isaac led her to the corner of the field with the plowed land to their right. He dipped his hand into his bag and cast a handful of seeds in a wide arc. He moved her a few feet forward. "You try."

Her seeds did not fly as far, but it was a worthy first effort.

Isaac walked back to the place he had cast. He drew a square shape in the dirt and counted the seeds, then did the same where she had cast hers. "Do you see the difference?"

Eva nodded.

"Yours fell too thickly. The plants will not thrive if they grow too close to one another, and we will run out of seed. You need to scatter them farther." He moved her a few steps forward. "Try again."

She did it correctly the second time.

"That is good. Cast a handful every few steps. I will do the same next to you. Then we will position ourselves and start new rows when we get to the far edge of the field."

Isaac walked a few feet over. He waited for Eva to cast a few times before beginning, so he could keep her in sight and ensure his swath of seed aligned with hers.

She looked back over her shoulder then faced forward and continued.

When they reached the edge of the field and turned around, Eva gasped. "The birds are eating the seeds!"

She tossed the first handful of the next row then paused, burying as many as she could with her boot.

"Do not stop to bury them," Isaac called. "The delay will reduce the harvest more than the birds."

She looked back at him and frowned.

"I will harrow the field at the end of each day. That will keep the birds from eating too many."

The sun was overhead by the time they'd seeded an acre. Eva had kept a steady pace, though she paused to rub the shoulder of her throwing arm from time to time.

"Stop," Isaac called when they were a few yards from the end of the row. He kept seeding his swath until he reached Eva, who was standing still, frowning at him again. "Go prepare lunch."

"But–"

"I will finish your row." He did that and sowed another swath before she returned with a bundle of sandwiches and two jars of tea.

Isaac removed his seed bag and set it next to Eva's. He sat on the quilt she had placed under a tree and relished the shade. His muscles relaxed as he ate, but his mind would not rest. Eva's speed had not improved enough with practice to finish the planting in time.

It would cause her shame, but the only way to seed four acres per day was for him to cast with both hands.

He felt watched and looked up.

Eva was staring at him, her head slightly ducked and a faint blush creeping its way onto her cheeks. "Regarding our conversation the day of the storm, I did not mean to offend you. I'm just trying to make a life for myself and..."

Isaac held her gaze and listened calmly. She was making an effort toward peace.

"Keith and I applied for this grant for the same reason our parents immigrated to this country—to escape poverty, oppression, and war. We wanted better for our children than we had. Most of the settlers on the wagon train did, too. Our desire was to raise our children in prosperity and live our lives in peace.

"There are thousands and thousands of unsettled acres," she went on. "I don't understand why immigrants and natives can't share the land and coexist."

He resisted the urge to argue and paused to digest her words.

Isaac set his tea aside and rested his hands in his lap. "Do you know of the great Indian Removal?"

"I know some. President Jackson signed a bill that allowed the government to negotiate with several tribes in the southeast."

"Negotiate so your government could take their land."

A flush of anger rose in her cheeks. "He gave them the *entire western half of the continent* and forbade settlers to cross that line."

"And yet, you are here."

The widow's face paled.

He spread his arms to indicate places far beyond where they were sitting. "These lands have been home to our people for as long as the stories of their ancestors can recount. Did you think the trees went unidentified until the white man came to name them? That directions could not be given until your people arrived to name the cities and designate the states?"

"I hadn't really thought about it," she said in a voice so soft it was almost a whisper.

"Many years before, a group of clans you know as Creek lived along the rivers in Alabama. There were warriors among them, but most were farmers and fishermen. They gave your government permission to widen the trail that ran through Creek territory, so American settlers could use it.

"Creeks welcomed white travelers who were passing through their lands. They operated outposts and inns, and served as guides and interpreters. All was well, at first, but the peace did not last.

"Whites began to settle on Creek land. Some Creeks welcomed the whites and their ways, but others called for war. Settlers and the sympathetic Creeks sought refuge at Fort Mims. Creek warriors attacked the fort, and your government declared war. The Creek Nation was defeated and forced to cede millions of acres of land."

Eva looked troubled. "I was told the Creeks were hostile... that they attacked settlers for no reason."

Isaac shook his head. "Most were peaceful. A few disagreed with assimilating whites, and it caused a civil war.

"The first group to be expelled was forced to make the long journey on foot, in winter, without any food or supplies. Men were arrested while working in their fields, and women and children were dragged from their homes. Soldiers prodded the old and weak with bayonets to make them walk faster.

"The removal took years. Thousands of Indians perished. They slept on the ground without blankets, exposed to the wind and rain. Some died from dysentery and disease. In the winter, they froze. In summer, heat and drought killed them. They buried their dead in graves along the way."

Tears shimmered in her eyes. "You were just a baby then," she said as she swiped them away. "How can you be sure?"

"Some of it was passed down through stories told by my people. Some I read. When I overhear whites speak of those times, they confirm it." The memories of settlers who passed through his people's lands, bragging and laughing about the atrocities, made his lip curl. "Whites often loosened their tongues in my presence because they did not think I understood their language. Now they do so because they think I am one of them."

Eva's eyes said she believed him, but her face looked tense and uncertain. "Do you wish to leave and live as you did before?"

He could answer truthfully with both *yes* and *no,* and that was the problem.

Isaac slowed his breathing and regained control of his emotions. "I am content to remain here and help you cultivate your land."

Eva's features wilted with relief. "I know I've been unkind to you at times, but I'm grateful for your help, and I'm glad you're here. I am also sorry for the barbaric acts of my government," she added with soft sincerity. "No one deserves to be treated that way."

Isaac could not find his voice to respond, so he offered her a nod.

Strands of her pale hair blew across her face on the breeze. She caught them with her dainty fingers and tucked them behind her ear. "It must sadden your people when they hear these things."

"I do not tell them, not everything."

"Why not?"

"The knowledge would stir hatred and make them attack whites. Violence brings war. Lives would be lost, and so would my people's land."

Isaac drank the last of the tea from his jar and pushed to his feet. He held out his hand to help Eva up. "Come. We have three more acres to seed before sundown."

The pain in Eva's right arm had become a constant burning ache. She massaged the muscles while Isaac hooked the wooden harrow to his horse's harness.

They had only seeded two more acres after lunch. They wouldn't have made two total if he hadn't started using both hands. She had talked him into letting her try, but she couldn't cast properly to her left.

Isaac looked up and made a shooing motion. "Go rest. This will not take long."

Eva gathered up the remnants of lunch and trudged to the dugout. She wished she could fall face-first onto her bed, but after working circles around her, Isaac would be hungry. She needed sustenance, too, which meant she had to cook. Worse yet, she had to find the strength to cast seed for another eight days.

The sabbath couldn't come soon enough.

Connor's horse was tethered in her yard, and its rider sat a few feet away, on Keith's bench.

Connor smiled and waved. "Good evenin'."

"Same to you! I didn't expect to see you or Mr. McKinnon for at least a week." They had heeded Isaac's advice, so the storm had delayed their seeding, too.

He pushed himself up off the bench with the help of his cane and pointed to a basket sitting next to him. "I ken this was yer first time tae seed a field, so I brought supper."

"Connor McDougall, you are a saint." Eva held up the empty tea jars. "Let me put these away, and I'll come back for the basket."

"Nae need. I can manage." He trailed behind her with careful, uneven steps and set the basket on the table.

Eva removed her bonnet and brushed the dust from her clothes. "I must look a fright." She smelled a fright, too. And, since there would be no time to do laundry, it would only get worse as the week went on.

Connor lowered himself into a chair at the table while she washed her face and hands. "How many acres did ye sow?"

"Only three between us."

"Ye'll gain speed with practice."

Eva let out a bark of laughter. "My arm disagrees."

The scent of fresh bread filled the room when she removed the cloth from the top of the basket. A mound of rolls had been tucked beside a stoneware crock. She lifted the lid and saw chicken, vegetables, and fat fluffy noodles swimming in a rich broth. "When did you find time to make this?"

"A man who had jus' claimed land a few farms over took pity on me an' sent his son tae help us plant. The lad was shocked tae see me casting right along with Mac. He'd never seen it done from tha saddle. He stayed, though, an' that freed me up."

Eva pulled two bowls from the cupboard and held up a third in silent question.

"Thank ye, but I willny be stayin'. I plan tae ride back an' eat with Mac."

"Stay for some tea, at least."

"I suppose I can linger a few minutes." He no doubt rued the painful walk back to his horse as much as she rued tomorrow's planting.

Eva served their tea and tried not to drool into her empty bowl. "Isaac best hurry if he wants his portion."

Connor paused with his cup half way to his mouth and smiled. "Have tha two o' ye made yer peace?"

"I think so. He's just... not what I expected."

"Is anyone? When ye truly ken them, I mean."

Eva tilted her head in concession. Isaac wasn't the person she'd assumed he would be, and what she'd been told about his kind wasn't accurate either.

Isaac came in the door and hung up his hat.

"Connor brought us supper," Eva said with a grin.

He sniffed the air as he went to rinse his hands. "What is his fee?"

Eva opened her mouth to scold him for his rudeness then noticed the twinkle of mischief in his eyes.

"Ten beaver pelts an' a stringer o' fish," Connor shot back with theatrical flourish.

"No deal."

Isaac dried his hands and joined them at the table as Eva finished filling their bowls. "How many acres did you and Mac sow?"

"Six, but we had help." Connor related the story about the neighbor's son. "Have ye encountered any more thievin' vandals?"

Isaac shook his head. "You?" Mac's farm had been untouched the night they'd returned from town, but that was no guarantee it would stay that way.

"Thankfully, no." Connor replied. "If ye'll excuse me, I'll be goin'." He pushed himself up from the chair. "Thank ye fur tha tea, Mrs. McCabe."

"Thank *you* for the rolls and the soup. It's delicious."

"Yes. Thank you," Isaac added.

Connor paused at the door. "If Mac an' I finish seedin' afore ye, we'll come help. G'night."

Isaac tucked into his meal, as did Eva. Judging by the way she had shed her manners, she was as hungry as he. He didn't comment, just watched her out the corner of his eye. A smile tugged at his lips when she sopped broth from the bottom of her bowl with the last shred of her roll.

Eva sat back and let out a contented groan. "That was the best soup I've ever tasted."

He held out a roll to her. "Be sure to get it all."

Her mouth dropped open, and she swatted his hand away. But then she blushed and smiled. "Connor has talent in the kitchen."

"He has talent for many things." Isaac spooned more soup into his bowl. "He also has fond feelings for you."

"I doubt that."

"He hides it well, but it is there."

"He's just being neighborly. His fond feelings are directed toward a lady back home."

"He never speaks of her."

"Probably because he sees no way to provide for a wife," Eva retorted. She sighed. "Connor and Mac were like brothers to Keith. They feel honor bound to look after me, that's all."

That was not all. She either did not see it or did not want to. "Does his infirmity repel you?"

"No. I admire him for living a respectable life in spite of it."

"Would you consider marriage to him if he asked?"

"I wouldn't turn him down because of his leg. But this conversation is pointless," she said, rising and collecting her bowl. "Connor would never put me in that position."

About that, she was probably right.

Eva's face was lined with exhaustion by the time she'd cleaned the dishes. "Would you be offended if I turn in early?"

"No. I am tired, too."

Isaac walked to the barn, feeling as if he'd been tasked with restraining the wind. He had explored Eva's feelings for Connor because he would not thwart a romantic pursuit by a man he respected. Her reaction was a relief and a scourge. Nothing stood between them to save Eva from him, or to save him from himself.

'*Content to stay*,' he had told her. Isaac let out a rueful chuckle over that lie. He was so ensnared he could not leave if his life depended on it.

Chapter Eleven

Eva set their lunch on a blanket under a tree and crumpled next to it. She and Isaac had worked from morning till night for six days, and they had only seeded twenty of the thirty-six acres. If she'd allowed them to work on Sunday, they wouldn't be so far behind.

Casting countless bags of seed had scraped her hands raw. Pain shot through her arm so intensely with every throw she had to grit her teeth to keep from crying out. Why had she been so headstrong? She should have known better than to stay and cultivate the claim.

Eva leaned her head against the tree and closed her windburned eyes. She was hungry, but she was too tired to eat. Tears stung as they collected behind her lids. They spilled out and wet a trail down her dusty cheeks.

She ducked her head when the familiar trod of Isaac's boots approached. He'd hunted and tanned all those pelts for nothing. He was probably wishing he hadn't agreed to stay. Maybe she should admit defeat and free him from his obligation.

His steps slowed as he neared the blanket.

She kept her eyes downcast and stared at his boots.

"Why do you cry?" he asked as he squatted next to her.

She looked up at him through her lashes. "My arm hurts so much I don't think I can finish seeding. We're already behind, and... I'm s-sorry I got y-you into this." Eva covered her face with her hands and wept.

"Do not cry." He handed her his handkerchief. "You are tired," he said on a sigh then stood and walked away.

Eva blotted her eyes as anger dried her tears. She was more than just *tired*. She was exhausted and in pain. She'd bared her feelings in a mortifying display, and he'd dismissed her as if it meant nothing.

Maybe she would fire him and hire someone else.

A mocking laugh bubbled up her throat. *With what money?*

Isaac returned as she was unwrapping the bread and cheese sandwiches she'd packed for lunch. "Drink this," he said, handing her a tin cup of murky water.

"What is it?"

"Herbs to help your pain."

She sniffed it and wrinkled her nose. Hopefully it tasted better than it smelled. "I'm sorry to be such a burden," she said with a generous dash of resentment.

Isaac sat cross-legged on the blanket and eyed her, as if taking stock of her mood. "You are not a burden."

"I heard you sigh when you walked away."

"I am annoyed with myself for overworking you." He opened one of the jars of cool tea she'd brought and reached for a sandwich then lifted his chin in the direction of the tin cup. "Drink."

Eva took a small sip of Isaac's medicinal concoction. The flavor reminded her of cut hay with an aftertaste of chewed clover leaves—not something she would choose, but not unpalatable. She drank it as fast as she could without burning her mouth then chased it with a generous gulp of the tea she had made.

"I will plant alone so you can rest," Isaac said between bites.

"But you said every day mattered."

"It does." He tipped his tea jar to his lips and took a long series of swallows.

"Then we both need to work."

"We have planted enough to feed your animals. Anything more is surplus."

"Yes—to sell, in case my herd doesn't increase enough to make a profit."

Isaac picked up the last sandwich and held it out to her until she took it. "Profit is not necessary to keep your claim. You must only cultivate the land. We will plant as much as we are able, but, so long as you grow enough crops to sustain you and your animals, you will not fail."

"I also have to buy next season's seed, and the next."

"We will have more pelts by then."

His reply angered her as much as it calmed her. The dratted man truly had an answer for every blessed thing. "Do you ever worry about *anything*?"

He shrugged. "Sometimes. But worry cannot change tomorrow. It only steals one's strength today."

"You sound like Keith," she muttered. "*Take therefore no thought for the morrow, for the morrow shall take thought for the things of itself.*"

"*Take no thought for your life,*" Isaac replied, "*what ye shall eat, or what ye shall drink. Behold the fowls of the air: for they sow not, neither do they reap, nor gather into barns; yet your heavenly Father feedeth them. Are ye not much better than they?*"

Eva's lips parted, and she stared at him in complete consternation. *I do not know this man at all.* "Do you believe in God?"

"Yes. I was taught the legends of my people and about the God my mother prays to."

"Do you pray to Him?"

"Sometimes."

"How can you believe in both religions?"

A crease appeared between Isaac's brows, and he blinked a few times. "The religion of my people is not like yours. It is not something carried in a book and taught to others. Mojave religion is passed down through stories and influenced by powerful dreams. It is something one experiences."

A church without a minister to oversee it would be chaos. "Is there anyone in charge? Do you have clergy?"

"There are leaders, but one cannot seek those titles. Positions such as shaman, chief, and counselor cannot be earned. People are chosen by the spirits to occupy those positions."

"How do you know who they are?"

"The chosen ones experience powerful dreams from infancy. It is how they receive their power and how the clan recognizes their status as they grow. Unlike the religions of whites, an outsider cannot convert and become Mojave."

"Not even someone like your mother?"

He shook his head. "All members of the tribe are connected to the creator by blood. Through years of patience and humility, my mother has been accepted by my father's people. Her presence has been woven into their history and will be passed down in stories for generations, but she can never be Mojave."

Eva pondered what life would be like, settling somewhere you would never be fully accepted. "Is she happy?"

"She was not at first, but that changed. She and my father have much love. Neither will ever leave the marriage."

Eva nibbled on her sandwich. She wanted to know more, but didn't want to cause offense.

Isaac narrowed his eyes at her. "Your mind is not satisfied."

She took a sip of tea and debated how to phrase what she wanted to say. "Many of my people think Indians are heathens who worship false gods and have no morals—no bible or rules to guide their behavior—and that is why they attack outsiders and steal from them."

His chest rose and fell with a measured breath. "It is true we have no written texts. That is because our traditions are passed down by way of songs and stories. We also have few rules. But that does not mean we have no sense of morality to guide our behavior." A look of condescension hardened his eyes. "White men of God come, waving their books full of rigid commandments, yet they treat our people as if they have never read them. Rules are meaningless if men are unwilling to follow them."

He drew another slow breath, and the blatant ire left his eyes. "Not all missionaries treat us poorly," he said in a softer tone. "Some show respect and try to understand our ways. But most view us as shallow and simple, which has turned many of my people deaf to hearing their message. If not for my mother, I would have spit on the white man's religion."

"I am sorry for the way your people were treated, and I'm glad you had the influence of your mother. Did she teach you about Jesus?"

"Yes." A smile tugged at the corner of his mouth. "Jesus would have been a good Mojave. He went into the wilderness to seek wisdom, and He was willing to die for His clan."

He leaned against the base of the tree and stretched out his legs. "Tell me about your husband."

He had answered her questions. It was only fair she do the same. "Keith was...shy. He listened more than he spoke. But he had a contagious smile. He also had a calming effect on everyone around him. It didn't matter how deeply ingrained the disagreement; he could often make peace with one soft-spoken sentence."

"Did he treat you as well as he treated others?"

Eva nodded. "He had a gentle soul." She smiled at a fond recollection of her husband putting a walnut shell over his nose, holding up large magnolia leaves in place of his ears, and braying like a donkey. "Whenever I became overly serious, he would do things to make me laugh. He had a boyish sense of humor that stood in contrast to how hard a worker he was."

Eva blushed. "Listen to me carrying on. What about you? Have you ever been married."

"No."

She didn't want to upset him again, but she was curious. "Do you have a lady friend, someone special you had to leave behind?"

Isaac shook his head. "Just my mother. My family."

"I can tell you miss them. I hope you'll see them again someday," she said sincerely.

"That is my wish, too," he replied just as earnestly, but his dismal tone implied he didn't believe it would ever happen.

Eva set her empty tea jar aside. She rubbed her right shoulder and moved her arm in a circular motion to test it. "The herbs helped. My arm doesn't hurt as much."

"I am glad, but you should rest today."

"I–"

"*Shh.*" Isaac held up his hand, palm out. "A horse approaches."

Eva tilted her head and listened. The faint trod of hooves thumped in the distance. How had he heard that over the noise of their conversation?

When the horse neared enough that she could recognize its rider, she stood and brushed the dust from her dress. "It's Mr. Kramer."

Isaac stood, as well.

Dwight reined his horse to a stop and looked down at them from the saddle. "Mrs. McCabe." He smiled and tipped his hat. "Mr. Shaw. Taking a leisurely nooning, I see."

"Guilty," Eva replied. "How are your crops? They had to be mere seedlings when the storm came. Did they survive?"

Dwight swung down out of the saddle. "A few washed away, but most of them made it."

Eva released a breath. "Good. Now that I know how much work goes into planting, I was praying you wouldn't have to do it all over again." She tied on her bonnet and tucked the loose strands of hair underneath it. "Forgive me for rushing you, but we must get back to work. What's the reason for your visit?"

"I came by to see if I could do anything to help,"—he cut his eyes to Isaac—"you getting a late start and all."

Isaac stepped forward and stood at Eva's side. "We do not need help."

She placed her hand on his forearm. "Perhaps not, but Mr. Kramer has come to offer his assistance. I'm inclined to take him up on it."

Isaac looked ask if he wanted to growl—at her *and* Mr. Kramer.

Eva ignored him, stood a little taller, and squared her shoulders. "I can't pay you for your labor," she told Dwight.

"I wasn't expecting you to."

"If you help, you can join us for meals."

Dwight grinned. "That'll be payment enough."

Isaac stalked past Dwight. "I will get another seed bag."

"No need," Dwight said, reaching into his saddle bag. "I brought my own." He shook the wrinkles out of the wadded cloth sack. "Just give me a moment to hobble my horse."

"Would you rather put him in the pasture? Gally would love the company, I'm sure."

"Well, all right. If you insist."

She gestured to Isaac, who was standing there, scowling. "Mr. Shaw can store your saddle."

Dwight handed his saddle and pad over, swapped the reins for a lead line, and set his bags under the shade of the tree. "Walk with me?"

"Yes," Eva replied with a smile. If she was going to string him along till fall, might as well pay him a little interest. Dwight winged his arm, and she accepted his escort.

He glanced back over his shoulder as they walked. "Your new farm hand is getting a little above his station, don't you think?"

"He's just protective of me."

"Well, that's a good thing, I suppose. Though why he feels the need to protect you from me, I can't understand."

Eva smiled at the ground and kept her counsel. "Perhaps it had more to do with the planting than with me. Some men pride themselves on their work and take an offer of help as a personal affront."

"Is he a good worker?"

"He is."

Dwight frowned. "Even so, I can't believe he's making you help with the seeding."

Eva stopped walking and let go of his arm. "Mr. Shaw isn't forcing me to work. I'm helping because I want to. Quite frankly, I'm helping because I must."

"Well, you won't have to anymore. I'll come seed every day until your spring crop is sown."

"I'm grateful for your help."

Eva started walking back to the field as Dwight opened the pasture gate and turned his horse loose, so she could stay a step ahead. His escort had been entirely proper, but physical contact of any sort would encourage him, and it would irritate Isaac.

Judging by the look on his face as they reached the field, it already had.

"You need rest," Isaac said to her as she slipped her seed bag over her head.

"I'll seed a row or two then go make supper."

Isaac gave one of his silent nods, but she could tell he was choking on the urge to argue. Being forced to share a meal with Dwight was stuck in his craw right beside it.

"I can cast two-handed," Dwight said to her as he put on his bag. "You don't need to stay."

"Oh, but I do. I want to assure myself the two of you can work side by side without it coming to blows." Eva ignored their slack-jawed stares and filled her bag with seed.

The scent of beefsteak wafting from the oven was heavenly. Eva smiled as she took two big juicy pies out to cool. Mac had paused his seeding long enough to slaughter a young cow and share his bounty, so she had baked an extra pie in return. She carefully lowered it into a towel-lined box and carried it over. If things went as planned, she would get it there before the men started making supper.

She met Mac and Connor walking up from the barn. *Perfect timing.*

"Well, hullo, lass," Mac said. "I dinnae expect tae see ye till Sunday."

Connor limped up, several steps behind, leaning heavily on his cane. He sniffed the air. "Is that whit I think it is?"

Eva grinned. "If you guessed beefsteak pie, then yes."

A wide smile spread across Connor's face, but it didn't hide his exhaustion or his discomfort. His leg must really be hurting.

Realization smacked the center of her chest and left it aching. Mac hadn't slaughtered because they needed the meat. He had sacrificed a day of seeding to give Connor a rest.

Mac went ahead of her and opened the door to his cabin. It had a dugout cellar in back, like hers, but the house itself was made from logs he had felled. "Make yerself comfortable. We'll be in as soon as we wash aff tha dust."

Eva put the pie on the table and filled two glasses with milk. She set out plates, cutlery, and napkins then looked around for anything else she could do to spare Connor from walking.

He hobbled in and dropped into his chair. "Eva McCabe, ye are truly heaven sent."

Mac walked up behind her and frowned. "Ye dinnae set enough plates."

"I can't stay."

"Vera well, but sit a minute an' tell us how yer faring with tha seeding." Mac said, pulling out a chair for her.

"We were falling behind," she said as she sat, "until yesterday, when Mr. Kramer came to help us plant."

"Whit does Isaac think aboot that?" he asked, placing a generous portion of the pie onto Connor's plate then one on his own.

Eva smirked. "He doesn't like it. But if they cover as much ground as they did yesterday, they'll finish today."

Connor chuckled. "Nothin' like pride an' spite tae get tha work done."

"What about you two? Did you seed all your acres?"

"No' yet," Mac said. "Another day er two, at most." He paused before digging into his pie. "Do ye think Mr. Kramer suspects anythin'?"

"No. I've caught him staring at Isaac a couple of times, but he hasn't raised any concerns. And as much as he resented me hiring a stranger, he would."

"Yer probably right. But Isaac should avoid lengthy encounters with anyone, especially Dwight. The man's got eyes fur ye an' yer land."

Eva emerged from the path that connected her land to Mac's just as Dwight was returning from the field. "Where's Isaac?"

Dwight removed his hat and blotted his brow with his handkerchief. "He stayed behind to harrow."

"Did you finish seeding?"

"We did."

Eva beamed. "That's wonderful! Come eat. Supper's ready."

Dwight swatted at his shirt and trousers, knocking loose an impressive cloud of dust. "I'll be in as soon as I wash up."

By the time he entered the dugout—wet hair slicked down, damp to his collar, and his cuffs rolled-back—she'd made coffee and set the table for three.

Dwight hung his hat on a peg then looked down at his trousers that were still tinged with lingering dirt. "I'm not fit to sit at your table."

Eva motioned for him to join her. "You're cleaner than the ceiling and the floor. Sit." She poured them a cup of coffee each and joined him. "Thank you again for helping us."

Pink glazed his cheeks. "'Tweren't nothing."

"Yes, it was. It might very well be the difference between failure and success for my crops."

Eva tested her coffee with a tentative sip then cooled it by adding a bit of cream. "I was glad to hear yours survived the deluge. It's a wonder those little seedlings weren't washed away."

Dwight nodded and touched his cup of steaming coffee to his lips. At his flinch, Eva held up the cream pitcher. He shook his head. "Thank you. I'll just wait for it to cool."

Eva fidgeted with the handle of her cup, changing its direction back and forth, then tucked her hand in her lap. She searched for something she could say, to make conversation about *any* topic besides Dwight's desire to court her. "You bought some hogs, correct?"

"I did."

"How do they fare?"

"Very well, as a matter of fact. But boy, are they smelly."

"I'm sure," she said with a laugh. "Though I never would've known you had them, had Mr. McKinnon not told me. You must've built their enclosure downwind. And for that, I thank you." That got a smile big enough to show off Dwight's dimples.

They disappeared as he took a cautious sip of his coffee. "So, this Isaac fella... Where's he from?"

"I... I don't know, exactly," she said, doing her best to hide the panic his question caused and quell the eddy he'd just set to spinning in her gut. "Mr. Shaw doesn't say much about himself."

"He said he's a friend of Mr. McKinnon. Mac didn't tell you about him?"

"He did," she said, spinning a tale she hoped wouldn't weave a different web than Isaac, "but not personal details. Mac recommended him on the strength of his abilities—and to act as my protector, after the incident with the men." She cast him a sheepish look and hoped the color in her cheeks cooperated. "I'm not usually given to such rash decisions, but Mr. Shaw seemed heaven sent, so I didn't press for more."

An odd look passed across Dwight's face. He opened his mouth to speak, but Eva pretended she didn't notice and glanced at the changing tint of the light coming through the window.

"Look how late it's getting," she blurted. "I'm a terrible hostess, making you wait so long." She brought the meat pie from its warm place on the stove and set it on the table. "I'm sure Mr. Shaw will forgive us for starting the meal without him," she said as she cut it and placed a hearty serving on Dwight's plate.

His eyes got big. "If that pie tastes as good as it looks, there won't be any left."

Eva laughed. "Well, then, for his sake, I hope he comes soon." She served herself and resisted the urge to dig in like a starving beggar. Supper had been tempting her since she'd dropped off the other pie at Mac's.

Dwight took his first bite and groaned his approval.

"Gmood?" Eva asked around a chunk of flaky crust.

"Mm," Dwight grunted, nodding his head and chewing.

They dove in and ate, too busy savoring the food to bother with conversation. Eva consumed her meal with such singular focus she started when the door swung open.

Isaac stepped inside and surveyed the scene with a sour expression.

She gulped down the bite she'd taken. "We waited supper on you for a while, but it was getting late." Eva laid her napkin on the table and rose to get him some coffee.

"Sit," he said, taking the cup from her hand. "I will get it."

She obliged him but put a large piece of pie on his plate while he was at the stove and looked to Dwight. "Would you like a second helping?"

"Please."

"I made two pies," she remarked to Isaac as she served Dwight. "I took the other one to Mr. McKinnon and Mr. McDougall."

Dwight brought his cup to his lips and peered at her over the rim. "What did they do to deserve such treatment? Tell me so I can do likewise."

Eva smirked. "Butcher a cow and give me half." She sipped her coffee and cradled her cup in her hand. "All kidding aside, I was returning a favor. They're still seeding. I took it so Mr. McDougall wouldn't have to cook."

Isaac stopped eating and looked up. "They are not finished?"

"No, but Mr. McKinnon said they would be in a day or two."

"I will go help them," Isaac said as he forked a bite of pie. He looked up and pinned Dwight with an unblinking stare. "Perhaps Mr. Kramer will also."

Dwight stopped chewing and looked back and forth between Isaac and her. He swallowed and cleared his throat. "Um. Sure. I can spare another day."

Eva needed a moment to recover, too. She was shocked that Isaac would choose to spend a moment longer with Dwight than he had to—much less a day.

She smiled at Dwight. "That's kind of you. I know they will be grateful." She looked over at Isaac. "Mr. Kramer is a godsend, truly. I was berating myself for resting on the sabbath and delaying the planting, but then he showed up. My obedience was rewarded so much that my cup overflows."

Isaac continued eating, spearing his pie with his fork as if he harbored ill will toward his sustenance.

Eva let him stew and turned back to Dwight. "Tell Mr. McDougall when you see him tomorrow that I'll provide lunch and supper for the lot of you."

The dimple in Dwight's left cheek reappeared. "Will do." He polished off his second helping of pie and drained the coffee from his cup. "Thank you, Mrs. McCabe. That was the best meal I've had in years," he said as he set his napkin on his plate. "If you'll excuse me, I'll collect my horse and head home. It'll be dark soon."

Isaac paused the slaughtering of his food. "Your horse is saddled and waiting for you in the yard," he said in a dismissive tone, gratitude nowhere in evidence.

Instead of swatting Isaac's knuckles with her fork—which was what he deserved—Eva rose and pasted on a pleasant expression. "I'll see you out." She followed Dwight to the place where his horse was tethered. "I apologize for Mr. Shaw's attitude. I don't know what's gotten into him."

"I dare say it's what gets into *any* man when he's around you."

Heat filled Eva's cheeks. She brushed his comment aside with a wave of her hand. "Mr. Kramer..."

"That wasn't some crafty pile of flattery. It's true. I've seen the way men look at you, Isaac included. He does a fine job, farming your land, but he seems awfully jealous. Are you sure you're safe with him here?"

"Mr. Shaw has proven himself trustworthy to my satisfaction. I think what you interpret as jealousy is just him being protective."

"Maybe so," Dwight said as he tightened his horse's girth. "Thanks again for the meal. Tell Isaac I'll meet him at Mac's after breakfast."

"I will," she said as he mounted. "Goodnight."

Dwight touched the brim of his hat and took off at a trot toward home.

Eva watched him go then walked back to the dugout, her irritation growing with each step. Something had most assuredly gotten into Isaac. Dwight had given them two good days' work and, as far as she knew, hadn't made any trouble. Yet Isaac was seething by the time they were done. He'd treated a good Samaritan rudely for no defensible reason.

She closed the door and rounded on him. "What in heaven's name is the matter with you!"

He looked up, his brow creased by a frown.

"I have *never* been so embarrassed," she went on. "Mr. Kramer gifted us with *two full days* of work in the field, and you treated him as if he was a smear of dung on your shoe. I don't know how it is with *your people,* but whites don't do that to our neighbors—especially when they go out of their way to give us aid."

Isaac stared at his plate and stayed silent, his lips pressed into a thin line, and a muscle at his temple twitching like a worm on a hook.

She drew a deep breath and got control of her temper. "Did Mr. Kramer bring this on himself?" She doubted it. The men were far from friendly, but they'd been working in harmony every time she'd ventured out to the field. "If he did something worthy of such poor treatment, then tell me."

Isaac rose without making eye contact.

"Well?" she prodded as he took his half-eaten supper to the dry sink. "What do you have to say for yourself?"

He braced his hands on the edge, his back to her and his arms straight and stiff, then turned around and pinned her with a furious glare. "That man is a jackal," Isaac spat. "He comes as a friend, but he is a trickster who will turn on you at the first opportunity."

"Only if I give him one."

"If? There is no *if.* You have welcomed a viper."

"Mr. Kramer might be a bit self-serving—who isn't? But he's no viper."

"Your feelings have blinded you."

"What feelings? Dwight is my neighbor, nothing more."

Isaac took a step toward her, his eyes churning like a storm-tossed sea. "He is more. You walk with him, smile at him, show him favor."

"I am quite aware of myself. I don't need you to tell me how I behave."

Isaac's nostrils flared with an indrawn breath. "You plan to marry him."

"I do not. I'm keeping my options open until I see how my crops and cattle fare," she said fidgeting with the edge of her cuffs. "Showing Mr.

Kramer a little attention from time to time will keep him happy. But this conversation is pointless." She lowered her arms and spread her hands out, indicating her black clothing. "I'm in deep mourning. I shouldn't marry anyone until winter, at least."

Isaac's hands balled into fists. "The viper wants your land."

"We've established that."

"He *is not good* for you."

"He–"

Isaac lunged toward her and grasped the nape of her neck. He towered over her, staring into her eyes, his chest brushing against hers with every ragged breath. He slowly lowered his head until his mouth was so close to hers she could feel his breath. He paused there, searching her eyes. Then he touched his lips to hers.

The kiss was gentle, yet it took command of her as his hand had taken control of her nape, tilting her head according to his will and holding her captive. His beard was all at once soft and rough against her face. A rush of prickles skittered over her body. She was boneless in his grip.

Isaac lifted his head and searched her eyes again. Fierce emotions had given way to smoldering banked coals. He released her and stepped back.

Eva's sanity returned with the loss of contact. A rush of shame and indignation came with it. She drew back her hand and hurled it towards his face with all her might.

Isaac caught her wrist midair. "Curse me. Hate me. Send me away. But do not strike me because of a kiss. Especially one that was shared."

"I'm in mourning! What you did was highly inappropriate."

"I gave you time to say no. You knew what was going to happen, and you did nothing to stop it."

Eva struggled against his grip. "Let me go. You're scaring me."

"I am not." He kept hold of her wrist as his gaze traveled over her face, her neck, then came back up and locked with hers. "The pounding of your heart, the blood warming your skin, the darkness filling your eyes...that is lust, not fear."

She drew back a leg and kicked him.

Isaac blocked it with his leg, but he released her. "You know that I am right. Dwight does not make you feel these things. And neither did your husband."

Eva gasped. "You bastard," she uttered in a low trembling whisper. Tears gathered in her eyes as Isaac took his hat from the peg and walked out. She grabbed her empty plate and flung it at the door.

Isaac did not regret speaking the truth, but the pain it brought to Eva's eyes had haunted his sleep all night. The dugout was locked the next morning, and no food waited. He should not have kissed her. She would certainly send him away this time. And if she did, she would be forced to give up her claim or marry Mr. Kramer.

He set the pail of milk on the porch and saddled his horse then led him down the path to Mac's. Maybe his absence would give Eva time to think about his words, to admit to herself that she was not as aware of herself as she thought.

It was plain to anyone with sight that Dwight Kramer did not arouse anything in Eva, except laughter, frustration, and occasional anger. But she was too restricted by the white man's ways to let that stop her from taking him as her husband. White women were taught to shun desire. Even in marriage.

When Eva had spoken about her late husband, the description she gave was that of a brother or a friend, not a man who stirred her passion. She longed to set those passions free whether or not she was willing to admit it.

Isaac often watched her from the edges of his vision—the way her gaze strayed to his arms, his chest, to parts of him that would cause her to glow with shame if she were caught. Eva was curious. Too curious for a widow.

Keith had not satisfied that part of her. If he had, her reaction would have been haughty anger, not tears.

Chapter Twelve

Dwight kept his word, and they finished seeding Mac's fields in one day. Eva kept her word, too, and fed them, but she did not stay to eat. By the time Isaac returned to her barn in the evening, she had already stabled her animals.

A locked door and empty porch awaited him when he brought the milk the following morning, so he made a meal of frybread and jerky from his hunting supplies. Eva needed her pasture fenced before she could take delivery of her cows, and he refused to be deterred. She would have to come send him away if she wanted him to stop working her land.

Isaac cut trees and hauled logs for several days, pausing from time to time to hew the cedar ones into posts, so his horse could rest. He ate frybread for breakfast, jerky for lunch, and roasted fish by the stream for supper. In the evenings, he bathed in the stream and washed his clothes. It was an existence to which he was well accustomed, but he missed Eva's company.

He finally caught a glimpse of her when he was splitting logs into fence rails and spreading them out to dry in the sun. She paused to look at him from beneath the brim of her bonnet on her way to the plot he had tilled for her vegetable garden. He could not see her features clearly at that distance, but he sensed her anger had not faded. He looked back down and tapped the next wedge into place.

Eva turned her head when the ping of metal striking metal sounded from the meadow. Isaac was splitting logs. She'd stopped feeding him, yet here he was, working just as hard.

Her throat still burned with anger over what he'd done. What had possessed him to kiss a widow in deep mourning then insult the husband she'd lost Eva could not fathom. Despite his assertions to the contrary, Isaac was not completely civilized, and he was much too bold.

She knelt by the first row of tilled earth and sifted through the packets of seeds in her apron pocket until she found the one marked *radish*. She would plant them on the opposite side of the garden from the carrots, as Isaac had advised. She'd heed his instructions, but only for the sake of her crops.

Who was she kidding? She'd heed his instructions and put up with his presence for the sake of her entire farm. She hadn't sent him away, because she couldn't. And that scorched her pride more.

What hurt most, though, was that he'd been right—about her and about Keith. Isaac had discerned her feelings of attraction to him and, worse, intimate details of her marriage, all from observation alone. Once she'd stopped throwing things and crying, she'd sat for hours, staring into the dark, mortified by what an open book she was.

Inching along on her knees, Eva made tiny wells with her finger and dropped in the seeds, then paused to cover them. Next, she planted several rows of cabbage. What didn't get eaten in summer could be preserved as kraut.

She paused to mop her face with her handkerchief and take a sip from her canteen. The days had been hot, of late, and the sun felt as if it was roasting her skin despite her clothes. Or perhaps because of them. Black made the heat more intense.

Eva straightened up and sat on her heels when bootsteps sounded behind her.

Isaac came and stood a few feet away, casting a cool column of shade in her direction.

She lifted her head but stopped short of making eye contact.

He stood silent, his arms by his sides. "I am sorry I made you cry," he finally said.

She raised her gaze higher when he turned and walked away, watching him go and mentally wading through the slurry of feelings the encounter had stirred. Even in anger, she was drawn to him—to his fit, masculine body and the mysteries it held.

Eva pushed herself to finish planting, debating whether her growing nausea was the result of the heat or her emotions. By the time she returned to the dugout, large patches of sweat stained her clothing, and she felt as if she might vomit.

She removed her dress and sighed as the air cooled her damp chemise. She wet a cloth and bathed her face and arms then changed into fresh clothes. Back home, women in deep mourning rarely went outside their homes or engaged in manual labor; but here, she had no choice. And the hottest months were yet to come.

Eva dropped into a chair and took a sip of water from her canteen. It stayed down, so she drank the rest in small swallows until she'd emptied it. By then, her digestion had righted itself. Isaac's apology had banked her anger, as well. Perhaps he deserved another chance. She'd all but starved him, and he hadn't deserted her.

When she prepared her supper, she'd make enough for him, too.

Eva debated welcoming Isaac back into the dugout for meals and decided against it. He was clearly struggling to restrain his passions. It was best not to tempt him.

She placed a roast beef sandwich, a jar of tea, and some dandelion salad in a shallow wood box and went to find him. A pail of milk sat on the porch, and the animals had been stabled, but he wasn't in the barn. He wouldn't go hunting this close to sundown, so Eva moved the pail of milk to the cool slab of slate in the cellar and ventured out to the fields.

He wasn't there either.

She was about to give up and turn back when she heard a chorus of cats meowing. The sound drew her to the stream.

Isaac was sitting cross-legged on the ground near a grove of willow trees, roasting fish over a small fire. An audience of yowling felines—her barn cats—formed a half-circle in front of him, like unruly spectators in a Grecian theater.

"Good evening," he called over the din. He frowned in the cats' direction. "Hush."

The yowls dropped to low feline whines and groans.

Eva sidled around the edge of them until she reached Isaac. His hand was occupied, holding the skewer of fish, so she set the box on the ground next to him. "I brought you some supper."

"Thank you. Have you eaten?"

Eva took a step back and clasped her hands in front of her. "Not yet."

He gestured to a stump a few feet away. "You are welcome to join me."

She wanted to decline, to save herself the embarrassment of being in the company of a man who could divine her deepest secrets with a glance, but she walked to the stump and sat. He had the same commanding influence over her as he did the cats. It was supernatural. It had to be.

Isaac lifted the cloth that was covering the food in the box with his free hand and peered inside.

"The sandwich is roast beef," she said, though he had probably figured that out from the smell.

Isaac lowered the cloth then examined the fish and held them over the flame a few minutes more.

Eva sat primly with her hands folded in her lap, but her insides were writhing like a bucket full of worms.

If Isaac felt any awkwardness, it didn't show. He looked the fish over again and used his knife to slide them off the skewer onto a smooth slab of wood then fanned them with his hat until they were cool enough to touch. He tore the flesh off one and tossed pieces to the cats, who had started up their yowling again. Within seconds, the only sounds were the crackling fire and the flow of the stream.

Isaac laid a whole fish on the cloth from the basket then stood and held it out to her.

Eva took it from him with some hesitation. Now she was committed to staying for the meal. But her mouth was incapable of forming a refusal.

"Did you finish planting your garden?" he asked as he sat back down.

"I did." Eva blew lightly on her fish then tore off a flaky white piece and tasted it. The fish wasn't seasoned that she could tell, but the smoky flavor from the fire made it delicious.

"I will wait until your seeds have taken root, then I will open the trench and give them some water."

Eva had a mouth full of fish, so she nodded her approval.

Isaac leisurely nibbled at his trout, while she picked hers clean in ill-mannered haste. How could he sit there calmly, as if they'd never shared more than a smile? Every time she looked at him, the memory of his kiss flashed through her mind like lightning and took her body by storm. It wasn't the kiss so much as him taking what he wanted in broad daylight, unashamed.

It was bold and uncivilized. And, God help her, that was the very thing she craved.

Issac popped a pinch of dandelion greens into his mouth then slid his knife from its scabbard and cut the sandwich in two. He held up half and raised a brow.

Eva shook her head. "I have one waiting back at the dugout." She rose and placed the trout-headed skeleton on the ground beside the box. "Thank you for the fish. Goodnight."

Before he could utter a reply, she'd spun and taken ten brisk steps in the opposite direction. It was rude, but she had to get out of his presence.

Eva went inside the dugout and closed the door. She dropped the bar into place then rested her forehead against the door and groaned. She'd forgotten to ask about the pasture fence. Mac wanted at least three days' notice when it was time to drive her cows home, and Isaac was the only one who knew when it would be complete.

She raised the bar and walked back to the stream.

The fire had been put out, and the area was deserted, except for the box she'd brought. Eva bent down and picked it up. She'd ask Isaac about the fence tomorrow morning.

Something big splashed in the water downstream.

Eva walked closer to the bank and peered past a willow tree, through its curtain of leaves. Her heart stuttered, and her lungs ceased to draw air.

Isaac stood nude in the center of the stream, facing away from her. Riparian trees formed a canopy above him, but the evening sun had dropped low enough to light them from beneath, shining its golden rays on his muscular form. His skin had been brown all over when he'd first arrived. Now his wrists and hands were the only parts of him that remained dark. His sculpted frame glistened in the slanted light, a testament to both his physical prowess and the demands of farm life.

He reached down and scooped up water with his large hands then poured it over his head. Rivulets cascaded down his broad shoulders, tracing the contours of his back and changing course as they ran over his muscular buttocks.

Eva stood, captivated by the sight. The sounds of nature—the rustling leaves, the distant calls of birds, the burbling flow of the water—intertwined with the thrumming of her heart and created a symphony of desire. The branches of the willow hid her, yet the veil bore witness to her stirrings of attraction, its beauty tainted by her fleshly yearnings.

She should shield her eyes and flee, yet she lingered, filled with need and unsettling shame. Isaac was handsome and virile, and she wanted him. More than she'd ever wanted Keith.

Eva choked on that traitorous thought as a wave of remorse made her turn and walk away. When she said her prayers tonight, she'd beg both God and Keith for forgiveness.

Isaac sped through morning chores, bolting down the breakfast Eva had left for him on his way to the pasture. He only had to build enough fence to keep the cows out of the fields—the side that bordered Mac's land could stay open—but the man who had sold Eva her cows would not board them much longer without increasing his fee.

He split three logs into rails and spread them out in the sun then dragged some older rails to the place he'd stopped construction and chiseled the ends.

Isaac smiled to himself when the sound of Eva's voice floated on the breeze in his direction. She was talking to her horse, telling him about the new cows that would come.

She lingered several minutes then came down the path and stood at the edge of the pasture, behind him. He did not need to look. Her footsteps told him where she was, just as they had the evening before.

Though he pretended otherwise, he had heard her return to the stream—her dainty steps, the change in the swish of the willow branches as they brushed against something solid—and knew she was watching him. He had kept his back to her but chose not to lower himself into the water. She needed to see what her body desired, to acknowledge her need, and she would not have watched if she feared being discovered.

"Mr. Shaw," she called.

Isaac stopped what he was doing and looked back at her, over his shoulder.

"How long until the fence is completed?"

"One week." At least.

She took a few steps toward him, the hem of her black dress skimming over the bright green spring grass. "We must retrieve my cows in five days, must we not?"

"To avoid additional cost, yes."

"Then I will help you. Tell me what to do."

Isaac finished securing the rail to the post and straightened up. Fence rails were too heavy for a woman to carry alone. The only aid she could give was lifting the opposite end helping him line them up with the holes in the posts. But it *would* increase the speed of his work some. Until she grew too tired and gave up.

"Come." He walked to the next post and pointed to the ground just past it. "Stand here." He retrieved a rail and set it on the ground, its ends near the posts it would be joined to. He repeated the action until three rails were lying side by side.

"I could have carried one of those?"

"No. They are too heavy."

Eva planted her hands on her hips. "How is me standing here helping the fence get built any faster?"

"I will show you." He gestured to the end of one of the rails, near her boot. "Grab it and lift when I tell you."

She bent over and wrapped her hands around the rail.

Isaac pointed to the top hole in the post. "We will lift it this high." He squatted and took hold of his end. "Ready?"

"Yes"

He gave a quick warning nod. "Now." He lifted his end slowly, keeping it lower than hers and taking the bulk of the weight. Still, Eva struggled to lift her portion.

They would need to fit her end first.

Still bearing most of the burden, Isaac lifted his chin to indicate the uppermost hole in Eva's post. "Line the end up and slide it in."

"I'll try," she said with a grunt. She widened her stance and aimed the chiseled end of the rail at the target. Her arms shook with the effort of holding it steady, but she lined it up and seated it enough to hold it in place.

"Let go," Isaac called. When her hands were well clear of the rail, he gave it a shove and pushed it in all the way in. Then he lined his up and jerked the rail back a few inches, until both ends rested far enough into the posts that they would stay.

They repeated the same process until all three rails had been seated.

Isaac had the endurance to keep working, but Eva had nearly dropped the last rail, so he paused and blotted his face with his handkerchief to give her a few moments of rest. If she lasted till lunch, it would surprise him.

She examined her hands and picked at a splinter.

"I will get some gloves," he said.

"I have some." She pulled a pair of leather work gloves from her pocket and put them on. They must have belonged to her husband. They were much too large.

Eva kept pace with him, though it was clear she was pushing herself to the limit of her endurance.

When the sun was overhead, she leaned against the fence and took a drink from her canteen. "If I keep helping, when will we finish?"

She had slowed with each section, but her assistance had increased his speed. "Four days." She would quit before that. "Maybe five."

Eva pushed herself off the fence. "I need to tell Mac. I'll bring lunch when I return."

Isaac spent the time she was gone setting posts. He joined her for a simple lunch of tea and corncakes under the nearest tree then got back to work.

They toiled under a cloudless sky, but the day was the hottest yet, and the sun shone so brightly it was blinding. Sweat coated Isaac's skin and dripped into his eyes. He wished he could strip off these white man's clothes and work in a breechcloth. But that was not wise. It would anger Eva, and the odd piece of clothing would raise suspicion. Going without his shirt would also reveal his tattoos and the scar on his shoulder.

He would not risk baring it in these lands until he knew the identity of the one who had inflicted it. And that day might never come.

Sitting in the shade of the tree had revived Eva. The pace of her work improved for a time. But then she began to slow, more so than before. Her movements grew sluggish, and her steps occasionally faltered.

She stumbled and caught hold of the fence.

"You should stop working," Isaac said.

"I'm all right." She let go of the beam and walked on then paused at the next post to drink from her canteen. She capped it and motioned for him to bring another set of rails.

Against his better judgment, he did. They seated the first one and reached to get the second.

Eva lifted her end, breathing heavily. She blinked and stared at the post but made no move to line up the rail.

"Mrs. McCabe?"

She dropped her end of the rail—barely missing her foot—then swayed back and forth and crumpled to the ground.

Isaac tossed the rail aside and ran. He knelt beside her and patted her face. "Mrs. McCabe." A thin powdery line edged the large patches of sweat that stained her clothing, and an odd pallor blanched the hollow beneath the red flush of her cheeks. He removed her gloves and examined her hands. They were hot and dry—too dry. "*Eva*," he said, jostling her shoulders. "Wake up."

She did not respond, so he scooped her up and carried her to the stream, to a place shaded by trees that was deep enough to reach his waist. He waded into the water, to the center, then bent his knees to get them lower.

The stream flowed over Eva's body, its current weaving through the folds of her dress. The black fabric darkened as it absorbed the cool liquid, making him wish he had rid her of it before wading in. The thin slip she wore beneath it would not have hidden her beauty from him.

Isaac held her steady, her shoulders and knees supported by his arms and her head lolled sideways against his shoulder, and waited for the water to wash the heat away. Visions of holding her this way had come to him many times in his dreams, and he savored the minutes that passed despite his worry.

Eva opened her eyes and blinked at the dappled sunlight filtering through the blurry leaves overhead. A heaviness weighted her limbs, and damp clothing clung to her skin. Her right side rested against something hard. It was someone's chest. Isaac's chest. He was cradling her like a baby.

She struggled to free herself.

His grip on her tightened. "Do not move. You will drown."

Eva put all her effort into focusing her eyes and figuring out where they were. It looked like the stream that ran through her property. "Why are we in the water?"

"The sun kicked you."

She looked up into his eyes and frowned. "It did what?"

"The sun made you hot while we were building the fence, and you fainted."

"Oh." She looked around again and wiggled her legs. "You can put me down."

"Not yet."

"I know how to swim."

"You are still weak."

She sighed and gave in. But only for a few minutes. Being cocooned in his strong arms was doing funny things to her insides that had nothing to do with her fainting spell. "If you're not going to let me go then take me ashore."

He frowned, but he began wading towards the bank. As the surface of the stream fell away, her clothes hung from her body like chain mail, sitting like a boulder on her chest and making her limbs feel like lead. Isaac's muscles bulged when he stepped from the stream up onto the sandy bank.

He looked down at her, still holding her like a child, as water sluiced off them and pelted the earth like rain. The lines around his eyes softened, but their centers burned a vivid blue.

Eva cut her gaze away. "Please, put me down."

He did as she asked, bracketing her shoulders with his hands until she'd proven she could stand unaided.

Eva gathered up a portion of her skirt and wrung the water out of it. She'd quit wearing stiff boned corsets when she came west, save for trips to town and formal events, but that might have been preferable to the quilted jumps she'd traded them for. It felt as if that one garment had soaked up more water than the rest of her clothing combined.

Isaac just stood there, as if his wet trousers were fresh from the ironing board. "Stay inside and rest tomorrow. I will work alone."

"I've already made plans with Mac to get the cows. And I refuse to pay a penny more for them," she said, picking up another section of her skirt. "Besides, women faint from time to time. We have special couches for that purpose. I'll be more careful in the future to take a break now and then."

"That will not be enough. You must wear less clothes and stop wearing black."

Eva let go of her skirt and glared at him. "*I can't.* The former would be indecent, and the latter would be irreverent—irreverent and disrespectful of my husband's memory."

"So, instead, you make yourself ill? Keith would not have allowed it, and neither will I."

"It's not your decision!"

"Yes, it is. Wear lighter colors, or do not come to the pasture."

He would refuse to work if she didn't obey. He was that stubborn.

Eva blew out a frustrated breath. "Isaac, you don't understand. I'm a widow in deep mourning. I'm expected to wear black. People will think poorly of me if I don't."

"Who? I would not. Mac and Connor would not either. No one but us sees you most days."

"But—"

"If no one is present to see, what purpose does it serve?"

"It serves a purpose for *me*. My husband deserves to be mourned."

"He does. But your heart is what mourns him, not your garments. Only you can know the depth of that."

She did. Every day. She could wear a hundred layers of the finest, darkest crape, and it would not convey the immense respect she had for Keith or the ache his absence had left in her heart.

"Wear black when you must," Isaac said, "but do not risk your life for the sake of etiquette."

Eva's spine lost its starch. His heels were dug in as deeply as hers had ever been. She was not going to change his mind.

"I won't be wearing *this* anywhere," she grumbled as she bent over and examined her hem. "It will take ten brushings to get out all the dirt." She lifted her waterlogged skirt—or rather, *skirts*; counting her petticoats, she had three—and tested the weight. "...If I make it back at all."

"I would tell you to lighten the load by removing some of your clothes," Isaac said with a twinkle of mischief in his eyes, "but I know better than to make that suggestion."

"Insolent man," Eva muttered. She lifted her soggy filthy hems off the ground and trudged back to the dugout.

Chapter Thirteen

She could stay here all day. Few things in life were this peaceful.

Eva stood at the new fence and gazed out over the pasture—her pasture—and her small herd of cows meandering on a carpet of vibrant green. She'd purchased all she could afford. But, God willing, the herd would double in size the first year. After that, it would grow exponentially, as more and more calves came into season.

The brown and white Herefords grazed methodically, save an occasional swat of a tail or flick of an ear, focused solely on the task of devouring the fresh spring grass. Their rhythmic munching added low notes to the morning birdsong filling the air.

Eva inhaled the earthy scent of dew-dampened land and said a prayer for the health of her herd. *May they live out their lives in peace, never knowing sickness or hunger.*

Isaac trotted up the path on his horse, riding bareback.

Eva looked up and shielded her eyes from the morning sun behind him. "Where did you run off to so early?"

"I went to visit Mac. Three of the cows are ready for his bull."

A sound that was part cough, part chuckle lodged in Eva's throat. Keith would've turned the color of a beet over that being said in the presence of a female.

Isaac, on the other hand, would no doubt invite her to the mating.

But that would be entirely fitting, considering her behavior of late. Not only had she put on light colors months before it was acceptable, she'd traded her quilted jumps for a thin cotton waistcoat, sinking further into an immoral state of dishabille. She might as well have thrown decorum into a sewer and stomped it.

Eva cut her eyes to Isaac as he dismounted and sent his horse into the paddock with a pat to the rump. "You're a bad influence on me, Mr. Shaw."

His brows drew together and dipped slightly "In what way? Your farm thrives, and so do you."

"Me?"

"Yes. You work in the heat without fainting, and you have put on weight since winter."

"Are you calling me fat?"

"I am saying you are no longer too thin."

Commenting on a woman's body was inappropriate, but lecturing him would be a waste of breath. "The crops are planted, and the cows are here. What do we do now?"

He gestured for her to walk with him then bent his elbow and offered his arm.

The courtesy was a shock, and she spent a full minute, pondering how to respond.

He must've watched Dwight and Mac and decided to imitate them. Might as well encourage good manners. She slipped her hand through and rested it lightly on his forearm.

"I had planned to walk the fields today," Isaac said, leading her at a leisurely pace back toward the dugout, "to check on the progress of the crops. Once that is done, I will fell trees and chop wood."

He had replenished the stolen firewood, but it wasn't nearly enough to last through winter. If he didn't chop the rest soon, it wouldn't have time to dry.

Eva slowed to a stop. "Will you teach me how to check the crops? If we divide the work, we can do the job faster."

"Come," Isaac said. "I will show you."

He stopped at the first field, where they'd seeded hay, and pointed to the sea of fledgling plants. "Look out over the entire field. The plants should cover it evenly and be the same size."

They were, as best she could tell.

"Your seedlings are of good size. If they continue to grow well, you will have plenty of food for your cows." He knelt beside the first section and pressed his hand into the soil then turned it palm up and rubbed the dirt that clung to his hand between his fingers. "Feel it," he said, pinching up some dirt and placing it in her hand. "The soil beneath the surface is not completely dry. We will wait for rain and check again in a few days if none comes."

"Must we check the entire field?" she asked as he stood.

"We must look at the plants, to check for pests and weeds, but we only need to test the soil every hundred feet or so."

He walked slowly, studying the plants, then stopped and felt the soil again. "Touch here," he said, pointing to the spot next to the print his hand had left.

Eva squatted down and pressed her open hand into the warm sandy soil. When she lifted it and turned it over, most of the dust blew away on the breeze.

"Feel the difference?"

She nodded.

"When the whole field feels like this, and no rain comes, I will pour water from the stream into the trenches."

They walked the remainder of the swath, scanning the plants, Isaac describing the various pests they might encounter and what could be done about them.

"Shall we split up?" Eva asked.

"Walk another section with me first."

She acquiesced and followed a few steps behind. She doubted she would remember all his teaching, but she listened with genuine interest.

Isaac stopped dead in his tracks and went silent. He dropped into a squat and examined a cluster of plants that didn't look like the others.

Eva crouched down beside him to get a closer look at the flat circles of lacy leaves. "Are those carrots?" she asked, reaching for one of the plants.

He grabbed her wrist before her fingers made contact. "Do not touch it. It has poison."

"What is it?"

"Hemlock."

Isaac stood and kept hold of her wrist, raising her up with him. "Come." He led her down section after section, scanning the ground and pointing out patches of the poisonous weed. They spread through half the field.

She and Isaac hurried to check her garden and the grain. Thankfully, neither was affected.

Isaac returned to the hay and pulled his work gloves from his pocket. "Bring the hoe and a piece of oilcloth."

"What are you going to do?"

"I must remove the hemlock so it does not taint the hay harvest. It will kill your animals."

Eva's heart stuttered. Then it pounded so hard she could hear it beating in her ears. "What about the pasture? The cows have been grazing there for days!"

"I checked it when I built the fence. There is nothing there that can harm them."

Once the strength returned to her knees, Eva hurried to the barn and brought the items he requested.

Isaac set the hoe aside and unfolded the oilcloth. "Help me spread this on the ground. I will use it to collect the hemlock so I can carry it away."

She watched him remove the first few plants, loosening them with the hoe then bending over and pulling them out by hand. Ridding the field of the poisonous invader was going to take hours. Maybe days.

Eva began putting on her gloves.

Isaac frowned at her. "What are you doing?"

"Helping you."

"No. It is too dangerous."

"The gloves will protect me."

"No," Isaac said firmly, shaking his head. "I will do this job alone."

Eva wanted to argue, but she relented. It was clearly a battle she would lose. She backed away and stared at the field until her thoughts made her eyes lose focus. "How did it get here? Was it mixed with the seeds I bought?"

"No. I checked the purity of every bag."

Then why was it only growing in the freshly planted field? "Could Mr. Kramer have done this?"

Isaac straightened up and rested his hands on the end of the hoe's handle. "I had the same thought but dismissed it. He did not seed this portion. Even if he had, I would not accuse him. Hemlock seeds can lay dormant for many months. They only sprout when conditions are right."

A chill rippled over the surface of Eva's skin. "Could the seeds have been put here last fall? When Keith was murdered?"

Isaac studied her with keen, assessing eyes. He apparently hadn't considered that. "It is possible. It is also possible that they were here when you arrived, and tilling the soil woke them."

Eva accepted his answer and turned to leave him to his work.

"Bring a bucket of water with the noon meal," he called over his shoulder, "so I can wash the poison off."

Eva set the food under their lunching tree and set the bucket a few feet away.

Isaac rolled back his dusty sleeves, laid his plant-stained gloves aside, and rinsed his hands before sitting down and picking up his food.

Eva inclined her head toward the bucket. "Where should I dump it?"

"Leave it here. I will wash again at the end of the day."

"Will you be able to dig it all up today?"

"I do not know. I will try."

"I wish you would let me help you," she muttered loudly enough for him to hear.

He didn't reply. Just ate quietly, staring at the field.

Eva stared at the pile of weeds on the oilcloth. If Isaac had left before the seeds sprouted... "Why did you stay?"

"Hm?" he replied, still staring at the field.

"I can't pay you, and you don't owe me anything. Worse still, I've treated you poorly when all you've done is help. Why did you stay?"

She had his full attention now. He stared at her, his face blank, but his eyes a window to myriad shifting emotions.

The window shuttered, and he stood. "Thank you for bringing the water. I must get back to work."

Eva stared at his retreating back then carried the remains of the meal to the dugout and busied herself with chores. She checked on Isaac's progress from afar, watching him pull weed after weed and carry them by the armload to the tarp. By late afternoon, his clothes were sweat-stained and filthy, so she took a clean shirt and pair of trousers to the hayfield after she'd milked Gwenie.

The tarp was gone and the field was deserted. The bucket of water still sat near the base of their lunching tree, full and mostly clear.

Eva called Isaac's name but got no answer. He must've taken the hemlock somewhere far away from the animals and the crops. He wouldn't take it to the place reserved for the orchard or anywhere near the stream and risk contaminating the water. An outcrop bordered the south edge of the property, outside the pasture fence. That was the most likely place he would go.

She set the clothes beside the bucket and went in search of him. As soon as she reached the far side of the fields, she noticed a column of light gray smoke rising into the sky near the border of her land.

Eva hurried on, until she found the source.

Isaac stood on a large flat slab of rock a few feet from the smoldering pile of hemlock. He turned when she called to him and held up his hand, as if to say *don't come any closer.*

She complied. But then she crept forward, to get a better look.

His hand quaked with a tremor, and his body swayed, as if he struggled to keep his balance.

"Mr. Shaw?"

"Stay... Stay b–" he mumbled as he turned around. His feet got tangled with each other, and he tumbled off the slab onto the field below.

"Isaac!" Eva ran to him and rolled him onto his back. A small cut on his forehead seemed to be his only injury, but nothing about him was right. Garbled words tried to push their way out over a thick tongue. His body trembled, and his pulse fluttered at the base of his throat.

He opened his eyes and stared up at her, unfocussed. He blinked and moistened his lips. "D... not...touch."

Eva let go.

Smears of green sap covered his clothes, and he smelled of smoke. That must be what was making him sick.

She grabbed his lapel and tore his shirt open, sending buttons flying, then yanked it off by the nearest sleeve. He gave a mumbled protest, which she ignored as she divested him of his boots and trousers also, leaving only his drawers and socks.

Eva stood, wadded his clothes into a bundle, and lobbed them onto the fire. She grabbed his wrist and tugged on his arm. "Get up."

"L... Leave me."

"No. I have to get you away from the smoke." She yanked harder. "Get up!"

He pushed himself into a sitting position, though it took several attempts. With her help, he rose awkwardly to his feet.

She caught him when he swayed and kept him from falling. "Hurry," she urged as she slung his arm over her head and around her shoulders. "We have to leave."

Eva stumbled under Isaac's weight but she refused to let him fall. Her chest was heaving from exertion by the time she'd led him back to their lunching tree.

His eyes rolled back, and his lids fluttered closed. He slipped from her grasp and slumped onto the ground. If not for his rapid breaths and the twitching of his limbs, she would have thought he died.

He still might.

Stories abounded of settlers foraging for wild plants and eating deadly ones by mistake. It had happened to a family on her and Keith's wagon train. The unfortunate couple lost a daughter and two sons, all because their longing for something fresh to eat had made them careless.

Fighting back tears, Eva tore a wide strip of cloth from her petticoat and began scrubbing Isaac from head to toe. He hadn't *eaten* the hemlock. Maybe if she washed the residue off his skin quickly enough, he would recover.

He still hadn't roused by the time she'd finished, so she lifted the bucket and poured the rest of the water on him.

He jerked in response and muttered something unintelligible.

Eva knelt on the muddy ground beside him and patted his face. "Isaac, wake up. Don't go to sleep. It's time to wake up."

His eyes opened partway, and he frowned, probably because dusk had settled in.

She ran to the barn and lit a lantern. After hanging it from the tree, she knelt back down and slapped his cheeks and his chest until he roused again. "Here," she said, lifting his head and holding her canteen to his lips. "Drink."

He choked on the first swallow. After coughing and sputtering, he tried again. The next few went down smoothly. Eva paused to give him a break then urged him to take more.

Isaac took a few more swallows and turned his face away. "Nuff." He lay his head back down and closed his eyes.

"You should have let me help you," Eva chided as much out of regret as reproof.

Isaac shook his head slowly back and forth.

"Yes, you should have."

"Y– You would...be sick, too."

"Maybe, but only by half."

He shook his head again.

"Stubborn man..."

Eva looked Isaac over again. His twitches were not as pronounced, and his breathing had slowed. She placed her palm on his chest to feel the beating of his heart. It had slowed some, too. Maybe he would live after all.

Isaac placed a hand over hers. A look of peace smoothed his features.

Touching a half-naked man should have sent her scrambling, but it didn't. Isaac's self-assurance, his comfort with silence and his own skin, had affected her. Instead of jerking her hand away and flouncing off in a fit of pique, she'd given herself time and permission to appreciate his physique, the mental image that had consumed her thoughts ever since she'd seen him bathing naked in the stream.

When she wasn't thinking about Isaac's body, she was pondering what it would be like to join with a man who didn't approach the act with shame, one who'd look his fill and take what he wanted eagerly and in broad daylight.

God help her, it was those thoughts that heated her the most.

Isaac's eyes flew open. He shoved her hand aside and rolled away from her. His body convulsed, and he coughed, gagging and retching, until all the water he'd drunk had spewed onto the ground beside him.

Eva rose up on her knees and placed her hand on his shoulder, consumed by shame for thinking about him in such a lascivious manner while he was laying on the ground, barely cheating death. "I thought you were getting better."

He pushed himself into a sitting position. "I am."

She tore another piece from her petticoat and wet it with water from her canteen. "Take this," she said, holding it out to him.

When he was done wiping his face, she offered the canteen so he could rinse his mouth.

Isaac swished and spit then set the canteen aside and rubbed the back of his neck.

"Please tell me you got it all. If you didn't, I'll pull the hemlock out myself—or burn the whole field and sell the cattle."

He looked at her with a frown that said he was trying to decide if she was teasing or crazy. "I g... got it all."

"Thank goodness."

Eva stood. "Can you walk?"

Isaac answered her by rising and taking a few halting steps. He looked at her mud-stained skirt and then down at his scanty attire and frowned again. "Where are my clothes?"

"They were covered in sap, so I burned them."

"You touched them?"

"I had to get them off of you."

"But–"

"I'm fine." She tucked the clean set of clothes under her arm, plucked the lantern from the tree, and held out her hand. "Come with me to the dugout. You're going to have to wash there."

"Why?"

"I used all the water, cleaning the poison off you."

He refused to lean on her for support, but he went without argument.

He detoured to the necessary and the wash bucket, then took the clothes and turned to walk in the opposite direction.

"Where are you going?"

"To the barn, to sleep."

Eva shook her head. "Your hands are still shaking, and your steps falter. You should stay in the dugout tonight, where I can keep an eye on you."

Isaac stared at her for a long moment. The same slurry of emotions that had filled his eyes when she'd asked him why he'd stayed churned again like a storm-tossed sea.

"Please," she entreated. "You seem better, but I want to watch over you. If something were to happen to you, I would never forgive myself."

He nodded and followed her in.

She turned her back out of habit, to give him privacy to dress, then chuckled to herself at the absurdity. "You should eat something," she said over her shoulder.

"I am not hungry."

She turned around to find Isaac standing there in only his trousers, his chest still bare. "What about some broth or tea?"

He motioned to the jars of dried herbs on the shelf, a duplicate set he'd made to match his personal collection. "Tea."

Eva pointed to them, one by one.

Isaac nodded at the third one over.

"The ginseng?"

"Yes."

She set it on the counter and kept going.

He nodded at the fifth jar.

"That's buckthorn. Are you sure?" Buckthorn was used to relieve a bound-up bowel, which, judging by the sounds that had emanated from the outhouse, he did not have.

He narrowed his eyes at the jar. "Uh... No."

She kept going, pausing at the elderberry, and again when she reached another herb whose name she couldn't pronounce, but one he'd said was thought to purify the blood.

Isaac chose them both.

She set them with the ginseng and put some water on to heat. By the time she wiped out a cup and found a spoon to measure with, Isaac had donned his shirt and was clumsily fiddling with a button, his hands shaking worse than when they hung and his sides.

"Let me help you with that," she offered with a reassuring smile. Eva smoothed the placket and began working the first button into its hole.

He reached up and stilled her hands. "I stayed because my heart will not let me leave."

Eva stared into deep blue eyes that were as weary as they were sincere and blinked at the sting of fresh tears. She'd battered Isaac's pride, over and over. Yet he'd humbled himself for her. He'd risked his life for her. She went up on her toes and kissed him, a superficial brush of the lips but one that lingered.

She didn't know what passions it might unleash, but she didn't care. She was tired of pretending.

Isaac wrapped his arms around her. Even in his weakness, he was strong, and she'd never felt so protected. He kissed her gently then broke the connection and rested his head against hers. "You tempt me."

"You tempt me, too. You have for a long time."

Reluctantly, Eva pulled away and went back to fussing with his buttons.

He stilled her hands again. "If it will not offend you, I would rather sleep without it."

Eva's cheeks warmed as she slipped the shirt off his shoulders and laid it across the foot board of the bed. "I've seen you in less." She'd seen him in nothing, but she'd keep that to herself.

She made the first cup of tea to his specifications then fixed a regular cup of her own and buttered a slice of bread.

"I wish you'd eat something," she said as she joined him at the table.

"Tomorrow."

Eva nibbled her bread until her tea cooled enough to drink. She was almost through, and Isaac hadn't touched his.

He must be afraid he'd spill it.

Eva scooted her chair around until their knees touched. She tested the heat of his tea then held it up to his lips. Little by little she fed it to him until it was gone.

"Thank you." He rose with a steadying hand on the edge of the table and looked around the dugout. "I will sleep on the floor."

"No, you will not."

His eyes snapped to her, brows raised.

"I– I want you close, so I can lay a hand on your brow in the night and hear you breathing." She gestured at the bed. "Sit."

Eva pulled off his filthy socks and helped him swing his legs onto the mattress. When he scooted to the other side and reclined, the reality of her choice sank in.

She looked down at her clothes and debated whether to remove any of them.

"Lie with me however you wish. I do not have the power for anything but sleep."

Eva removed her boots and, with her back to him, slipped off her outer garments and her petticoat. Her chemise was thin but not sheer, and her cotton waistcoat kept her top half thoroughly covered and contained. She took the pins from her hair but left it braided.

When she turned around, Isaac was lying atop the quilt with his hands resting on his waist, staring at the ceiling.

"Do you want a blanket?"

"No." His gaze slid her way tentatively. "I am accustomed to sleeping without one."

She blew out the lamp and climbed in under the covers by the faint moonlight that filtered through the window paper. She lay on her back and stared at the ceiling, too, but she didn't share Isaac's sense of peace. In the quiet stillness, her thoughts ran amok, and her fears grew. They always did when there was no daylight to chase them away.

Isaac's condition was better than when she found him, but what if she hadn't gotten the poison off him in time? The tremors had improved, but they hadn't left him.

Eva closed her eyes and prayed the damage wasn't permanent. More fervently still, she prayed for his life. Poison didn't always cause death right away. He could still succumb in the night.

Isaac didn't deserve this—any of it. This *uncivilized native* had behaved more Christian-like than most whites she knew.

A rueful tear trickled down the side of her face at the memory of him lying beaten and bloody in the snow. She'd been so full of hate that she'd left him all night in the cold and wished for animals to drag him away. She didn't deserve his help or his loyalty.

If he died...

The mattress shifted, and a shaky finger touched the trail the tear had made. "Why do you cry?"

Eva drew a slow breath to steady her voice. "I'm worried I didn't get the poison off soon enough. And I'm ashamed of the way I've treated you." She rolled toward him, more tears gathering in her eyes. "I had such hate in my heart when we met."

"To hate, one must first love. The hatred you have for your husband's killer is a measure of how much you loved Keith."

"But I wrongly aimed it at you."

He brushed the moisture from her cheeks. "Your tears have washed all that away. Let us think about it no more."

Eva placed her hand over Isaac's heart, reassured by its slow steady beat.

He placed his hand on top of hers, as he had done in the field. "Does this cause you guilt?"

"What?"

"Kissing me... Lying with me."

"A little." She debated whether to tell him the truth until Isaac turned his head and looked at her. Even in the muted moonlight, his eyes bore into hers with persuasive intensity. "It should pain me more, but I think it's what Keith wants," she finally said. "He's been coming to me in dreams, telling me it's all right to move on, all right to love another."

"Hm."

"At first," she admitted, her cheeks growing hot, "I thought the dreams were borne of my own desire, my body trying to convince me to give in to my sinful yearnings. But the same dream has repeated itself almost every night. That last one was so real I tried to reach out and touch him."

Isaac searched her eyes. "You should accept his words," he said, turning his head back to face to the ceiling. "He has given you permission to put aside your mourning."

"Perhaps."

Isaac patted the hand that rested on his chest. "Sleep, Eva McCabe. All is well."

Chapter Fourteen

Isaac awoke to the smell of steak and eggs frying, and to Eva bustling around the kitchen, fully dressed. The sun had risen, but only barely. He sat at the side of the bed long enough to assure himself of his strength then got up and slipped his arms into the sleeves of his shirt.

She met him as he rounded the end of the bed with a cup in her hand and embarrassment filling her cheeks. "I made coffee, but if you'd rather have more of your special tea, I'll fix that for you instead."

"I will drink coffee."

She lifted the cup, as if to bring it to his lips.

Isaac carefully took it from her. "I can hold it."

Eva stepped back and watched him drink. "Your hands aren't shaking anymore." The relief in her voice was clear.

"It appears I will live," he said partly in jest; his insides were not yet as steady as his hands. He lifted his chin in the direction of the stove as she flitted about and smoothed the coverings on the bed. "Do I have time to do the milking?"

Eva gasped and threw her hands in the air. "The eggs!" She hurried to the skillet. "I already milked Gwenie and fed the horses," she tossed over her shoulder.

Anger sparked in his chest upon hearing that she had done his work, but he breathed it away. She still feared for him and was giving the sickness time to leave his body.

Visions had come to him last night before sleep had, flashes of Eva finding him by the fire and leading him to safety. She had put on fierceness and bravery, but beneath it was terror.

Also beneath it was affection. Her kiss left no doubt that it was him she feared losing, not the laborer.

The prickle of being watched crept up the back of Isaac's neck.

Eva had placed the platter of steak and eggs on the table and was standing there, staring, but not at his face. Her eyes were focused lower, on his open shirt.

Isaac walked closer. He lifted her hand and placed it on his chest. "You spoke of yearnings last night. What do you desire? Tell me."

Her eyes widened in shock, but they danced with everything from curiosity to hunger. "I..." Desire swept across her face like wildfire, then shame snuffed it out. "I can't."

At the sound of a horse riding into the yard, she jerked her hand away.

Isaac fastened his shirt and tucked the tail of it into his pants while Eva smoothed her clothes and glanced around nervously. She went for the door at the sound of the knock, but Isaac was closer.

He opened it, expecting Mac or Connor. "Mr. Kramer."

Dwight's smile fell. "What are you doing here?"

"I live here."

Eva joined them and beamed at Dwight. "What Mr. Shaw means is he takes meals with me. We were just sitting down to breakfast. Come join us."

"I don't want to impose."

Yes, you do.

"It's no imposition," Eva said, hastily slicing some bread she had likely intended to save for lunch. "My flock is laying more eggs than we can eat. There's plenty."

Dwight hung his hat by the door and stood by an empty chair, glaring at Isaac, who had already taken a seat at the table. He aimed a kinder face at Eva when she served his coffee.

"Please, sit while I get you a plate."

Muumayk 'ilyhwe.

The *invited skunk* remained standing until she took her seat anyway.

Isaac made use of the Skunk's delay to slide a piece of steak from the platter onto his plate, to go with the eggs he'd already purloined.

Eva bowed her head and gave thanks then spread her napkin in her lap and aimed another bright smile at her neighbor. "What brings you by, Mr. Kramer?"

"I saw smoke yesterday evening. I was concerned there might have been more trouble."

Isaac grunted. "Yet you waited until morning." *And spent far too much time on your appearance before coming.*

Dwight cut his eyes to him. "Noone came for help, so I figured it could wait. Besides, there's not much can be seen or done after dark."

Eva pushed the platter closer to him and gestured for him to serve himself. "I'm grateful you stopped by, though you needn't have. Isaac was merely burning some hemlock he found in the hayfield."

"Poison hemlock?"

"Yes. Thankfully, he got it all."

"Mrs. McCabe asked if someone put the seeds there on purpose," Isaac interjected, locking gazes with Dwight long enough to make the man visibly uncomfortable.

"I can't imagine who," Dwight said.

"Neither can I," Eva added, watching the interchange with nervous curiosity. "Mr. Shaw said they were probably here when Keith and I settled, and that the tilling of the soil caused them to grow." Her brows dipped with concern. "You haven't found any on your land, have you, Mr. Kramer?"

"No. But I'll take a closer look next time I walk my fields. Can't be too careful."

Eva wrapped her dainty fingers around her fork. "I agree." She nibbled at her eggs then set her fork down and picked up her coffee. "How do your crops fare?"

Dwight paused cutting his steak. "Very well, thank you."

Silence fell over the group as they ate, Eva and Dwight exchanging polite glances from time to time.

"Since all is well here," Dwight said, pushing his plate away and sitting back to finish his coffee, "I'll go ahead with the hunting trip I planned."

"Where to?" Eva asked.

"I've been invited to travel several miles south, to a claim that's thick with elk."

"How nice," she said. "How long will you be gone?"

"A few days. It should prove to be a bountiful hunt. Your hand is welcome to join us." he added with a glance in Isaac's direction.

Eva's face fell to a look of indecision.

Isaac took the burden from her and replied to an invitation that should have been extended directly to him. "Thank you, Mr. Kramer, but I must decline."

"Are you sure? I dare say Mrs. McCabe can manage without you for a few days."

"I am certain."

"Well, suit yourself. I was planning to bring some game back for Mrs. McCabe anyway. Perhaps she would agree to have me over for supper in exchange for an elk." Dwight lifted his cup in Eva's direction. "You've taken to wearing lighter colors. Gives a fella hope," he added with a smile.

Eva blushed. "My choice to put on half-mourning was for practical reasons, I'm afraid. Black is too hot to wear in the fields. I apologize if my attire is in any way misleading—or offensive. I certainly hope you won't think less of me."

"Of course not," Dwight replied with a smile that had dimmed from optimistic to obligatory. "I'm patient to wait for your answer. My friends, however, don't have that luxury. Grants are being snapped up left and right, and they're half the size they were in 1850. I'll need an answer soon—if you're going to barter with them for your claim, that is."

Eva glanced at Isaac. The color faded from her cheeks as she looked back to Dwight. "I told you I've decided to stay."

"I understand. But why toil in the fields if you don't have to?" The regard in his eyes softened. "Is it because of Keith...because he's buried here?"

Eva's face flinched slightly at the question.

"Who are these friends?" Isaac demanded.

Dwight shot an irritated glance his way. "Henry Combs and John Whiteworth."

"How do you know them?"

"We met while working a railroad job back East."

"Why didn't they come west with you?"

Dwight looked to Eva, his hand turned out and his lips parted, as if to ask why she was letting her hired hand interrogate him.

To Eva's credit, she held his gaze and waited for an answer.

Dwight relented. "I had already been working for a year when they joined the crew," he replied in a tone that sounded more defeated than irritated. "They stayed behind to save more funds."

"When will they need an answer?"

"In a few weeks... August at the latest." He sat forward and looked into Eva's eyes. "If you marry me, I could forfeit my claim and prove up yours instead. You wouldn't have to move. You could visit Keith whenever you wished and leave the heavy work to the men."

Isaac feigned nonchalance as he laid his verbal snare. "Why involve your friends at all? Mrs. McCabe and I are managing. Why not wait until she proves up and marry her then? You would own all of it, your claim *and* hers."

Dwight's eyes lit with interest that belied the way he shrugged off the suggestion. "That's another way to go about it, I suppose."

"And since her claim is twice the size of yours," Isaac added, "you could show your gratitude by allowing her to retain ownership of half."

Dwight's jaw tightened. "Perhaps."

Isaac's mouth twitched with the impulse to grin. The Skunk had walked straight into that trap and clearly did not like it.

Of course, laying it had required suggesting Eva marry the self-serving fool, and the thought of that soured Isaac's stomach. He had said those things to see Dwight's reaction—to let Eva see Dwight's reaction—but maybe he shouldn't interfere.

She would have a much easier life married to a white.

Eva rounded on Isaac the moment the thud of hoofbeats faded into the distance. "What was that all about?"

He frowned at her over the rim of his cup. "I wanted to know more about Mr. Kramer's so-called *friends.*"

"Don't you dare feign ignorance. Barely one month ago, you called Mr. Kramer a *viper* and told me he was not good for me. Now you're trying to pair us up and march us down the aisle."

"I am not."

"That's what it sounded like to me."

Isaac stood and took his plate to the dry sink. "I said those things so you would see his reaction, see that it is your land he wants."

"I am well aware of Mr. Kramer's schemes."

He turned and faced her. "Are you? You treat him like a favored guest."

"He *is* a guest. And a neighbor who has come to my aid during difficult times. I treat him with the kindness and hospitality he deserves."

"Does that hospitality include accepting his offer of marriage?"

"I haven't accepted it."

"You have not turned it down."

"I explained that to you. I'm waiting until I see how my crops and cattle fare."

"Your farm thrives."

"It does at the moment. But no one—not even the clever, optimistic Hatchoq—can predict what will happen tomorrow."

Isaac turned and headed for the door, muttering something in his language.

"What was that? Speak English."

His shoulders rose and fell with several breaths before he turned around. "You are like a child with fire."

"I am not a child. I am a *full-grown woman* who is trying to survive in this perilous country and keep her husband's dream alive."

Fire blazed behind his icy glare. Isaac crossed the room in three swift strides. "Tell me he makes your blood run hot and your body yearn," he said, his dark eyes shifting back and forth, searching hers. "Tell me you want him—or *any* white—and I will walk away."

Eva swallowed, her throat dry and her heart pounding. The only man who made her feel those things was Isaac.

His large strong hand grasped the nape of her neck. He lowered his mouth to hers, but he didn't pause this time. He kissed her with boldness, as if he were claiming her as his own. His tongue skimmed her trembling lips, seeking entry. And God help her, she gave it.

His greedy mouth took possession, his hand tilting her head at his will. Blood hummed through her veins and pooled low in a primitive throb, that aching twinge of anticipation she'd felt so many times but never sated.

With a rumbling groan, Isaac dragged his mouth from hers. His hot lips traced a trail along her jaw and down her neck, to the sensitive place where it met her shoulder. Her body was quickly turning traitor at his tender assault, stealing her wits and annulling her morality. Then he swiped his tongue along her flesh, leaving a hot tingly trail that wrenched a moan from her as it cooled.

"Isaac..."

He backed her against the dry sink and pressed his hard body to hers. "Tell me what you desire," he said against the tender skin just below her ear.

"I..."

His free hand slid up her bodice and closed around her breast, and she lost all reason. "You enjoy being kissed and touched. That is clear. What else do you desire?"

Her lips tried, but she couldn't form words.

"Shall I strip you bare and gaze at you...?" he asked, cupping both breasts and flicking at her bodice's buttons with his thumbs. "Tell you how much the sight of you pleases me?"

Yes.

His right hand stole around back, cupped her buttock, and pressed her pelvis closer. "Shall I touch the place that yearns for me the most?" he asked, moving against her so that his erection grazed her in a tempting overture.

Eva's eyes fluttered closed. Even dulled by the layers of their clothes, the sensation made her head spin. She parted her thighs in an effort to get closer. She was mortified at her shameless behavior, but she couldn't stop herself.

Isaac shifted his hips and broke contact. He sank his fingers into the braid that was pinned in a coil at her nape and gently tilted her head back. "Look at me."

Eva did as he asked and found herself gazing into eyes as heavy lidded as her own.

"I want you," he said in a low, raspy voice that left her breathless. "Lay with me. Right now."

"I can't," she whispered.

"Is it because I am not white."

"No. It's because I'm a widow in mourning. Keith–"

"Has given you permission."

"Even if he has, we're not married."

"So, marry me."

Eva let out a laugh then sobered when she realized he was serious. "The nearest preacher is forty miles away."

"We do not need one. Among my people, when a couple decides to marry, they simply do. It is God who joins us, not man." He cradled her face in his hands. "Marry me, Eva. I want you as my wife. My heart will not let me leave."

Eva stared into eyes so earnest it stole her breath. What Isaac asked flew in the face of convention—broke every rule of English propriety she'd been taught. But it was what her heart wanted, too. "Yes. Stay. Be my husband."

Isaac claimed her mouth again. The kiss was bold, yet it bared his heart and had an edge of tenderness that brought tears to her eyes.

He removed his shirt and tossed it in the direction of the bed. "You stare at my chest when it is bare," he said, lifting her hand and placing it on the firm expanse between his nipples. "Touch me and satisfy your curiosity."

Eva's cheeks burned, but she didn't pull away. She brushed her fingers lightly over the small patch of hair in the center then over the brown disks on either side. The tiny buds responded to her touch. Isaac stood motionless as her hand traveled lower, tracing the firm mounds of muscle that lined a furrowed path to his navel.

The ridge straining against his breeches tempted her, but she stopped short of touching it and lifted her hand to the scar on his shoulder instead. *It's a wonder he hadn't died from the wound or the weather. What if she hadn't brought him into the dugout when she did?*

Isaac removed her hand from his scar and kissed the tips of her fingers. "What do you desire?"

"Things I shouldn't."

"I will decide if you should or should not. Tell me."

The thought of saying such intimate things aloud twisted her stomach into a nervous knot. She could never speak that way to anyone but Isaac. "I want us to lay without clothing...to feel your skin next to mine."

"I want that, too," he said as he began unfastening the buttons of her dress. "What else?"

"I want you to..." She had started to say 'not act embarrassed,' but Isaac was clearly unashamed. He was standing there, undressing her with the morning sun lighting up the room.

His hands stilled, and he locked gazes with her. "I must ask you something, and I want you to tell me the truth."

"All right."

"Are you a virgin?"

"How could I be? I'm a widow!"

"It is possible to be both. Did Keith ever lay with you for more than sleep?"

"Of course, he did."

Isaac cupped her face with his hand and caressed her cheek. "I did not mean to anger you. In many ways, you behave..." He mumbled, as if searching for a word. "Innocent. If you were yet untouched, more care would need to be taken."

"Oh."

He removed her dress and began unfastening her waistcoat.

"We had a real marriage," she explained. "Keith was just bashful. He never saw me completely disrobed."

"Hm," Isaac grunted more than said.

"When he... joined with me, he'd push the hem of my gown up just far enough to manage the act." Then he'd quickly finish, mutter his thanks as he rolled off, and leave her wanting but too embarrassed to tell him so. "He was careful not to hurt me, but he behaved as though I was barely present."

"Did he prefer men?"

She cast him a mildly insulted look. "No. He was just modest. Even though Keith knew he was well within his rights as a husband, he still felt as if he was imposing."

Isaac tossed her waistcoat on the foot of the bed, near where his shirt had landed, and carefully pulled the pins from her hair. The thud of her braid falling against her back sent a shiver down her spine. He swiped it over her shoulder and began working the locks loose. "I desire to see your hair unbound."

She would never have believed the simple act of freeing her hair could be so sensual. Her head ached where the coiled braid had been attached, but the shifting roots caused a myriad of delicious tingles. When Isaac finally reached the top and scrubbed the tips of his fingers over her scalp in a slow massage, Eva groaned and leaned into his touch. "That feels *good*."

He chuckled then plucked the bow of her chemise loose and slid the neckline off her shoulders and down to her waist.

Eva's hands flew up to cover her breasts. "What if somebody comes?"

"No one will come," Isaac said, grasping her wrists and removing her hands. "Mac and Connor have gone to buy lumber, and The Viper won't be back for days." He grazed her nipples with the palms of his hands. "There will be no shame in our bed. Tell me what you desire."

"I... I want you to take your time. To kiss and touch and..." How could she explain the way to quench a yearning that had never been fulfilled?

"You want things you do not have words for."

She nodded.

"You do not need words. Your body will tell me."

Isaac divested her of her last piece of clothing and stepped back until he no longer shadowed her. Blue fire smoldered in his eyes as his gaze traveled the length of her, lingering on the places her hands longed to conceal.

Eva's feverish skin prickled with every tiny draft. Her English breeding screamed that standing nude for a man's perusal—even a husband—was wicked and worthy of shame. But she had never felt so alive.

"You are beautiful," Isaac said in a husky, hypnotic voice. Taking her by the hand, he led her to the bed and coaxed her to lie back on the quilt.

He shed his breeches then climbed on and straddled her with his knees. She was immediately transfixed by his burgeoning arousal. She had never seen one before, only felt one inside her. No wonder the marital act was always tinged with discomfort.

"Do you wish to touch it?" Isaac asked.

She wanted to say yes, but...

His mouth curved into a half-smile as he took her hand and placed it there.

Eva brushed her fingers over his hot skin then grew bolder and wrapped his shaft with her hand. It felt like velvet covered oak. She stroked her hand up and down, captivated by the juxtaposition of textures.

A shuddering groan rumbled in Isaac's chest.

He removed her hand and kissed her knuckles then proceeded to explore her upper body with his fingers. After weeks spent in the fields, her hands were almost as dark as his, but the rest of her was the color of cream. She stared at the contrast until the tide of sensations swept her away and made her close her eyes.

He bracketed her shoulders with his arms, dipped his head, and teased her lips open with his.

Eva stroked his beard and threaded her fingers into his hair as she joined in.

Isaac kissed her thoroughly, with skill and exasperating patience. Then his mouth moved from her lips to her jaw to her neck, nipping and tasting, as if cataloging every curve. She gasped when he closed his mouth around her nipple, and curled her fingers around strands of his hair. "Oh! Isaac..." Eva's lower half throbbed with every tug of his mouth, and she trembled in anticipation.

He showered attention on her breasts until she thought she'd go mad. Then his weight shifted on the mattress, and his hand grazed her curls. "Open yourself to me."

Eva parted her thighs like a wanton, drunk on desire and stripped of all restraint. She sighed as his callused finger parted her folds. The sigh died in her throat and came roaring back as a high-pitched moan when he began stroking her tender flesh. It was exquisite, and it was intense. She clamped his hand between her thighs.

He stilled. "Open, Eva."

She relaxed and released his hand.

Isaac nudged her thighs farther apart and moved his legs so that he was kneeling between hers. She couldn't close them now. The alarm she felt must've shown on her face, because he kissed the tip of her nose and whispered, "Trust me."

Isaac flattened his palm over her curls and rubbed in a circular motion. The sensation was dulled, but the pressure felt good.

Eva's hips lifted of their own accord. "Isaac, please…"

He gave her some of his weight, fitting his lower body to hers and rocking his hips so that his shaft stroked the most intimate part of her in a steady glide, up and down. Every time he thrust his hips, she whimpered. The sensation was exquisite.

A purr-like growl vibrated deep in Isaac's throat, mixed with words she didn't understand. His hips pressed into her more firmly, and the tempo of his movements increased.

Eva clutched the tattoos that encircled his biceps. Her thighs pressed against his in a futile effort to come together. Isaac was driving her to a frenzy of passion, and he hadn't even entered her. God in heaven, she would explode in a blaze of shameless rapture if he did.

A storm of sensation gathered until her whole body quivered with its intensity. Part of her wanted to fight it, and part of her wanted to chase it.

Isaac leaned down, closed his mouth around her nipple, and suckled so firmly it hurt. The feeling shot straight to the place his shaft touched, and Eva's world shattered into a million glorious pieces.

His hips slowed to a stop, sending fading ripples of bliss all the way to the tips of her toes. As the fog began to lift, she was dimly aware of him looming over her, draping her legs over his thighs, and pressing his large hot shaft against her entrance.

Isaac paused to position himself then pushed until he was fully sheathed. Eva's guttural groan of pleasure enveloped him along with the tight wet heat of her body, and he stilled himself instead of giving in to his primal urge. Self-control was a skill he had mastered growing up in his clan. During hunts and battle, he could lie in wait for hours, enduring bites of insects and extremes of weather without moving or uttering a sound.

Taking his weight on his elbows, he began to move. The gentle thrusts nudged Eva's limp body, drawing sighs and groans from her that eventually changed to *ohs* and *ahs* and syllables of his name. He knew when she fully returned to herself. She wrapped her legs around his waist and her arms around his shoulders, all four limbs clutching him tightly. Pleasure was building in her just as it was in him.

Isaac nuzzled her neck and nibbled the tender pale flesh, reveling in her mews and the clench of her muscles around his erection. The time for gentleness was over.

He pressed his shaft in deep, wrenching a sob of delight from his bride, then withdrew far enough to drive it into her with some force. "Tell me if I hurt you," he ground out through a mouth that was rigid with the effort it took to postpone his release.

"Ah!" Her nails dug into his flesh. "*More.*"

He thrust harder. Faster. "This— is what— you desire."

"Yes. Yes!"

He pounded into her until she cried out and her muscles clutched him like talons. He nearly lost himself with her, but a vision of clarity struck and pulled him back from the edge.

That was Eva's choice to make.

Retreating when he wanted to bury himself deep was torture. With a growl, he yanked his shaft free and spilled his seed between their bodies.

They collapsed in a spent, panting pile.

Isaac reached down and patted the bed until his groping fingers found his shirt. He raised up enough to wipe his seed off her skin then tossed the shirt away.

He drew Eva against his chest and rolled them onto their sides. He held her close and stroked his hand up and down her back. "Are you all right?" he asked once the pounding of her heart had slowed.

"Oh, Isaac," she said in a breathy, awe filled voice. "I... There are no words...."

He smiled against her dewy forehead. "I will take that as a yes."

She lay relaxed in his embrace for a time, then the starch returned to her limbs. Eva tilted her head back and looked into his eyes. "Why did you withdraw?"

He chose his words carefully—not with any intent to deceive, but because she deserved the truth. "I did not deal fairly with you. I aroused your passion then persuaded you to marry me while you were weak. It does not matter that I did not set out to trap you. I still did."

"You didn't trap me. You made me face my true feelings. But I still don't see what that has to do with this."

"I can pass for white, but it is something I will never be. There may come a time when the truth is discovered. I did not give you time to consider that... Nor that any child I sire will have Mojave blood."

The last traces of contentment disappeared from her face.

"I have much love for you, Eva. But if you do not want to spend your life with me or bear children fathered by a half-breed, I will understand. You are free to end our marriage and send me away."

She hugged him close and pressed her cheek to his chest. "I could never send you away."

Her words soothed his soul, but he would honor the pledge nonetheless.

Isaac pulled the edge of the quilt over her when she shivered from the cooling of her skin then ran his fingers through her flaxen hair.

He was chilled, too, but in his mind, not on his skin. Eva wasn't the only one who had decided to wed during a time of weakness.

He now had a wife and a home, but his spirit remained restless. He was a man with a foot in two worlds, being forced to choose. He despised that he must deny one in favor of the other.

Something wet his chest. Tears.

He drew back so he could see Eva's face. "Why do you cry?"

She met his gaze with shimmering eyes then ducked her head. "I feel as if I've betrayed Keith," she whispered.

Isaac held her close, but he remained mute. How could he reassure her when he felt a similar shame, knowing that his body and his heart desired a white.

Chapter Fifteen

The warmth of the late-July sun heated Eva's shoulders as she surveyed the pasture from beneath the brim of her bonnet. The cows lay under a grove of trees, languidly flicking their ears and swishing their tails in the shade.

She was free to be as lazy. For the remainder of the month, there wasn't much to do. Her cellar held several crocks of meat, and she'd add crocks of kraut once the cabbage was harvested. The carrots, onions, and potatoes would follow shortly after. By winter, her cellar would be full.

Stores of food had been put up for her animals, as well. Both the grain and hay were in. Despite the delay in seeding, the yield had been high. The breeding of her cows had gone well, too. God willing, calves would start dropping at the end of February.

Isaac came walking up the path from the barn.

Eva sensed him before she saw him. Her eyes riveted themselves to his lean, panther-like stride and traced every flex of muscle beneath his clothes. She couldn't help herself. Every stolen glance held a promise of unexplored passions.

Isaac kept his distance when he reached her and showed no signs of familiarity, save the smolder of appreciation in his eyes.

Eva did the same. Though she had to grip handfuls of her skirt to keep herself from throwing her arms around him.

To everyone else—even Mac and Connor—they were still widowed employer and farm hand. She couldn't show Isaac any favor unless they were concealed and alone. "Would you please fill the wood box in the dugout, Mr. Shaw?"

A half-smile was her answer.

She went to start lunch and left the door ajar.

Several minutes later, he shouldered in, carrying an armload of firewood. He stacked it in the box, dusted off his hands, and took a seat at the table.

"What's the word for gnat?" she asked.

"In my language?"

"Yes."

"*Smalykaapak.*"

"I can't pronounce that," she said, setting a cup of tea in front of him. "What do you call someone who sneaks into a woman's house and won't leave."

The corner of Isaac's mouth twitched with another half-smile. "*Makach suuduurvm.*"

Eva frowned but attempted to repeat it. "Muh-kak soo... muh-kak soo-doo-r... I can't say that either—even though that's what you are."

He grinned and stuck out his chin in a look of playful hubris. "Then call me *maqualachiisk.*"

She planted her hands on her hips. "That's too long for a nickname."

His grin faded to a look of pleasant sincerity as he lifted his cup and took a sip of his tea. "How about *posh*?"

"Posh?"

"Yes. Posh."

"What does that mean?"

"Cat."

Well, he did move like one. "Why cat?"

"From the time I arrived, I fed your cats bits of fish any time I caught some. Their motive is selfish, but they kept me company when I was lonely, and they have come to my aid more than once."

Eva's heart pinched at the memory of them lying on him when he was injured and near death. Though he had no recollection of that day. "How?"

"By keeping the barn free of snakes and rats, and by warning me of danger." Isaac stood and gave her a peck on the cheek. "Hearing the name will remind me that it is wise to be kind and make friends."

She held her hand out to take his cup.

"Pack our lunch and ride with me to the clearing," he said as he handed it over.

Eva beamed. "You'll never have to ask twice."

He walked out the door, chuckling, while she indulged her craving for the sight of his masculine form and watched him go.

Eva tied up their meal in a cloth and carried it to the yard, where Isaac waited with the horses. He held the bundle while she mounted then tied it to her sidesaddle, grabbed a shock of his horse's mane, and swung himself onto its bare back. They took off at a trot towards their new favorite place—a sizable-but-sheltered clearing near the southern border of her land.

He had discovered it weeks ago, a swath of tall trees that parted down the center and contained a long stretch of meadow several yards wide. It wouldn't be of much use in winter, but thickened by the lush bushes and invading vines of summer, it shielded its contents from view on all sides.

Eva clutched the bundle to her chest and made her way through the underbrush while Isaac staked their horses in a cove-like recess nearby. She retrieved their lunching quilt from the makeshift closet Isaac had built in the base of a hollow tree—the place he also stored his quiver and bow between hunts—then shook it out and spread it on a patch of soft grass in the shade.

Isaac emerged from the foliage and set their canteens next to their lunch on the quilt, then pulled off his boots and socks, and tossed them beside it. He went barefoot every chance he got. He removed his shirt and laid it across a nearby bush to air. He'd been doing that ever since they found the clearing. The sun had darkened his skin to the same luscious brown it was when they first met.

"Come," he said, taking hold of Eva's hand. "Practice first." He stood her at one end of the long clearing, handed her his bow, and gestured toward a leather target he had fastened to a tree at the opposite end.

Eva flexed her fingers and gathered her strength. She chose an arrow from the quiver, nocked it against the string, and drew back with all her might, aiming it just as Isaac had taught her. Her shoulders burned with the effort it took to hold the string taut as she lined up the shot. Eva held her breath and released the arrow, exhaling once it pierced the target... several inches too low.

"Try again," Isaac said.

She nocked another arrow and aimed. It flew high this time.

"Again," Isaac said.

Eva waited for the fire in her biceps to fade then lined up a third shot. The arrow found its mark and pierced the target dead center.

"Very good. Your aim is improving."

"Maybe," she said, handing him the bow. "But it takes me three shots, at least, to hit the bullseye."

"If you wish," Isaac said as they returned to the quilt, "I can make a smaller bow for you."

"Would that help?"

"Yes."

Eva admired the ripple of muscles across Isaac's back as he bent down to retrieve their lunch. The sight of him always made her heart flutter. He unwrapped the simple fare of bread and roasted beef and set it in the center of the quilt. They sat across from each other, his knees apart and ankles crossed as he always sat, and her legs folded to the side, underneath her skirt.

They ate in comfortable silence, the only sounds the chirping of birds and the rustling of leaves overhead. The dappled sunlight filtered through the canopy above, creating a dance of shadows on Isaac's face as he savored each bite.

Eva stared. She couldn't help herself.

He gestured to the sandwich resting on her lap that only had a few nibbles missing from one corner. "You didn't eat much."

"I'm not hungry," she said as she held it out to him. "Do you want it?"

He shook his head, so she wrapped it up in the cloth and set it aside. The gentle breeze played with loose tendrils of her hair as she took a sip from her canteen. Its cool touch on her skin felt good.

Isaac stretched out his legs and leaned back on his elbows.

"I wish we could stay here all the time," Eva said on a wistful sigh.

Isaac smiled and relaxed back onto the quilt. He held his arm out in invitation.

Eva scooted closer and nestled her head on his shoulder, listening to the steady rhythm of his heartbeat as they basked in the tranquil solitude of their secret clearing.

"Are you happy?" she asked. "Living here, with me?"

His chest stilled, then he drew a slightly deeper breath. "I am content."

"What would you be doing, right now, if you were still with your family?"

He turned his head and glanced down at her. "I would be helping the other men plant crops near the river and going on hunts."

"You said you helped wagons cross the river, too."

"They arrive later in the year." He covered her hand that was tracing random shapes on his chest and stilled it. "Why do you ask these things?"

Eva wiggled her hand until she'd intertwined her fingers with his. "Because I'm curious." And because Isaac held part of himself back, secrets she wanted to explore. "My father's father used to play his fiddle in the evenings and tell us stories about his childhood. We'd heard most of them before, but he told them so well, we didn't mind hearing them again." She sighed. "I miss my family...the familiar routines. Even the tasks I used to dread. Don't you miss yours?"

"I do. But I now live as a white, with you. This is what I have chosen and how it must be."

Isaac was an expert at self-sacrifice, and at ending a conversation he didn't want to have. Eva wanted to hug him and hit him in equal measure.

"Teach me a word in your language."

"I taught you posh."

"Teach me something else."

He drew a breath laced with longsuffering. "*Mahwakanyuutat alyuuvach.*"

"What does that mean?"

"Wild pig."

She tried to imitate him, but when she formed the first glottal syllable, she sounded as if she were choking on a fish bone.

He hadn't. His deep, firm voice made the words sound rich. Exotic.

Isaac repeated the words more slowly, but she ducked to hide her heating cheeks and shook her head.

"You can learn it if you try. My mother did. ...But perhaps I should not teach you. You might slip and say the words in public."

"No one would understand."

"That is true. But they would recognize it as the language of an Indian, and that is all that would matter. We both would be in danger if anyone learned of my past." A self-deprecating sort of growl rumbled from within his throat. "This is why I should walk away. You would have a better life if you marry a white. Even one like Mr. Kramer."

"I don't want another man, especially Mr. Kramer. I will keep your secrets."

Eva raised up on her elbow and looked Isaac in the eye. Her words had soothed him, but not as much as she'd hoped they would. "This is what I have chosen, and this is how it will be." She leaned in for a kiss then slid her hand down and fumbled with the buttons of his falls.

The corner of Isaac's mouth quirked up. "You yearn for me again so soon?" They'd already engaged in carnal delights before rising from bed that morning.

"Yes." *Constantly.* Ever since their first joining, her body craved more. She felt like a tame attendant of the lustful woman hiding inside, tasked with keeping lunging animal spirits contained, using tattered, brittle leashes.

Isaac removed her hand from his trousers and rolled her to her back, stretching out over her, one hip resting on the ground next to hers.

Eva reached up and untied the leather cord that queued his hair. She tossed it aside and ran her fingers through the dark shoulder-length locks then traced the tattoos that encircled his arms. She wished she could see him clean shaven, as he'd been when they first met. Combining that memory with his unbound hair and muscular chest, she could see the warrior, even if no one else could.

Isaac kissed her thoroughly, sending shivers down her spine. "Open this," he said, tugging at buttons that held the bodice of her dress closed. When she did, he untied the ribbon cinching the top of her chemise and pulled it down to expose her breasts.

She playfully squeezed his biceps. "What's your word for this?"

"*Iisaly.*"

She knew he was humoring her, but he was doing it with an impish glint in his eyes, so she kept going. "And this?" she asked, touching his chin.

"*Iiyatakwatha.*"

That was one she'd never be able to learn. "And this?" She touched his nose.

He leaned down and kissed the tip of hers. "*Iihu.*"

"Ee-hu?"

"Um hm. *Iiya halyame,*" he said, planting kisses on each of her cheeks. "*Iiya kwah'uur,*" he went on, melding his lips with hers in a toe-curling kiss.

"Rr... Repeat that one," Eva said, breathlessly. "I don't think I caught it the first time."

Isaac chuckled and caressed the swell of one breast. "*Nyama.*" He closed his warm moist mouth around her nipple and drew on it, making her flinch. "*Nyama iido.*"

Eva slid her hand between them and caressed the firm bulge in his pants.

"*Muudar,*" he said in a husky voice.

He pushed himself up off the ground then gathered the hems of her skirts. "*Mat kalyaym,*" he said as he nudged her knees apart and knelt between them, flicking the buttons of his falls loose and shoving her skirts to her waist. As he almost always did, Isaac sat back on his heels and looked his fill without an ounce of shame, his appreciative gaze taking in every part of her.

Eva often pondered if delighting in her self-wed husband was a sin, but at times like this, she was too drunk on desire to care.

Isaac stroked her thighs with his large callused hands, murmuring more words she didn't understand. Next, he took her breasts in his hands and molded them gently. He smoothed his palms over the firm tips then rolled her nipples between his thumb and fingers.

Eva pulled away. "Ouch."

Isaac withdrew his hands. He looked her over again, but this time with an analyzing gaze, not a heated one. "Are you with child?"

Warmth filled her cheeks. "I think I might be."

His throat rippled with a swallow. "Are you ashamed that I am the father?" The question had been asked with casual boldness, but vulnerability lurked behind it.

"No. I love you, Isaac."

The apprehension in his eyes turned to blatant desire. "I am sorry I hurt you," he said as he bracketed her shoulders with his arms and came down over her. "I will take more care."

Isaac stared down at Eva draped across his chest, sleeping. She was carrying his child. It changed nothing, and it changed everything. He had said his decision to stay with her and live as a white was firm. Now his words were being tested.

It felt as if he was creeping through the lands of his enemies on a moonless night, unable to see the threat, but knowing it was all around him. Even within. Strong passions besieged him more than ever—fear and hate and love. They came in many forms, swapping one for the other and sneaking up on his senses in ambush.

He did not hate his wife, but he despised being forced to choose between his way of life and hers. The Mojave in him wanted to strip off his disguise and flee back to his clan.

But that was impossible.

And even if it wasn't, it was wrong.

"Eva..." Isaac said, gently patting her shoulder. "Eva, wake up." The light had taken on tones of amber, and the air was beginning to cool. It was time to return to the dugout.

She lifted her head and rubbed her eyes. "How long was I asleep?"

"Two hours. More, perhaps."

She sat up and began fastening her clothes. "You should have woken me sooner."

"You needed rest." He buttoned up his trousers and began pulling on his socks and boots. He wished he could leave his feet bare as he did when he lived with his clan.

The cry of an eagle sounded. Isaac looked up as it flew overhead and landed on the tallest tree. He couldn't see its eyes from that distance, but he knew it was looking at him, just as the eagle had done the day he killed his brother.

Isaac stared at the eagle until it flew away then finished putting on his boots.

"Are you all right," Eva asked.

He nodded, afraid that if he spoke, she would recognize the lie. "I will get the horses."

Eva's hand on his arm stopped him from rising, but it was the timid look in her eyes that froze him in place. "Can we stay a few minutes more? I have something I need to ask you."

Isaac crossed his legs and sat so that he faced her. "What is it that worries you?"

She gave him a shaky smile. "Is it that obvious?"

"Yes."

Eva moistened her lips. "I'm proud to be your wife," she said, smiling again, "and to bear your children…"

"But?"

"But I worry about the way we were married. The laws for whites are different. If a couple isn't legally married, their offspring are not considered legitimate."

"They are called bastards."

"Well, yes," she said, her face flushing with embarrassment.

Isaac studied her, the way her hands gripped each other tightly in her lap, the way tension bracketed her lips. She still had more to say. "What else worries you?"

The color in her cheeks paled, and moisture collected in the corners of her eyes. "When whites make their vows, it's binding until death. But since we didn't marry that way… I worry that you'll fall in love with someone else and decide to leave."

Isaac took her hand in his. "I have much love for you. I will not leave the marriage."

She stayed quiet, but he could see that was not enough.

"If we marry by your laws," he explained, "everything you have will become mine. I would be the owner of it all, even you."

"I know."

"I thought you wanted freedom. To choose how you will live. To own your land."

"I did, but…"

"When I said I did not want your land, I meant it."

"I know. And that's why I trusted you enough to marry you. I knew you'd deal fairly with me."

Isaac scrubbed a hand over his beard and considered her words.

"You've put as much work into proving up my claim as I have," Eva said. "You've earned it."

The hopefulness in her eyes made him want to agree and ease her mind, but this was not a decision to be made in haste.

"I would like to think on it," he said as gently as he could. "I will give you an answer soon."

"All right," she replied, but his answer had dimmed her gleam of hope.

Chapter Sixteen

Isaac watched Eva over the rim of his cup at breakfast a few days later. She pushed her food around her plate without eating much. Her condition was to blame for her lack of appetite, but so was his reluctance to marry her the white man's way.

He would not make her wait for an answer any longer.

Isaac set his coffee aside. "I have made my decision."

Eva locked gazes with him, staring with the eyes of a frightened child trying to be brave.

"When you asked me to marry you in the way of your laws, I did not hesitate to give you an answer because of any lack of loyalty or love. I would stay with you forever either way. I postponed my answer because I wanted time to dream. Just as when Keith came to you and freed you to love another, I sought confirmation for my choice."

"Did you get it?"

"Yes. I am willing to grant your request. But there is much I must tell you before you bind yourself to me for life."

Eva sat back and appeared to mentally fortify herself.

Isaac did, as well. It was not in his nature to speak about himself, or of things that brought him shame. "When you first took me in, I told you I killed someone."

"You said you killed a member of your clan to save some settlers."

"I did, but he was not just a clan member." Isaac paused to consider his choice one last time. Once the words were spoken, he could never take them back. "The word I said was not inches. It was *inchen*. It is the word in my language that means *older brother*. The man I killed was my brother."

Eva's composure faltered some, but she held his gaze. "What was his name?"

"Mahwat. He was the son of my father and his first wife, my father's favored son."

Emotions flickered in her eyes and wove their way through her brow, as she fought to reconcile a man who sat before her with one who would kill a member of his kin. "You did it to save innocent people. It was justified. Though I'm sorry you were put in the position to take the life of your brother. That couldn't have been easy."

It had been easier than she thought. "Mahwat and I were close as boys, but he turned cruel and ambitious as we grew. When we were nearing manhood, I told him of a dream I had. I was excited that I might be a leader in the clan, in spite of my mixed blood.

"Before I could tell our father, Mahwat presented the dream to him as his own. The events of the dream came to pass, and Mahwat was elevated in the clan instead of me."

"Did you tell your father the truth?"

"No."

"Why not?"

"It would not have changed anything. I had no way to prove the dream was mine."

The look of frustration on her face reminded him of the anger he had carried for years.

"Does your clan know you killed him?"

"They know he is dead. I tied his body to his horse and sent it in the direction of our village."

Eva scooted her chair closer and laid her hand on his. "I am sorry this happened, but it doesn't change the way I feel about you. I still want you as my husband."

"You honor me with your loyalty, but there is more.

"The day I killed Mahwat, an eagle appeared and followed me back to the river. It stayed until I sent his body away. The same eagle has been coming to me in dreams. Then one perched above the clearing the day you told me of our child."

"What does it mean?"

"I believe it is urging me to return to my people and tell my father about Mahwat."

Eva's eyes filled with fear, and her fingers tightened around his hand. "What will they do to you?"

"I do not know. But it is something I must do."

"When will you go?" she asked in a voice that was just above a whisper.

He stood and helped her up then encircled her with his arms. "Not for many months. I vowed to help you farm your land, and I will keep that promise." He would also sell pelts and leave an inheritance for his child. "You have much time to think and wait for answers to come in your dreams."

Eva hugged him and clung tightly for a long moment. "I do not need time to think or dream," she said, pulling away and looking up into his eyes. "You are my husband and the father of my child. I will go where you go and stand by your side."

Isaac's throat tightened so much he couldn't speak. Eva was brave, but her unwavering devotion in the face of the things she feared most—losing a spouse and venturing into Indian lands—sliced into him like an arrow, straight to his heart.

"Hullo, the house!" a male voice called from outside.

Eva quickly smoothed her clothing and swiped at the moisture that had gathered in her eyes. "That sounds like Mac," she said as bootsteps sounded in the yard, coming toward the porch.

"And Connor," Isaac added.

"How do you–?"

"I can hear his uneven steps and the thump of his cane."

Isaac opened the door and welcomed them in.

"I hope we're no' intrudin'," Mac said as he hung his hat on a peg.

"Mornin'," Connor said, limping in behind him. "Apologies fur comin' unannounced."

"Nonsense," Eva said as Isaac pulled out the other two chairs and gestured for them to sit. "Have you eaten?"

Mac chuckled. "More than we shuid."

Eva served coffee all around and joined the men at the table. "You two are beaming like boys on Christmas. What has you all excited?"

Connor looked to Mac. "Ye shuid be tha one tae tell it."

A smile so broad spread across Mac's face it made his eyes twinkle. "I sent fur ma Allison. She'll be here afore tha first snow."

"Oh, Mac," Eva exclaimed. "That's wonderful!"

"And three o' ma brothers are comin' with her," Connor added, smiling just as grand.

"That is good news," Isaac said.

"It is," Eva agreed. "I'm so happy for you both."

"Where will your brothers claim land?" Isaac asked.

"We're still workin' out tha details," Connor replied. "If they must settle on Mac's land fur a time, then sobeit."

"They're keepin' ma Allison safe on tha journey. I'll pay any price they name."

Isaac caught Eva's eye and raised a brow.

She answered with a similar look.

"Whit wis that aboot?" Mac asked.

Eva tucked an errant strand of hair behind her ear and cast the men a timorous look. "We have some news, as well."

"Told ya," Connor said to Mac under his breath.

Mac circled his hand in Eva's direction. "Oot with it, lass."

"Isaac and I... We've decided to get married."

"Ha!" Connor blurted. "I knew it!"

"Congratulations," Mac said, clapping Isaac on the shoulder. "When's tha weddin'?"

"Well," Eva replied, "that's the odd part. We're already wed—in the way of Isaac's people. Now we want to say vows before a preacher and make it legal in the eyes of mine."

"There'll be a preacher in Beckinsdale all week," Mac said. "That's only eight miles away. Ye shuid go."

"If ye go on tha morrow," Connor said, "Mac an' I can be there tae witness yer nuptials."

"Aye," Mac agreed. "We're ridin' tae tha next town over, tae buy some pigs. Ye could travel with us as far as Beckinsdale an' say yer vows, then return home while we travel on tae Murston."

Isaac looked to Eva. "I am willing if you are."

"The sooner we do this, the better."

"'At's the spirit," Connor said with a chuckle.

Mac narrowed his eyes at Eva. "There's more tae this story, isn't there, lass?"

She nodded, color rising in her cheeks and her gaze dropping to the table. "Isaac and I are expecting a child sometime early next year."

"Well, now," Mac crooned. "That *is* cause fur celebration."

Eva looked up at him. "You're not disappointed?"

"No, lass. Many a couple 'ave bound themselves with a handfast when they couldnae wait fur a man o' tha cloth, an' many more 'ave welcomed an eight-month bairn."

Isaac helped Eva down from her horse and secured their mounts to the hitching rail next to the tiny church in Beckinsdale.

"Do I look all right?" she asked, swatting the dust from her dress.

"You look beautiful." He had only seen Eva wear black, gray, and a pale shade of purple. The bright blue dress she'd chosen drew attention to her eyes and made them sparkle like stars on a cloudless night.

Eva beamed at him and smoothed the lapel of his borrowed suit. "You look very handsome in that. I must buy some wool suiting and make you one of your own."

Mac sauntered over, clearly bridling his steps so Connor could keep up. He gestured at the line of people forming. "Ye best secure yer place afore more arrive."

"He's right," Connor said, shooing them with his free hand. "We'll catch up."

Isaac offered his arm and escorted Eva to the end of the line, where waiting couples flashed nervous smiles and offered friendly greetings. He nodded and did the same. His ancestry was a source of shame and frustration, but not his bride. He was humbled that Eva had chosen him and proud to have her by his side.

It took them an hour to reach the doors of the church. By then the line had grown so long it curled around the side of the building. Voices quieted as they inched their way inside and waited for their turn at the altar.

Eva's grip on his arm tightened as the couple in front of them said their vows and hurried out past them.

"Next," the minister called, barely looking up. He scribbled something on a piece of paper then looked their small group over. "Which one of you is the groom?"

"I am," Isaac said.

"What's your full name?"

"Isaac Bartholomew Shaw."

"And yours?" he asked Eva as he wrote Isaac's name.

"Eva Rose Attwood McCabe."

He scribbled hers. "Are you both of age?"

"Yes," they answered in unison.

"Are either of you married to anyone who yet lives?"

"No."

"Very well. Repeat after me." He indicated Isaac should do so first. "I, Isaac Shaw, take you, Eva McCabe..."

Isaac took Eva's hands in his and looked into her eyes. "I, Isaac Shaw, take you, Eva McCabe, to be my wife...to have and to hold from this day forward...for better and for worse... for richer and for poorer...in sickness and in health...to love and to cherish, till death us do part, according to God's holy law."

"I, Eva McCabe, take you, Isaac Shaw...."

Sunlight slanting through the windows lit Eva's hair as she spoke, but Isaac's gaze was fixed on her face, an unfamiliar tightness creeping into his throat. Her lips formed each word with a quiet resolve, and though he had known her voice for months, it felt foreign in its gravity, as though she were speaking directly to his soul.

Something swelled inside him, a sensation he had not expected, rising with each line she uttered. His pulse sped, but not of nervousness. The cause was something firmer, more rooted.

He had agreed to marry Eva the way of her people only because she had asked it of him, and to refuse would have caused her distress. Now he regretted dismissing the ritual as unnecessary.

Her eyes held his, and in them, he saw pure devotion—a future he had somehow never fully grasped until this moment. He stood outwardly the same, while inside, something had shifted, permanent and undeniable.

"I now pronounce you man and wife," the minister said.

Isaac lifted Eva's hands and kissed them.

"*Meal do naidheachd!*" Mac said, clapping.

"Aye," Connor said. "Congratulations!"

Eva folded the cornflower blue dress she'd worn for the wedding—one of the few she'd brought west that hadn't been dyed black—and carefully returned it to her trunk. She spent a few minutes admiring the marriage certificate given to them by the minister then placed it on top of the dress. She was now and forever more Mrs. Isaac Shaw.

Isaac came in with the pail from Gwenie's evening milking, and Eva closed the trunk and smiled. "Supper will be ready shortly."

He set the pail in the cellar then examined the borrowed suit that was draped over the drying rack. "Has this aired enough to be returned?"

"Yes." She'd hung both garments outside as soon as the morning dew had evaporated and hadn't brought them back in until later afternoon. "I plan to return it to Connor tonight. I told him and Mac to come eat with us. I doubt either one of them will feel like cooking after driving pigs for twenty miles."

"You might decide to feed them on the porch once you smell them."

"Issac Shaw!" Eva was seconds away from delivering a grand setdown when she saw the mischief glinting in his eyes. She gave his arm a playful slap and hugged him instead. "You're a shameless scamp, but I love you."

Isaac took a seat at the table and worked on a bridle he was mending, while she checked on the rabbit stew. She moved it to the back of the stove to keep it warm. Mac and Connor had miles to travel and would be slowed by the pigs, so she took up her mending and waited.

When the sun had dropped so far behind the trees that she would be forced to light a candle to see, she set the garment aside and went to Isaac. "I'm getting worried. They should have been here by now."

"They are probably ridding themselves of the stench and the dust before joining us, but I will go there to be certain."

Isaac rose and lit a lantern then paused. "Horses approach." He peered out the corner of the window and nodded to Eva to open the door.

The men shuffled in, stinking of sweat and swine, and wearing grim expressions.

Eva's blood ran cold despite the August heat. Mac was in a state she'd never seen him in before. A strange pallor blanched his skin, and his eyes looked bleak. "What's wrong?" she asked. "Did something happen to Allison?"

He shook his head and dropped into a chair.

Connor did likewise.

"Take a seat," Mac said to her with a hollow, exhausted voice.

Eva lowered herself into a chair, dreading what he might say.

Mac lifted his windburned eyes to Isaac, who stood behind her with his hand on her shoulder. "Ye, too. Ye'll want tae be sittin' down fur this."

Isaac hesitated then pulled his chair close to Eva's and took hold of her hand below the table.

"I can scarcely believe whit I'm aboot tae tell ye," Mac went on, "but I heard it with ma own ears, so I know it tae be tha truth. Connor heard it, too."

"Aye," Connor muttered darkly.

Mac drew a labored breath and looked at her and Isaac. "After ye left fur home, Connor an' I went on tae Murston an' rented a room fur tha night. It was on tha ground floor, a stone's throw from tha saloon.

"Connor an' I were laying there, tryin' tae fall asleep in tha blasted heat, when we heard voices. A small group o' men had gathered near our window, an' one o' them was Dwight."

"What was he doing in Murston?" Eva asked.

"I dinnae ken. We slipped out o' town tha next mornin' without crossing his path." A look of dread mixed with pity wilted Mac's expression. "Brace yerself, lass." He looked directly at Isaac. "An' don't ye take aff in a fit o' rage afore ye've heard everything I came tae say."

"I will listen."

Mac looked back at Eva. "Dwight boasted that he has been tryin' to scare ye aff yer land fur some time. It wis he who broke yer fence an' stole yer wood."

"That evil trickster!"

"That's tha least o' it. He wis also tha one who dumped Isaac in yer yard an' left him fur deid."

Isaac's stoic façade broke into a look of utter shock. "Does he know who I am?"

"I dinnae believe so. He spoke o' 'tha widow's man, Isaac' later, as if speaking o' someone else." Mac's expression darkened. "He said he invited ye tae come along on a hunt with tha intention o' killing ye."

Eva gasped.

"He reasoned that if Eva didnae have ye tae work her land, she'd be forced tae forfeit."

Horror twisted her stomach. What if Isaac had accepted Dwight's invitation?

What if she'd married him instead?

Mac reached across the table and touched her arm. "Catch yer breath, lass. There's more." He looked as if he'd rather be anywhere but there. "Dwight lamented over a watch he'd jus' lost in a card game. He went on tae tell tha tale o' how he acquired it. It wis yer husband's.

"Keith, rest his soul, wasny murdered by an Indian. Dwight Kramer took his life."

"But the tracks, his scalp—"

"Dwight made it look that way tae escape suspicion."

Eva bolted from her chair and retched into the chamber pot. She'd shared meals with her husband's murderer. She'd invited the devil himself into her home!

Isaac came up behind her and handed her a cloth to wipe her face. She leaned against his chest and wept.

"I'm sorry we didnae see tha evil," Connor said, his voice thick with regret. "Tha degenerate fooled us all."

Isaac's arms tightened around her. "I will show him how it is to be murdered by an Indian," he snarled.

"I share yer rage," Mac said, "but ye have a wife an' a bairn on tha way. Eva needs a husband, no' a felon. Even if ye dodged tha noose, yer past would surely be revealed." He scrunched up his lips in a disgusted grimace.

"We dinnae ken tha identities of tha men he was talking tae, besides. If he wis willin' tae confide in them o' murder, I dooubt they have any more humanity than he."

"Mac's right," Connor said. "Dispatching tha miscreant to hell—though supremely satisfying—is much too risky."

A growl rumbled through Isaac's chest.

"Fate has a way o' punishin' men fur their crimes," Connor went on with menacing certainty. "A man cannae farm with fractured limbs. He needs tools, oxen, an' a hail body tae prove up a claim."

Mac laid a staying hand on his brother-in-law's arm. "Tha more pressing concern is Eva's safety," he said to Isaac, "an' yers, as well. The two o' ye are tha only things keeping Dwight from this claim."

"I can defeat him easily," Isaac said.

"Whit o' his friends? Ye cannae win a battle if ye dinnae ken who is yer enemy."

Isaac guided Eva over to the table and sat with her, his air of defeat palpable. "What do you suggest?"

"I think ye'd be wise tae leave as soon as ye can."

"What about our claim?" Eva asked.

"It'd be safer without ye," Connor said. "Dwight cannae take yer land, so long as ye live tae challenge 'im. The law disnae require ye tae reside on yer claim year-round. Ye have tha necessary structures an' tha cultivation. So long as ye are no' gone fur more than six months at a time, ye can still prove up."

"But what about the cows?"

"Ma brothers can care fur them. They'll be here afore long. Mac an' I can manage until then."

"That will put you and your family in danger."

Mac shook his head. "We have no claim on this land, an' tha herd we'd be carin' fur is an asset. Dwight has no motive tae harm us."

"Trust us, lass," Connor said. "Provin' up yer claim will be a sweeter revenge. Then it'll be yers tae occupy or sell, as ye see fit."

Isaac looked down at her. "We could travel south and find a place to stay through winter then return for a visit next year."

"We could take that trip you spoke of." Traveling into the lands of Isaac's people was likely safer than staying where they were.

"Perhaps."

Eva's throat tightened as she worked up to asking her next question. "What if we're unable to return?"

"We'd say we saw ye here on tha required days," Connor assured.

Mac cast Connor a solemn glance. "I think she refers tae something darker."

"Ah."

"Ye can write a letter afore ye go, signin' yer claim over tae us," Mac said. "We'll only use it if we must."

Eva stayed silent, debating. As if she had a choice.

Mac peered into her eyes with an earnest gaze. "I swear a vow tae ye—an' I'd swear it tae Keith, were he standin' here—I willnae rob ye of yer claim. Tis only a last resort tae keep it outta Mr. Kramer's bloodstained hands."

Eva looked to Isaac. At his nod of approval, she turned back to Mac and Connor. "All right. But I want you to have it regardless. I'll not let your family work my land for free."

"Vera well. However it goes, wages or a sale, we'll settle on a fair price."

And he would. A better friend and neighbor she'd never find.

Eva looked around at the home she and Keith had made. She wasn't sure she had it in her to start over again. "I don't know how we'll manage the trip. I still have our wagon, but Keith cut the tarp into pieces when he finished building the dugout."

"Ye can have ours," Connor said.

Eva served the soup and savored one last meal with neighbors she considered family.

Blinking back tears so they wouldn't fall and smear the ink, she wrote a transfer of the claim and slid it to Isaac to sign. She sanded it and stared at it as it dried then threw her arms around Mac's neck and hugged him tight. "I'm going to miss you, Mac McKinnon."

"And I ye, lass," he replied in a rough voice, hugging her so tightly he lifted her off the ground.

Eva pulled away and gave Connor a kiss on the cheek. "I wish I could be here to welcome Allison," she said, dabbing her eyes. "I wish we could stay and be neighbors."

Connor cleared his throat. "As I said, fate has a way o' makin' things right. A year or two from now, it might be safe fur ye tae occupy yer land."

"Even if ye sell," Mac countered, "ye can still visit. Afore long," he said, waving his arm to and fro, "rail lines will cover tha country like a web o' an ambitious spider. Trips'll be reduced from weeks tae days."

She smiled at their efforts to cheer her, but inside, her heart lay broken.

Chapter Seventeen

Eva packed the essentials into the wagon with Isaac's help, looking over her shoulder at every turn. Not only did she fear that Isaac might seek revenge if Dwight Kramer walked into the yard, it would be better for all involved if he didn't see them leave or learn they were wed. Once word got out that she and Isaac were gone, the story Mac and his family would tell is that Eva had taken a trip to care for an ill relative, and Isaac had gone along as her protector.

Eva walked into the dugout and took one last look around. The bed had been stripped of its covers, and the cupboards emptied of most of their contents. The stove would stay behind for Connor's brothers to use, and for them, if they were ever able to return.

"I'm done in here," she said to Isaac. "Do you need help with the barn?"

"No. All that we are taking from it has been packed, and Gwenie is with Mac." He had parked the wagon behind the barn, in a place shaded by trees, so it would be shielded from view until they drove it out onto the open road.

Eva slipped her arms around Isaac's waist and rested her weary head against his chest. "Tell me we're doing the right thing. It feels as if we're letting Mr. Kramer win."

He hugged her close. "We are not surrendering. We are being wise in battle and choosing the best strategy."

Eva followed Isaac out of the dugout and closed the door. The bench Keith had built still sat where he'd placed it under the tree. She wanted to take it with them, but that would arouse suspicion.

She walked with Isaac to the pasture where their horses were grazing

"Houyhnhnm," Isaac called to his horse. "Come." He had been training his horse to respond to English commands since coming to work on her farm, but he hadn't changed the horse's name.

"What does ho-an-um mean?"

"Intelligent horse. It is not a Mojave word. It is from *Gulliver's Travels*."

Isaac led Houyhnhnm out and refastened the gate. "I must retrieve the items from the clearing."

"Can I come, too?"

"I have already packed your saddle."

"If you help me mount, I can ride without one."

He swung himself up onto Houyhnhnm's back and held out his hand to her. "Ride with me." They clasped arms. Then, in one swift motion, Isaac lifted her off the ground and set her in front of him.

Houyhnhnm didn't sidestep or indicate in any way that he disliked carrying a second rider.

Eva stroked the horse's broad neck. "You're intelligent and well behaved."

Isaac had placed her with both legs hanging off one side of the horse. He held her steady with an arm around her waist as they began to ride. She wanted to lean against his chest and tuck her head in the curve of his neck, but she couldn't take the chance of being seen. Riding double with her hired man was scandalous enough.

Isaac guided his horse the long way around, giving her one last look at the cows and the crops.

"I wish we could spend one more day, lunching in the clearing," Eva said wistfully as the southern border of it came into view.

"I do, as well." Isaac patted her hip where his hand rested. "There will be time for lunches on the quilt, once we go far enough from these lands."

Houyhnhnm tossed his head, and Isaac murmured to him.

"We'll be traveling south, not west," Eva said. "Will there be trails wide enough for the wagon?"

"Yes. There are roads."

Houyhnhnm lifted his nose. His ears turned back, and he tossed his head again.

"Easy, boy," Eva crooned. "We're almost—"

"*Shh.*" Isaac drew Houyhnhnm to a halt and sat very still. He leaned down with his lips near her ear and whispered, "Horses. Behind us."

Eva strained to hear, but she could barely make sense of the sounds.

Isaac murmured something in his language and gently adjusted the reins. Houyhnhnm began stepping sideways, slowly and soundlessly, until they were deep beneath the canopy of an oak tree.

The distant noise grew closer and more defined. The thumping of hooves, the low hum of male voices, and the jingle of tack—a group of men, riding.

Eva leaned into Isaac's embrace and prayed whoever approached was friendly. The vegetation that concealed the hidden clearing was too dense for Houyhnhnm to pass through, and open meadow surrounded it. If they rode away, they'd be seen.

The limbs above them spread wide and hung low. Maybe, if she and Isaac stayed still and quiet, they wouldn't be noticed.

"No matter who we encounter," Isaac whispered, "pretend all is well."

Eva nodded. Feigning ignorance if she came face to face with her husband's killer seemed impossible, but she had no choice. Multiple horses approached. If it *was* Dwight, he wasn't alone.

The horses entered the meadow, a few yards away. They'd soon round the copse of trees and reach the place she and Isaac were hiding.

"What's the plan?" a man asked.

"Get rid of 'em both."

Eva clamped her hand over her mouth to stifle a whimper. "It's them," she whispered as Isaac frowned and locked gazes with her. "The men who beat you and threatened me."

He looked in the direction of the voices then turned Houyhnhnm the opposite way and signaled him to walk.

"What are you doing? They'll see us."

He urged Houyhnhnm into a trot and steered him toward the hidden clearing. "Go," he told her in a harsh whisper, slowing his horse at the edge of the dense vegetation and brusquely setting her on the ground. "Hide yourself while I distract them."

"But—"

Isaac spurred Houyhnhnm into a gallop and took off.

"I heard a horse," one of the southern men blurted.

Eva didn't pause to look back. She picked her way through the bushes and vines as quickly as she could then crouched behind a dense fir tree at the inner edge of the clearing.

"Look. There he is!" the other southerner called.

Hooves pounded the ground as they galloped past her hiding spot. She wished she could see how many there were. She wished even more that she'd brought her gun, but Isaac had packed that, too.

Eva stood and walked into the middle of the clearing, turning slowly and listening, trying to determine the direction Isaac had gone. Maybe his plan was to circle around to the opposite side and hide in the clearing, too. But what about Houyhnhnm?

The horse had found his way back to Isaac after he was beaten. Perhaps he was smart enough to keep himself safe.

Eva clasped her hands in a nervous ball and scanned the bushes for movement. They remained completely still as the sounds of all the horses faded away.

Silence was worse than being hunted. Not knowing if Isaac was safe was more than she could bear. Eva's whole body trembled, and tears began to sting her eyes.

Please, God. Don't take another husband from me.

Many agonizing minutes passed. Then she heard a single horse approaching at a full gallop. Maybe Isaac had outrun the men and put enough distance between them to circle back and hide.

Eva turned as the horse sped around the outside of the clearing, keeping her ears trained on the sounds. Suddenly, hooves skidded to a stop and reversed course.

A moment later, she knew why.

A group of horses thundered by, their riders yelling, "Hurry!" and "We got him now."

The blast of a gun made Eva jump.

No, no, no! Isaac was unarmed, except for his knife. He would surely lose to men with guns.

Eva ran to the hollow tree. She slung Isaac's quiver over her shoulder and grabbed his bow. The sounds had faded again, but, a few minutes later, they returned. She crept through the brush and peered out of a space between the leaves.

She'd been right. It was the same three men who'd beaten Isaac and later returned to threaten her.

One of the riders was gaining on Isaac. He lifted his gun and fired.

Isaac dove from his horse just in time. He rolled away, seemingly unhurt. But he'd lost his advantage. The three riders swiftly closed in and dismounted.

Eva nocked an arrow and aimed it at the man who'd fired the gun. She'd give her presence away as soon as she let it fly, but she didn't have to think twice. Isaac would die unless she joined the fight.

She lined it up, waited for him to slow his movements, and released.

Her arrow missed, but it diverted the men's attention away from Isaac.

Eva ducked back into the foliage as the men turned to look her way. They scanned the meadow's edge for such a long moment she feared they might come to investigate.

Something moved beside the men. Isaac leapt up behind the closest man, grabbed his hair, and drew his knife across his throat.

The other men stared at him in shock. They charged toward Isaac, yelling obscenities, so Eva let a second arrow fly.

It missed.

This time, the men paid it little mind. Isaac had disarmed the gunman with a well-aimed kick and had engaged them hand to hand.

Eva crept closer and kept shooting, whenever she was able to let an arrow fly without risk of hitting Isaac. Except for the occasional thud of a foot or fist making contact, the battle was eerily quiet. Isaac's knife arced through the air, each thrust of his arm driving his enemy backward. Her arrows flew with a soft swoosh but silently landed in the dirt.

Eva reached for the next and pulled one of the remaining two arrows from the quiver.

The battle had shifted, and the men had the advantage. One of them—the mean one with the northern accent—ran to his horse and pulled his rifle from its scabbard. As he turned to rejoin the fight, he spotted her. He lifted the rifle and aimed it at her.

Eva dove and flattened herself in the knee-high grass, losing her hold on the bow, and braced herself to be fired upon.

The man lowered the barrel, even though she could glimpse him between the blades, which meant he could see her. A sinister smile spread across his face, and he walked back toward Isaac.

Eva crawled to the bow, grabbed it, and got to her feet. She paused to recall Isaac's lessons, when everything in her screamed for her to hurry. She and Isaac would both lose if the next arrow didn't find its mark.

She nocked it then quieted the chaos in her head and suppressed her fear. Hitting her target was the only thing that mattered.

Isaac landed several blows that had the man nearest him stumbling backward. She decided to shoot him first while she had the opportunity, to give Isaac a chance to catch his breath. But then the other man lifted his gun. She changed tac and let her arrow fly to him instead.

The arrow pierced his neck instead of his heart, but it felled him and caused his shot to miss.

Reducing the number of opponents to one gave her a moment of relief, but Isaac was still in danger.

The deaths of the third man's companions had turned him vicious. He kicked the knife from Isaac's grasp and charged him, knocking loose the cord that queued his hair, and tearing at his clothes. Isaac was truly in a battle for his life.

The quiver held one last arrow. But, with the men fighting in such close contact, Eva was unable to use it.

She set the quiver and bow aside and scanned the ground for Isaac's knife. If she could somehow get it back to him, he would have a better chance.

A horse and rider galloped up from the direction of the hay field. Dwight.

"What's this?" He swung down from his horse, his revolver in a holster at his hip. "I thought I told you not to come back," he yelled at the man fighting Isaac.

The man stopped fighting and stared at Dwight with a perplexed expression.

"You heard me. Back away."

His performance made Eva sick and released the lock on her tongue. "You can stop pretending," she spat at Dwight. "I know you're the one who killed Keith."

He smiled at her and chuckled. Why had she never heard the deranged notes lurking in his laugh?

Issac growled at Dwight, his hair flowing about his face like a fierce warrior.

The other man peered at Isaac's arm then gave his torn sleeve a yank, fully exposing the tattoo on his biceps. "Shoot him, Whitey! He's the injun!"

Eva swallowed the bile rising in the back of her throat—Dwight was Whitey. He knew the men who'd attacked Isaac.

Dwight began closing the distance between them. "I knew something about you was familiar," he said to Isaac, his lips still showing a hint of his former smile. "You've changed since I dumped you by the widow's woodshed."—Dwight's gaze shot to her—"The body *you* told me had been thrown over the falls. Who'd've ever thought you'd be a sympathizer to injuns, Mrs. McCabe. Your hired man must be doing more than farming for his pay."

Eva's blood boiled over, and her fingers itched to grab him by the throat. "He's not my hired man, you degenerate pig. He's my husband."

Dwight's face went slack, and his eyes turned icy. By the time his hands had fully fisted at his sides, his whole body vibrated with rage.

If she'd been within arm's reach, he would have struck her.

Isaac used the distraction to snatch his knife from the ground and stab the last man deep into his chest. The man's eyes opened wide, and so did his mouth, but the only sound that came out was a gurgling wheeze. Isaac tossed the body aside and assumed a stance ready for battle, blood dripping from his blade.

Dwight drew his revolver and leveled it at Isaac. "I'm going to enjoy killing you more than I did her first. It will be supremely satisfying, ridding this claim of a rival *and* a savage with one shot."

Eva ran to Isaac's bow.

Uttering a growl that didn't sound human, Isaac charged Dwight as she nocked the last arrow and pierced her enemy straight through the heart.

Eva's spirit roared, but her body went limp with overwhelming sadness. She'd won, but there was no prize. Killing Dwight couldn't bring Keith back. And now she risked losing Isaac.

Isaac tore his sleeve all the way off and used it to wipe the blood from his blade and his hands. "You were very brave," he said, sheathing his knife and wrapping her in a tight embrace.

Eva clung to him. "What now? When people find out about this…" She ducked her head and cried until his shirt was damp with her tears.

"Shh," Isaac soothed. "It will be all right." He kept holding her close and lifted his head. "Houyhnhnm," he called in a loud voice. "Come."

The horse trotted up several moments later and stood next to his master. He swished his tail calmly. Then he lifted his head and perked up his ears.

Isaac's grip on her tightened, and a new alertness stiffened his entire frame. "More horses approach," he said softly, pointing in the direction of the dugout.

Eva's heart sank, even as its cadence took off like a frightened hare. "I used all your arrows."

Isaac snatched the revolver from Dwight's lifeless grasp and handed it to her. By the time she'd prepared herself for another fight, he'd retrieved all the arrows, slung the quiver onto his back, and readied his bow.

He stared down the first arrow's length as two riders came into view.

Eva followed suit and raised her weapon.

The riders halted and lifted their hands in a show of surrender.

"Wait," Eva said, lowering the revolver and placing a staying hand on Isaac's arm. His hearing might be keener, but she knew the silhouette of her neighbors by heart. "It's Mac and Connor. They must've heard the shots."

Eva pocketed the gun and waved.

"Gracious, lass," Mac said when he reached them. "Ye near gave ma a cooranary." He took note of Isaac's appearance then gestured in the direction of the bodies that lay beyond Dwight's. "Who are they?"

"They're the men who beat Isaac and returned to threaten me," Eva said. She recalled the way the last man spoke to Dwight and seemed to know him. "Could they have been the ones Dwight was talking to in Murston, outside the saloon...? Two of them spoke with a southern accent," she added at Mac's and Connor's contemplative frowns.

"I cannae be certain," Connor said. "Dwight did most o' tha talking."

Eva shared a worried look with Isaac. Their greatest enemy was dead, but there was no way to know if these were the sum of his accomplices.

They might never be safe.

Her body turned so weary she feared she might drop where she stood.

"Let Isaac take ye back tae tha dugout so ye can rest," Mac said to her as he and Connor dismounted. "We'll take care o' this."

Isaac hoisted himself onto Houyhnhnm's back and lifted her up in front of him, as before. "I will bring shovels."

"Dinnae bother," Connor said. "We'll feed 'em tae tha swine."

"Ack, nae!" Mac retorted with a look of abject horror. "Those swine will one day be our supper."

"No' *our* swine, ye dullard." Connor kicked Dwight's body with the toe of his boot. *"His."*

Eva slid to the ground when Isaac paused by the wagon to retrieve a fresh shirt and trousers, so he could change out of his bloodstained clothes. "I can walk."

He eyed her as she took her first few steps. "I will return my horse to the pasture and meet you inside."

Her answer was a nod. She'd lost the strength for words.

Eva slumped onto the bed, the only piece of furniture left on which to sit, and stared into the cold empty hearth. Together, she and Isaac had taken four lives. The killings were justified, yet they gouged pieces from her soul.

And what was left for them now? Isaac was alive, and the world had been ridded of a few evil men. But Keith was still gone, Isaac faced discovery, and the memory would forever taint the way she felt about her land.

Eva dragged her unfocussed gaze away from the hearth and looked over her shoulder as Isaac came in, carrying a bucket of water.

He removed his torn shirt and used a clean portion of the tail like a rag to wash the rusty stains from his skin. "I think it is beyond repair," he said, holding the shirt up by its yoke.

Eva nodded and stared blankly at the floor in front of her. In the fringe of her vision, she saw Isaac pause then remove his trousers and put on the fresh clothes he'd brought from the wagon.

He came and squatted down before her. "Have I caused you shame?"

"No."

His gaze roamed over her face as if assessing the truthfulness of her statement. "The first time a warrior engages in battle, it brings much pride and also confusion. He wins by taking lives, and his people celebrate his victory when he returns to the village. But in quiet moments alone, if the warrior has a heart, he knows the depth of what he has done." Isaac reached up and took her hand. "I am grateful you were with me, but I am sorry you were drawn into the fight."

Eva's eyes burned with the sting of fresh tears. "I couldn't let them kill you."

He kissed her hand then sat next to her on the mattress. "Do not cry. I am well, and so are you. The men left us no choice. We did not seek the battle out. We defended ourselves against invaders."

He was right.

Eva rested her head on his shoulder. "What do we do now?"

"I still wish to visit my clan, if you are willing."

"I am." Isaac's words had restored her strength enough to manage a day's journey in the wagon.

"Come," he said, rising and assisting her to stand. "Mac and Connor have returned."

Isaac carried the bucket out for them, but they didn't need it. Both men were clean and damp.

"It's done," Mac said as he and Connor dismounted. He lifted a blanket, revealing a bundle of bloody clothing tied to his saddle, and lowered his voice. "Once we burn that an' give tha swine a few more hours tae feast, there willnae be any trace o' Dwight Kramer."

"Or his evil companions," Connor added, limping over to Keith's bench and dropping onto it with a weary thud.

Isaac handed his torn shirt to Mac. "Add this."

Mac took it and tucked it into the bundle.

"Tae compound his sins," Connor remarked as Isaac seated Eva on the bench next to him, "Dwight lied aboot his crops. His fields are shockingly sparse. Tha rain washed away more than 'a few' o' his seedlings."

"Why didn't he just reseed afterwords?" Eva asked.

"I dinnae ken," Connor said. "Perhaps he could no' afford tae."

Isaac brought crates from the porch for himself and Mac.

Mac raised a brow and looked hopeful. "Shall we unpack tha wagon?" he asked as he sat.

Isaac shook his head. "We have not changed our plans."

Connor flashed a sad smile. "Ma heart wants tae argue, but it goes against ma better sense."

"Aye," Mac agreed. "It wis a foolish question. We cannae be certain tha threat is over."

"It wasn't foolish," Eva countered. "Staying crossed my mind."

Mac's lips curved in appreciation, but his massive shoulders drooped. "Me an' ma kin will care fur Dwight's farm in his absence, but we cannae take over his claim without waiting a respectable time fur our *missing neighbor* tae return. His friends who offered tae buy out Eva's claim might vera well show up. If they do, we will have tae turn his land over ta them, or at least offer. Squatting on it now would be tantamount tae admittin' knowledge o' his death."

"I know you will do what is best," Isaac said. He looked to Eva. "If we are to begin our journey today, we should go."

Eva smiled at her friends and tried to hold back her tears. "I'm going to miss you both."

Connor cleared his throat and patted the solid oak plank on which they sat. "Yer free tae take this with ye now."

Eva smoothed her hand over wood so well-crafted it gleamed. She'd miss the remembrance of Keith, but Connor needed it more. "I've decided to leave it. Keith chose to place this here, and here is where it belongs. God willing, I'll return to sit on it one day."

Chapter Eighteen

It took forty-five days to reach the lands occupied by Isaac's clan.

Eva posted several letters to Mac along the way, telling him of their adventures and assuring him they both were safe and well. In the last one, she'd told him, until further notice, to address any correspondence to them care of a trading post half way between Fort Yuma and Santa Fe.

"What are the Mojave people like?" she asked Isaac as they rolled along the dusty trail edged with cactus, gnarled trees, and scrubby clumps of grass.

"They are the same as whites in many ways. The men plant and hunt. The women cook and care for the children. At night, we gather together to sing and tell stories."

"Do they look and dress like you—when you first came to my farm, I mean?"

"The men have more tattoos than I. Some are covered with them." He looked sideways at her. "My people do not wear much clothing. The women do not wear shirts."

Eva couldn't conceal her shock. "What about your mother?"

"She dresses like you."

That was a relief.

"And your sisters?"

"The oldest one, Mary Elizabeth, dresses in the clothing of whites. But she does not live with the clan anymore."

"Why?"

"It was her choice." He paused and steered the team around a washed-out section of the road. "Three summers ago," Isaac went on, once they were back on the rutted path, "a white man was badly injured when his wagon crossed the river on the way to California. My mother offered to care for him until he was well enough to travel. His bones needed time to mend, and he was with us for many weeks. The man decided he loved Mary. He asked her to marry him and go with him when he left."

"I'm surprised your parents allowed it."

"They rejected his proposal at first. But they returned to their hearts, because of Mary's feelings. She has light hair and eyes, like our mother, and very pale skin. Our father even changed her name to *Nyamuuraa* as she grew, because she so closely resembles a china doll.

"Mary always felt out of place, even though she is accepted by the clan. By the time she left, we had all agreed. Mary belongs among whites."

Isaac slowed the wagon as they topped a rise and started down a slope. "My second sister, Ruth—or *Mataha*, as she is known among my people—married a man in our village."

"What does her Mojave name mean?"

"Wind."

"Does she look like Mary?"

"No. Ruth has dark skin and eyes, like my father. She wears the clothing of our people, but she covers her chest out of respect for our mother.

"It is the same with my third sister, Cora Jane, though she has not married yet. She is fourteen."

"What is Cora's other name?"

"*Halakuuk*, which means *she is happy*."

Isaac turned quiet and guided the horses a few more miles. He chose a place to camp far enough from his clan's village that they wouldn't be discovered.

Eva fixed a simple supper then bedded down with Isaac next to the wagon. He molded his body to her back and draped an arm about her waist as he usually did, but tension kept his muscles firm.

"Talk to me," she said, resting her arm atop his and massaging some of the stiffness from it. "I can feel your worry."

"I am planning how I will keep you safe."

"I thought you said your clan is peaceful."

"They are, but Mahwat had many friends. I do not know how my visit will be received."

Eva scooted so that she was on her back, looking up at him. "Your hair is past your shoulders now. Will you shave your beard and go as they remember you?"

"I have not decided that. I have only decided that I will go alone."

"But–"

"You will be safe here. If things go well, I will return and tell you. If I do not return, you can drive the wagon to the trading post and send word to Mac."

"Why would you not return?"

His glaze skittered away.

"Are you planning to leave me?" That got his attention.

"No."

"Are you ashamed that I'm white?"

"*No.*"

"Then the only thing left... You worry they might harm you."

He splayed his hand over the slight bulge of her abdomen that was barely large enough to fill his palm. "I do not fear for myself. It is your future and that of our child that concerns me."

"I don't want a life without you, Isaac. If you can't promise they will not harm you, then we will go together."

He clearly didn't like that idea.

Eva covered his hand that was on her belly and threaded her fingers with his. "What would your people do if a white couple walked into their village, unarmed?"

"They would remain calm and attempt to communicate."

"Then it's settled. Keep the beard. You've proven you can pass for ko. Even *I* didn't recognize you at first. We should go together, dressed as we are."

"If I speak, they will know my voice."

"Then I will do the talking. Tell me what to say."

After breakfast, they stowed the wagon in a secluded location and rode the horses as close to the village as they dared. Isaac put his looking glass to his eye and surveyed the area.

"What do you see?"

"The men must be hunting... Only a few are in camp." He scanned the area further. "And the women are calm, not anxious as they would be if the men had ridden into battle."

"Is you father with them."

"I do not know."

"Remind me of what I am to say." He'd gone over it the night before, but she needed to get it exactly right.

Isaac lowered the looking glass. "Ask for my mother by her Mojave name, *Kuku Chapuuk*, dove who blows out water."

Eva repeated the words softly several times.

Isaac tied the horses to graze, looking more conflicted by the minute.

Eva went to him and took his hands in hers. "We can still turn back. I won't think less of you if you change your mind."

"I do not want to turn back. I am not afraid. My dreams have shown me this is the path I am to take. But you have once again been drawn into my battle."

"As it should be. You're my husband, which means we're allies for life."

Isaac searched her eyes. "*'Amuhank*," he uttered as he sealed his lips to hers and kissed her deeply.

"I love you, too," Eva murmured against his lips as they parted.

He clutched her to his chest then stepped back and offered her his arm. "Let us go."

Eva slipped her arm around his and walked with him toward the village.

Two Mojave men rode out to meet them as they reached the outskirts.

The men wore only loin cloths. Rows and rows of blue lines covered their faces and upper bodies. One assessed them cautiously, a bow resting across his lap. The other man glared at them, holding a club, and spoke in short curt words she couldn't understand.

Isaac leaned down and whispered, "They ask why we are here."

Eva patted his arm reassuringly then slipped hers free and walked a few steps closer. "I am looking for *Kuku Chapuuk*."

The cautious one raised his brows, and the other frowned and scrutinized her.

"*Kuku Chapuuk*," Eva repeated. "Dove who blows out water. Is she here?"

The frowning man said something to the cautious one, prompting him to turn and ride back into the village.

He returned with a white middle-aged woman in a plain blue day dress and five more scary men. The woman studied them with brilliant blue eyes as she neared, a warm breeze teasing the wavy strands of gray-blond hair that framed her face.

Eva recognized Isaac's mother from the drawing, but she asked anyway. "Are you *Kuku Chapuuk,* dove who blows out water?"

"Yes," the woman replied, clearly surprised but equally curious. "Who are you?"

Eva resisted the urge to look at the menacing group surrounding them and said a silent prayer for mercy. "My name is Eva Shaw, your daughter-in-law."

The woman's eyes widened and darted to Isaac. She walked closer, her hand coming up and covering her trembling lips.

Isaac removed his hat and the cord tying his hair. "It is me."

His mother wrapped her arms around him and held him in a long embrace. "I've missed you, Isaac."

"I have missed you, too," he said, returning her hug.

Isaac's mother pulled away, smiling and dabbing her eyes. "Forgive my manners. It's nice to meet you, Eva. Call me Loraine."

Eva opened her mouth to speak, but Isaac stopped her with a touch of his hand as he scanned the group of villagers that had gathered. Some looked happy to see him, but most wore stern expressions. A few had murder in their eyes.

"I wish to speak with my father," he said, followed by a few words in his language, which she assumed was the same phrase repeated.

"I will get him," Lorraine replied. She turned toward the village but halted after the first few steps.

A man—an older, darker version of Isaac—was coming toward them.

"This is my husband, *Kumadha,* Isaac's father," she said to Eva when the man reached them.

Eva smiled up at him. "Pleased to meet you." She should have had Isaac teach her greetings in his language, too.

Loraine gestured to Eva and spoke fluently to Kumadha, then she indicated Isaac and spoke some more.

Kumadha remained mute, at first, but his stony expression softened as his wife continued speaking. Long moments later, he gave a single silent nod that was so much like Isaac's, Eva had to bite the inside of her lip to hold back a grin.

He walked past Eva to Isaac, waving off the men who started to follow him, and went with him to sit in the shade of a nearby tree.

The clan members let them go, but their expressions hadn't changed.

Eva sidled up to Loraine. "Will they harm Isaac?"

"No. His father has agreed to speak with him, and Kumadha is a respected member of the clan." Loraine flashed a kind smile. "You must be tired and thirsty. Come rest in my house while the men have their meeting. We can chat over tea."

What must've been the entire population of Isaac's clan, minus the men who were hunting, was standing behind Eva when she turned around. Children stared at her from the spaces between their mothers, who nearly all held a baby resting on one hip.

Loraine said something to them in their language, the only word of which Eva understood was her own name. "I introduced you and told them who you are."

Eva's polite impulse to smile and nod clashed with the urge to duck her head and shield her eyes from the rampant nudity—among the women especially. They stood unashamed, wearing nothing more than grass skirts and jewelry made from beads and shells. Some had tattoos that were as extensive and ornate as the men's.

Loraine motioned for two of the young women to come closer. They looked and dressed like the other women in the tribe, except for beaded, dicky-like sashes that completely covered their chests. "Eva, these are my daughters, Ruth and Cora Jane."

"Hello," Ruth said in a soft tone that Eva wasn't sure whether to interpret as a reserved nature or compulsory politeness.

Cora Jane wore a full, genuine smile. "Welcome, Eva!"

"Thank you. I am pleased to meet you, Mataha," she said to Ruth, "and you, too, Halakuuk."

Ruth seemed pleased by the use of her Mojave name.

Cora Jane practically beamed. "I wish our other sister, Mary, was here. She would have loved meeting you."

"Thank you. I wish that, too."

"Cora Jane," Loraine said, "go help prepare for the return of the hunters. Eva and I are going to visit over tea."

"Yes, *intay*," she responded cheerfully.

The crowd parted for them as Loraine led her through. Eva focused her attention on people's faces, but hers still flamed.

"Their state of undress is disconcerting to outsiders," Loraine said, taking in Eva's hot cheeks. "I felt the same way when Isaac's father brought me here."

"But you didn't adopt it."

"No. I prefer to stay covered. And," she added with a conspiratorial smile, "I think Kumadha prefers me that way, too—a package only he is allowed to unwrap." Loraine laughed. "I've embarrassed you more. Forgive me. I've been living away from whites too long."

She stopped at one of the larger houses in the village and led Eva across a large section of ground that was framed by poles and covered with a thatched roof. The day was hot for late September, and the shade felt good.

"Come in and make yourself comfortable," Loraine said as they passed through the door into a large room that had a pile of animal skins near a simple hearth and a few kitchen furnishings. "I was making tea when you and Isaac arrived." She gestured to a set of four chairs in one corner that surrounded a small table. "My husband's people do virtually everything sitting on the ground. I 'do as in Rome' most of the time, but I insist on a few comforts. The table and chairs, my tea," she said as she carried a wooden tea tray with a full ceramic service over and set it between them, "and a chamber pot."

Eva took in the room, which was primitive with touches of culture. "Are you happy here?" Heat climbed her cheeks again. "I'm sorry. That was rude."

"No. Not rude at all. Honey?" Loraine added some to Eva's tea at her nod. "I'm sorry there's no cream."

Eva stirred the honey in. "This is perfect."

"Has Isaac told you anything about me?"

"A little. He said you came to live here after Indians from another tribe killed your first husband."

"I was newly widowed and quite shaken when Kumadha first brought me here." Loraine said, sitting across from her. "Neither he nor his clan mistreated me in any way, but I couldn't communicate with them, and I had lost everything that was familiar. For many months, I simply wanted to die.

"A few of the women fed me and encouraged me, until I began to work alongside them and learn their language. Later, when Kumadha asked me to be his wife, I realized love is what matters. One can be content almost anywhere if they have someone special by their side."

A sudden rush of empathy flooded Eva's heart. "My first husband was murdered also. I can't imagine what it would have been like, mourning Keith among strangers."

"I noticed you were wearing half-mourning colors, but I didn't want to pry."

"I should still be in black." Eva said, shamefaced. "Keith has only been gone a year. I put on lighter colors at Isaac's urging, because black was too hot for working in the fields."

"We all do what we must," Loraine said without a hint of judgment. She picked up her cup and cradled it in her hands. "May I ask how you met my son?"

Eva took a sip of tea to buy time to think. She wasn't sure how much Isaac would want her to reveal. "I hired him to help me cultivate my land."

Loraine studied Eva with keen eyes, but she didn't ask for details.

"Isaac is a hard worker and a good man," Eva volunteered, feeling the need to say something more. "I'm grateful his path crossed mine."

Isaac removed his hat and shirt and set them aside. His father eyed the scar the bullet had left on his shoulder as they sat on the ground, across from each other. Time had etched more lines in Kumadha's face during the ten months they had been apart.

"An eagle has sent me to speak to you," Isaac said in his clan's language.

"Then I will hear what you came to say," his father responded in kind.

Isaac had spent the entire journey choosing his words. Now, those words fled. "I have been living among the ko and took a wife."

"You came to tell me things I can see?"

"No." Isaac braced himself. "I came to tell you that I am the one who killed Mahwat."

His father did not flinch so much as an eyelash. His only reaction was a slow rise of his chest. "I saw it in a vision. What I did not see was why."

"After we helped the lone wagon cross the river, he refused to honor the trade. He followed the man and his woman, readying himself to kill them and steal their horses. I could not let him do it."

A look of grim resignation spread across Kumadha's face. He was aware of Mahwat's increasing lawlessness, so Isaac chose not to shame him by speaking of it.

"There is more I wish to tell you," he went on.

"You may say it."

"During the year of the locusts, I had a dream about a caravan that would come with twenty-two mules. When I came to tell you about it, you already knew. I assumed one of the elders had the same dream, but that was not the truth. Mahwat told me he had gone to you and claimed the dream was his. He took pleasure in stealing it from me."

"Why did you not tell me?"

"The mules had already come. I had no proof I saw it before it occurred."

"You are a dreamer," Kumadha muttered, his dark eyes going unfocused. "A half-breed and a dreamer..."

Isaac had to pause and clear his throat of emotion. His father finally knew the truth, but it likely did not matter. "Because of what he did, my heart is divided," he said, once he could speak without shaming himself. "I cannot deny the satisfaction that came from killing my brother, but I did not enjoy taking your son from you."

Kumadha lifted his gaze, humble eyes that reluctantly connected with Isaac's. "I want to be angry at you, but I cannot. You are not the only one who has felt satisfaction in killing outside of battle.

"The story of how your mother came to be with our clan is not truth. I did not get her in a trade. I spotted her in a camp of the Comanche, while I was on a hunt. I was drawn by her beauty and wanted her for myself."

"I thought your love for her came later."

"It did, and it did not. I tried to abide by the ways of the clan once she lived among us, but I desired her too much."

Isaac gave a grunt of commiseration. It had been the same with Eva—passion that overrode good sense and challenged honorable behavior.

"My reasons were not all selfish," Kumadha continued. "I feared the Comanche would not agree to trade her, and I knew what she would endure if she stayed with them, so I crept in at night and stole her. I killed two of their men to accomplish the task.

"You are the only one I have told," he added. "Our clan believes I traded for her, and the Comanche do not know who took her or where she was taken. I have chosen to live with this lie to guard your mother's safety."

"I will live with it also."

Kumadha narrowed his eyes. "The guilt that hung like bear skin around your shoulders when you arrived has left you, but your spirit is still restless."

"I made this journey to speak with you, but also to remove my wife from danger. It is not safe to return to our home."

Kumadha gestured at Isaac's bare upper body. "Has your ancestry been discovered?"

"Not by men who would betray me. Eva and I were attacked by a group of ko who wanted our land. We killed them."

"We?"

"Yes. Eva proved her loyalty and her skills with my bow."

Kumadha raised a brow and nodded in appreciation. "Who threatens you now?"

"We believe more members of the group exist. If they kill us, they can steal our land."

"Can they not steal it better if you are gone?"

Isaac shook his head. "So long as we remain alive, we can challenge them for ownership."

"Where is this land?"

"It is in Oregon Territory, near Fort Hall."

"That is the land of the Shoshone," Kumadha said firmly. An unspoken *how can anyone own it?* hung in the air.

"The white man's government is granting portions of land to settlers in exchange for them farming their portion. To make room, they are moving clans to other sections of land called reservations. It has only just begun, but it will happen more and more. The clans can fight, but the white man's army is large. They will not be stopped."

Kumadha grimaced as if he had tasted bad water. "The clans must hunt to survive. They will die if they cannot roam the land and follow the herds."

They might survive if they adopted the white man's ways, but Isaac held his tongue and let his father's words go unchallenged. The clans had been there long before outsiders came and were the rightful keepers of the land.

They were not uncivilized, just misunderstood. Their bible was the songs and stories they passed down, and their religion was keeping the earth in balance and living in harmony with the land. How could they negotiate with invaders who did not know this and did not want to understand?

A mighty storm was coming, and it grieved Isaac's heart. The best he could do was warn his clan and help them evade it as long as they could.

"As I appear now," he said, "I am able to move among whites easily. Their tongues are loose in my presence, and their language is not foreign to me." He lifted his arms from where they rested on his knees and turned out his hands. "I did not come, expecting our people to welcome me with a feast, but if they will allow me to sit among them, I can tell them what I have learned."

"Our war chief will want to strike first, to gain the advantage."

"Then decide for yourself what the clan should and should not know. But hear me, father. Dealing peacefully with whites is the only way to save our people. Killing them brings soldiers, and soldiers bring war."

Kumadah's face remained solemn, but moisture glistened in his eyes. "I have heard you, Hatchoq. I will consider all you have said."

Eva looked over her shoulder when a knock sounded at Loraine's door.

"*Mahavk*," Loraine called. "That means enter," she told Eva in a softer voice.

Isaac walked in, carrying a stack of pelts and a sack of gifts they had brought for his clan.

Eva looked from the bag to him, hopeful. "How did it go?"

"My father heard me. He has gone to speak with the elders."

"Would you like some tea?" Loraine asked. "I can warm it up for you."

"I will drink it as it is," Isaac responded, sitting in the chair between them. He dug around in the sack while his mother poured him a cup then handed her a tin of tea leaves and a folded piece of peach and green calico fabric tied with twine. "We brought these for you."

"Thank you." Loraine sniffed the tea with relish then smoothed her palm across the surface of the fabric. "It's beautiful!"

"There's enough for a dress," Eva said then laid a hand on Isaac's arm to halt him from setting the bag aside. "And thread."

He dug around some more and pulled out the spool.

Perhaps the meeting hadn't gone so well. It wasn't like him to forget such a detail.

His mother noticed, too. Her gaze briefly connected with Eva's before aiming a kind smile at him. "I've gotten to know your wife. Now I feel I must do the same with you."

"I dress as ko, but I am still Mojave in my heart."

Eva reached across the table and took hold of her husband's hand. "Isaac sacrificed much to help me. He has had to make some difficult choices."

Empathy weighted Loraine's expression so completely it choked off Eva's next breath and erased any doubt about her love for her son. "He's been making difficult choices all his life." Her smile returned, and she sat back in her chair. "I'm glad you're here—both of you. Do you plan to visit long?"

"That is a question for the clan," Isaac replied.

"I can't speak for the elders," Loraine said, "but I have faith in them. Regardless, your father has invited you into his home. You are welcome here."

He needed to quit dwelling on his worries.

Eva patted Isaac's hand to get his attention. "I've tested your mother's patience with replies almost as short as yours," she said in a teasing tone that had Loraine smirking. "Perhaps, now that you're here, you can satisfy her curiosity."

"What is it that you wish to know?" he asked.

"Did you leave because of Mahwat?" Lorraine asked in a gentle tone devoid of any judgment.

"Yes," Isaac replied.

"Where did you go?"

"I traveled north, to Oregon Territory. That is where I met Eva."

"How long have you been married?"

"Since June, in the manner of our clan. Since August, by the white man's way."

Mirth flitted across Loraine's lips.

"What amuses you?" he asked.

She shook her head. "You are so much like your father it unsettles me sometimes."

Isaac frowned.

"Forgive me for having fun at your expense, *humay*. You and your mate are splendidly matched. You have chosen well."

The smell of wood smoke and food cooking drifted in from outside. Eva sniffed the air and hoped that meant they would eat soon. The tea had calmed her appetite for a time, but she was getting hungry.

The scents grew stronger when Kumadha opened the door. He approached the table and towered over the group, giving Eva a view of his many tattoos up close.

She was torn between staring and looking away. His only garment was a loincloth. Even his feet were bare.

The dilemma was solved when he began speaking. She couldn't understand his words, so she watched Isaac's and Loraine's expressions for clues. Understanding nods and no sign of disappointment—that was good, wasn't it?

Kumadha turned to Eva and said, "Come. The clan will meet."

"My husband speaks a few words in English," Loraine said to her. "That was his effort to include you in the conversation."

Eva shrugged. "I'm afraid the only word I know is Isaac's nickname, posh. And ko," she amended as the three of them rose to follow Kumadha.

Eva paused and grabbed the edge of the table. The room felt as if it was tilting, and spots appeared before her eyes. She quickly sat back down to keep from falling.

Isaac knelt in front of her and looked up at her with concern. "What is wrong?"

"I'm all right. I just got dizzy."

Loraine said something to Kumada in his language then asked Isaac, "Shall I fetch the healer?"

"No," he said, rising and helping Eva to her feet. "She is not ill. She is carrying my child."

"Oh, Isaac!" Loraine exclaimed. "That's wonderful!" She spoke excitedly to Kumadha, who reacted with a sudden look of surprise that quickly melted into a smile.

Loraine circled the table to Eva. "It's half a mile to reach the center of the village, but then we'll be sitting the rest of the time. Do you feel well enough to go?"

"Yes. I feel better now." She took hold of Isaac's arm, once he'd secured the sack to the stack of pelts and slung the bundle over his shoulder, and went with him out of the hut.

His parents flanked him on the other side as they walked, Loraine striding along, arm in arm with her husband, as if he wasn't one stiff breeze away from being naked.

She turned a curious look on Isaac. "Why does Eva call you cat?"

"Because she couldn't pronounce the other word I suggested."

"Actually, I could," Eva explained, "but it was too long for a nickname."

"What was it?" his mother asked.

Isaac hesitated as if he didn't want to answer. "*Maqualachiisk.*"

Loraine's mouth dropped open, and she swatted his arm. "Isaac Bartholomew Shaw!"

He flinched and grinned.

Kumadha was chuckling.

Eva looked back and forth at them. "What does *maqualachiisk* mean?"

Loraine rolled her eyes. "It means very handsome."

The hunters had returned.

Isaac seated Eva with his parents then looked from clansman to clansman as he carried the bundle of pelts to the place where the elders gathered. A few still simmered with anger, but most—the ones who acknowledged what his brother had become—had regret and understanding in their eyes. He laid the gifts on the ground before the elders and returned to his family.

When the entire clan had gathered, the hunters donned skins and danced around spits of roasting meat, singing of a successful hunt. Women carried the food they had prepared and placed it all around until everyone was served. Then the reciting of the story cycles began.

His mother translated it to Eva, who was nibbling on a piece of roasted rabbit and taking it all in with childlike eyes.

Isaac wished to feel as carefree. The familiar rituals and soulful chanting soothed him, but he could not forget he was sitting in the midst of his people, guilty of killing one of their members and dressed in white man's clothes.

Kumadha rose, causing a hush to fall over the gathering. "Hatchoq has obeyed the eagle and returned," he said to the crowd, his wife repeating the words softly in English to Eva. "He has been gifted by the spirits. He is a dreamer who has spoken truth to me, and I welcome him."

A reverent murmur of *sumach a'hot*—he is gifted—rippled through the crowd.

The men with rancor in their eyes appeared humbled. They might never accept him, but they would not defy the spirits. And they would not stand against him when his own father—the one whom he had wronged—did not turn him away.

"I have given my son a different name," Kumadha went on. "Dog of two packs is his old name. It hurts him. Call him by his new name, *Hatchoqnych Meramerk.*"

"What does that mean?" Eva whispered.

"Dog that is loyal."

Epilogue

March 1, 1853, late afternoon

Isaac rode toward his people's village on Houyhnhnm, trailed by a riderless Sir Galahad loaded with supplies from the trading post. His parents had convinced him to stay with them until Eva gave birth. Once she was strong enough to travel, they would choose where to make their home.

Nuume, a trusted friend who had welcomed him back into the clan with a grand smile and a hearty embrace, ran up to him as he entered the village. "*Mamuuvilyk! Mamuuvilyk!*"

"Tell me," Isaac replied in his language. "Why must I hurry?"

"You are a father. Your wife gave birth!"

"When?"

"Early this morning, before dawn."

Isaac dismounted and stared at the horses in dismay. They had traveled far with heavy loads. They needed rest and food and water.

"Go," Nuume said, shooing him. "I will care for them."

Isaac rinsed the dust from his face and hands with water from his canteen, thanked his friend, and hurried to his parents' hut.

He paused at the door and listened to the sound of his baby's voice coming from within. "I am home," he said, opening the door.

"I'm glad," Eva said, smiling up at him from their bed mat. "I've missed you."

Isaac looked around the otherwise empty room. "Where is my mother?"

"She went with Cora Jane to fetch some water."

"I'm sorry I wasn't here to help you through your labor," he said as he squatted down beside her and caressed her face that was paler than he remembered. "Are you well?"

"I am." She pushed the edge of the blanket aside. "Look. We have a son."

Isaac's heart swelled at the sight of his child's precious face. The baby's skin was fair, but dark hair covered his head, and Mojave blood had clearly molded his features. "He is handsome and healthy. I am pleased." He leaned down and kissed Eva's forehead then touched the infant's hand with his finger.

She stroked the baby's cheek. "He's demanding when he's hungry, but the rest of the time, he gazes about peacefully or sleeps." Eva looked up at Isaac. "Have you settled on a name?"

She was referring to the Caucasian names they had discussed, as Mojave names were not chosen until well after the baby was born. His people believed talents and abilities were given to a child by way of dreams that came to them while they were still inside the womb. It was only as the child grew that the abilities were revealed.

Isaac shook his head. "Have you?"

"I think he looks like a Thomas. Thomas Isaac Shaw."

"That is a good name. So is Thomas Keith."

Eva's lip trembled. "You're going to make me cry."

"I suggested including your late husband's name to honor him. I thought you would like it."

"I do. Very much. That's the problem." Eva let out a note of a laugh that sounded as if it had nearly been a sob.

She sniffled and regained her composure. "I have a suggestion for the baby's Mojave name," she said, mischief dancing in her eyes. "How do you say *sneaks in when his father is away?*"

Isaac laughed. "You could not pronounce it."

"Believe me," Eva said between giggles. "I would try."

She shifted her position and grimaced.

"Are you hurting? I can bury hot coals beneath the mat."

"I'm all right...just stiff from lying in one place."

"I will help you." Isaac folded a blanket and wedged it behind her upper body then sat beside her. "A letter from Mac was waiting at the trading post," he said, pulling it from his pocket.

Eva's face lit with eagerness. "Open it."

He unfolded the letter and scanned the first page. "It says they all are well... Allison is expecting..."

"What! Give me that," she said, snatching it from him. "I want more than a summary."

"'Allison is expecting," Eva read. "'The bairn should arrive sometime in August, I am told. I have never been so thrilled and terrified in all my life.'" She shook her head and chuckled sympathetically. "Poor Mac.

"'Our neighbor is still missing,'" she read on, pausing to cast him a knowing look. "'The friends he mentioned never arrived. They must've gotten his letter, telling them that you decided to stay and work your claim.'"

Isaac frowned. "How can a dead man send a letter?"

"Don't ever repeat this, but Connor has always fancied himself an expert forger. He only employs his skills for fun and pranks, but he is good."

She tilted the paper toward the fading sunlight. "'Your farm thrives. Connor's brothers have done a fine job of caring for your land in your absence. I hope you and Isaac will return.'"

Eva lifted the page and found a second. "Look. Allison enclosed a note, too.

"'Hello, Eva. We have never met, though I feel I know you. Mac has told me of your kindness and your bravery on more than one occasion. He misses you, and, as strange as it sounds, so do I. I hope you and Isaac will return to claim your land.'

"'But if you don't, Connor will buy it. And if he doesn't, Mac will buy it for him. My childhood friend, Moira, came west with me. She has been in love with Connor since they were wee. Connor brushes the subject aside whenever I bring it up to him, but the affection is mutual.'

"'He never pursued a mate, because he doubts his ability to provide. I told him he cannot claim that anymore. Your Isaac taught him to tan, and now that Connor has us women to cook and run the household, he can devote enough time to hunting and tanning to earn a generous wage. Mac swears if Connor doesn't ask for Moira's hand soon, he'll betroth them.'"

Eva laughed. "He'd do it, too!" She lowered the letter. "I miss them so much."

The longing in his wife's expression felt like the current of the river, pushing Isaac a different way than he wanted to go. He had planned since leaving the trading post to discuss something with her as soon as he arrived home, but now...

My direction has finally become clear, just when Eva has the option to move back and safely occupy her land.

Isaac stretched out beside her on the mat, propping himself up on one elbow so he could see her face and that of his son. "There is something I must tell you."

She refolded the letter and set it aside. "I'm listening."

"While I was traveling, I had a dream. In it, I saw cows wandering in a wheat field. I did not understand the meaning at first, until I recalled our conversation when you were deciding what to do with your land. Remember when I told you that your land was good for cows and crops, that you could not make a bad choice?"

She nodded.

"I realized the same is true for me. I have always lived with a foot in two cultures, thinking I must choose one or the other. The dream showed me that I can choose both. In the past, I viewed my mixed blood as a shameful misfortune, but now I see it as a gift that can be used to help my father's people."

"It isn't shameful. It's one of the things I love about you," Eva said, brushing back stray strands of his hair. "Being raised the way you were has allowed you to view life from a better perspective. It has made you humble and wise."

Isaac took her hand in his. "I promised my father I would bring news to help the clan avoid war and remain on their land. It can be done if we return to our claim, but it will be easier if we live closer to the village, near the trading post.

"Regardless of where we make our home, we will visit those we love, and I will build you a proper house."

Eva stared down at the folded letter, still resting on the cloth their son was swaddled in.

"Your desires matter to me," Isaac said. "Which do you choose?"

She lifted her gaze and looked at him the way she had so many times when they'd lain together in the clearing, her eyes content and full of love. "You are my husband. Being with *you* is what I choose. I told you I would go wherever you go and stand by your side, and I meant it."

Isaac kissed his wife, hoping she could feel the love and gratitude that was overflowing from his heart. Then rested his forehead against hers and sighed. Living among whites would always carry a certain amount of risk, but he would be doing that regardless. And, though he wanted his children to hear clan stories and learn their ways, he missed Mac and Connor almost as much as Eva. "The decision is not easy."

Eva cradled his face in her hands. "There's plenty of time to choose. Let's dream on it."

Notes from the author

Thank you for reading *Battered Pride*! If you enjoyed the story, please tell your friends about it and leave a review.

www.amazon.com/dp/B0DJ1MRFDZ

About *Battered Pride*

When I created Hatchoq's character in *Come Back*, I never intended for him to appear in anything but one scene. You fans changed that. Your requests for him and other characters to get their own books turned a standalone debut into a series and sent me down a rabbit hole of research. Hatchoq's story has been the most requested one of all. I hope it meets your expectations.

On Mojave language

Because of a scarcity of resources and the fact that forming Mojave sentences is so different from that of English, some creative license was taken when writing *Battered Pride*. I apologize to any native speakers if putting reader experience above complete grammatical correctness is in any way offensive.

On Scottish accent & language

Creative license was also taken when writing scenes with my Scottish characters. My goal was to give their dialogue the flavor of the accent without making things difficult for the reader. Below is a glossary of the words and phrases used.

Aboot (about)
Aff (off)
Afore (before)
Aye (yes)
Bawdy (rabbit/hare)
Canny (can't)
Didnae (didn't)
Disnae (doesn't)
Dinnae (don't)
Fur (for)
Hevny (haven't)
Heid (head)
I dinnae ken (I don't know)

Jus' (just)

Ken (know)

Meal do naidheachd (congratulations)

Mibbe (maybe)

Ma (my)

No' (not)

Nae (no)

Oot (out)

Shuid (should)

Tae (to)

Wee (little/small)

Whit (what)

Wis (was)

Ye (you)

Yer (your)

Ye're (you're)

Ye're aff yer heid (you're crazy)

On historical accuracy

If you've read previous books in this series, you know I strive for historical accuracy all the way down to the etymology of the words I use. I've touched on sensitive topics before, but because the hero in *Battered Pride* is half Native American, this book marinates in it.

I have always enjoyed studying life in the 1800s, and I enjoyed studying the Mojave people of that day. They were a relatively peaceful group of clans who lived and farmed along the Colorado River. That said, not every scholarly source I found was as pleasant.

Humans are complicated mixtures of noble and sinful. So is history. It doesn't fit neatly into pretty boxes, no matter how hard we shove. During the research phase of this novel, I learned many things. Some facts surprised me.

Contrary to popular perception, Native Americans were not all existing peacefully before outsiders showed up. Anthropologists have documented extreme and prevalent violence among indigenous peoples long before the arrival of Spanish- and, later, European explorers and settlers. The advent of trade actually settled things down.

Native Americans owned both European and African slaves. Some tribes, such as the Comanche, engaged in acts of torture so heinous I could barely stand to read about them.

By no means are whites blameless. While many settlers simply wanted the opportunity to escape tyranny or famine and build a better life for themselves and their descendants, others ignored federal boundary laws and engaged in mistreatment of indigenous peoples, the U.S. government ultimately becoming the worst offender.

Treaty or no, tribes were forced off their lands, and that is a regrettable tragedy.

In literature and film, Native American characters are often divided into *savage warrior* or *noble chief* stereotypes. What a mistake. They are unique beings with strengths and flaws, who feel happiness, hatred, generosity, greed, love, and jealousy, just as anyone else. Early immigrants who took time to get to know the 'Indians' discovered that many were kind and had a great sense of humor.

My goal with this book was to weave an engaging story around a satisfying romance, and to portray the characters and setting as true to history as possible. I hope I succeeded.

Also by Melissa

There are currently four novels in the Forging America series. In order, they are:

Come Back
Precious Atonement
Fool's Iron
Battered Pride

These novels can be read as standalones, but they are best enjoyed if read in order. The entire Forging America series can be found on Amazon.

Forging America Series
www.amazon.com/gp/product/B09X4GRLS6

To be notified of new releases, you can follow my author page and or sign up for my newsletter. Newsletter subscribers get a FREE, exclusive book when they sign up!

Melissa's Author Page

www.amazon.com/stores/Melissa-Maygrove/author/B00JL4UPCY

Newsletter Sign-up & Free Book

www.dl.bookfunnel.com/uonrrvm6ze

Do you read other genres?

I write contemporary romance as Scarlet Knight. Currently, there is a paranormal romance duet available, The Sweetwater Duet, that has a historical element.

www.amazon.com/gp/product/B09WLTRHLR

These books can be read as standalones, but, because the second one continues the story of the first, I encourage you to read them in order.

An Honorable Man
To Have & To Hold

About the author

NAMED ONE OF HOUSTON'S 100 CREATIVES
FOR 2014 BY THE HOUSTON PRESS &
MENTIONED IN 'WHO'S WHO AMONG TEXAS
AUTHORS'

Native Texan Melissa Maygrove is a mother, nurse, freelance editor, and romance author. When she's not busy caring for her tiny NICU patients, she's hunched over her laptop, complicating the lives of her imaginary friends and playing matchmaker. Melissa loves books with unpretentious characters and unforgettable romance, and she strives to create those same kinds of stories for her readers.

Helpful Links

Bookbub Author Page

www.bookbub.com/authors/melissa-maygrove

Melissa's website

www.melissamaygrove.com

Melissa's Goodreads Author Page

www.goodreads.com/melissamaygrove

Printed in Dunstable, United Kingdom